'I first read this twenty years ago, and have never forgotten the wonder and fury it kindled at the time. Anyone who talks about the glory of war has obviously never read it. A beautifully detailed and intensely personal account of a conflict which lasts for over a thousand years, as told by the one grunt who lives through it all. Only a writer as skilful, and knowledgeable as Haldeman could use war's dark glamour to lure the reader in and then deploy that same fascination to show just what kind of effect this orchestrated barbarism can have on the human soul.' *Peter F. Hamilton*

'[*The Forever War*] deserved a Pulitzer, for it is to the Vietnam War what Catch-22 was to World War II, the definitive, bleakly comic satire' *Thomas M. Disch*

'An almost polemical work, frighteningly convincing in its descriptions of future military technology. The novel is both a product of a particular historical moment and a work of contemporary relevance' *Waterstone's Guide to Science Fiction, Fantasy and Horror*

'A vastly entertaining trip' *The New York Times*

'His prose is as clear and engaging as his ideas' *The New York Times Book Review*

'Among the best ... *The Forever War* has all the authenticity of a good war novel – the dialogue, people, training and barracks mentality' *Newsday*

'An engrossing, poignant epic ... Mandella is one of the most memorable characters science fiction has ever produced' *San Francisco Examiner*

'A brilliant novel' *Booklist*

Also by Joe Haldeman

NOVELS
War Year (1972)
The Forever War (1974)
Mindbridge (1976)
All My Sins Remembered (1977)
Worlds (1981)
Worlds Apart (1983)
Tool of the Trade (1987)
The Long Habit of Living (1989)
The Hemingway Hoax (1990)
Worlds Enough and Time (1992)
1968 (1995)
Forever Peace (1997)
Forever Free (1999)

SHORT STORY COLLECTIONS
Infinite Dreams (1979)
Dealing in Futures (1985)
None So Blind (1996)

THE
FOREVER
WAR

Joe Haldeman

The right of Joe Haldeman to be identified as the author
of this work has been asserted by him in accordance with
the Copyright, Designs and Patents Act 1988.

This edition published in Great Britain in 1999 by
Millennium
An imprint of Orion Books Ltd
Orion House, 5 Upper St Martin's Lane, London WC2H 9EA

This edition reprinted in 2004 by
Gollancz
An imprint of the Orion Publishing Group

13 15 17 19 20 18 16 14

A CIP catalogue record for this book is available
from the British Library.

ISBN 13 978 1 85798 808 6

Printed and bound in Great Britain by
Clays Ltd, St Ives plc

The Orion Publishing Group's policy is to use papers that
are natural, renewable and recyclable products and
made from wood grown in sustainable forests. The logging
and manufacturing processes are expected to conform to
the environmental regulations of the country of origin.

www.orionbooks.co.uk

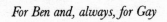

For Ben and, always, for Gay

THE
FOREVER WAR

AUTHOR'S NOTE

This is the definitive version of *The Forever War*. There are two other versions, and my publisher has been kind enough to allow me to clarify things here.

The one you're holding in your hand is the book as it was originally written. But it has a pretty tortuous history.

It's ironic, since it later won the Hugo and Nebula Awards, and has won "Best Novel" awards in other countries, but *The Forever War* was not an easy book to sell back in the early seventies. It was rejected by eighteen publishers before St. Martin's Press decided to take a chance on it. "Pretty good book," was the usual reaction, "but nobody wants to read a science fiction novel about Vietnam". Twenty-five years later, most young readers don't even see the parallels between *The Forever War* and the seemingly endless one we were involved in at the time, and that's okay. It's about Vietnam because that's the war the author was in. But it's mainly about war, about soldiers, and about the reasons we think we need them.

While the book was being looked at by all those publishers, it was also being serialized piecemeal in *Analog* magazine. The editor, Ben Bova, was a tremendous help, not only in editing, but also for making the thing exist at all! He gave it a prominent place in the magazine, and it was also his endorsement that brought it to the attention of St. Martin's Press, who took a chance on the hardcover, though they did not publish adult science fiction at that time.

But Ben rejected the middle section, a novella called "You Can Never Go Back." He liked it as a piece of writing, he said, but thought that it was too downbeat for *Analog's* audience. So I wrote him a more positive story and put " You Can Never Go Back" into the drawer; eventually Ted White published it in *Amazing* magazine, as a coda to *The Forever War.*

At this late date, I'm not sure why I didn't reinstate the original middle when the book was accepted. Perhaps I didn't trust my own taste, or just didn't want to make life more complicated. But that first book version is essentially the *Analog* version with "more adult language and situations", as they say in Hollywood.

The paperback of that version stayed in print for about sixteen years. Then in 1991 I had the opportunity to reinstate my original version, which now appears in Britain for the first time. The dates in the book are now kind of funny; most people realize we didn't get into an interstellar war in 1996. I originally set it in that year so it was barely possible that the officers and NCOs could be veterans of Vietnam, so we decided to leave it that way, in spite of the obvious anachronisms. Think of it as a parallel universe.

But maybe it's the real one, and we're in a dream.

Joe Haldeman
Cambridge, Massachusetts

THE
FOREVER WAR

PRIVATE
MANDELLA

1

"Tonight we're going to show you eight silent ways to kill a man." The guy who said that was a sergeant who didn't look five years older than me. So if he'd ever killed a man in combat, silently or otherwise, he'd done it as an infant.

I already knew eighty ways to kill people, but most of them were pretty noisy. I sat up straight in my chair and assumed a look of polite attention and fell asleep with my eyes open. So did most everybody else. We'd learned that they never scheduled anything important for these after-chop classes.

The projector woke me up and I sat through a short tape showing the "eight silent ways." Some of the actors must have been brainwipes, since they were actually killed.

After the tape a girl in the front row raised her hand. The sergeant nodded at her and she rose to parade rest. Not bad looking, but kind of chunky about the neck and shoulders. Everybody gets that way after carrying a heavy pack around for a couple of months.

"Sir"—we had to call sergeants "sir" until graduation—"most of those methods, really, they looked ... kind of silly."

"For instance?"

"Like killing a man with a blow to the kidneys, from an entrenching tool. I mean, when would you *actually* have only an entrenching tool, and no gun or knife? And why not just bash him over the head with it?"

"He might have a helmet on," he said reasonably.

"Besides, Taurans probably don't even *have* kidneys!"

He shrugged. "Probably they don't." This was 1997, and nobody had ever seen a Tauran; hadn't even found any pieces of Taurans bigger than a scorched chromosome. "But their body chemistry is similar to ours, and we have to assume they're similarly complex creatures. They *must*

3

have weaknesses, vulnerable spots. You have to find out
where they are.

"That's the important thing." He stabbed a finger at the
screen. "Those eight convicts got caulked for your benefit
because you've got to find out how to kill Taurans, and be
able to do it whether you have a megawatt laser or an emery
board."

She sat back down, not looking too convinced.

"Any more questions?" Nobody raised a hand.

"OK. Tench-hut!" We staggered upright and he looked
at us expectantly.

"Fuck you, sir," came the familiar tired chorus.

"Louder!"

"FUCK YOU, SIR!" One of the army's less-inspired
morale devices.

"That's better. Don't forget, pre-dawn maneuvers tomorrow. Chop at 0330, first formation, 0400. Anybody
sacked after 0340 owes one stripe. Dismissed."

I zipped up my coverall and went across the snow to the
lounge for a cup of soya and a joint. I'd always been able
to get by on five or six hours of sleep, and this was the
only time I could be by myself, out of the army for a while.
Looked at the newsfax for a few minutes. Another ship got
caulked, out by Aldebaran sector. That was four years ago.
They were mounting a reprisal fleet, but it'll take four years
more for them to get out there. By then, the Taurans would
have every portal planet sewed up tight.

Back at the billet, everybody else was sacked and the
main lights were out. The whole company'd been dragging
ever since we got back from the two-week lunar training.
I dumped my clothes in the locker, checked the roster and
found out I was in bunk *31*. Goddammit, right under the
heater.

I slipped through the curtain as quietly as possible so as
not to wake up the person next to me. Couldn't see who it
was, but I couldn't have cared less. I slipped under the
blanket.

"You're late, Mandella," a voice yawned. It was Rogers.

"Sorry I woke you up," I whispered.

" 'Sallright." She snuggled over and clasped me spoon-fashion. She was warm and reasonably soft.

I patted her hip in what I hoped was a brotherly fashion. "Night, Rogers."

"G'night, Stallion." She returned the gesture more pointedly.

Why do you always get the tired ones when you're ready and the randy ones when you're tired? I bowed to the inevitable.

2

"Awright, let's get some goddamn *back* inta that! Stringer team! Move it up—move your ass up!"

A warm front had come in about midnight and the snow had turned to sleet. The permaplast stringer weighed five hundred pounds and was a bitch to handle, even when it wasn't covered with ice. There were four of us, two at each end, carrying the plastic girder with frozen fingertips. Rogers was my partner.

"Steel!" the guy behind me yelled, meaning that he was losing his hold. It wasn't steel, but it was heavy enough to break your foot. Everybody let go and hopped away. It splashed slush and mud all over us.

"Goddammit, Petrov," Rogers said, "why didn't you go out for the Red Cross or something? This fucken thing's not that fucken heavy." Most of the girls were a little more circumspect in their speech. Rogers was a little butch.

"Awright, get a fucken *move* on, stringers—epoxy team! Dog'em! Dog'em!"

Our two epoxy people ran up, swinging their buckets. "Let's go, Mandella. I'm freezin' my balls off."

"Me, too," the girl said with more feeling than logic.

"One—two—heave!" We got the thing up again and staggered toward the bridge. It was about three-quarters completed. Looked as if the second platoon was going to beat us. I wouldn't give a damn, but the platoon that got their bridge built first got to fly home. Four miles of muck for the rest of us, and no rest before chop.

We got the stringer in place, dropped it with a clank, and fitted the static clamps that held it to the rise-beams. The female half of the epoxy team started slopping glue on it before we even had it secured. Her partner was waiting for the stringer on the other side. The floor team was waiting at the foot of the bridge, each one holding a piece of the

6

light, stressed permaplast over his head like an umbrella. They were dry and clean. I wondered aloud what they had done to deserve it, and Rogers suggested a couple of colorful, but unlikely, possibilities.

We were going back to stand by the next stringer when the field first (name of Dougelstein, but we called him "Awright") blew a whistle and bellowed, "Awright, soldier boys and girls, ten minutes. Smoke'em if you got 'em." He reached into his pocket and turned on the control that heated our coveralls.

Rogers and I sat down on our end of the stringer and I took out my weed box. I had lots of joints, but we were ordered not to smoke them until after night-chop. The only tobacco I had was a cigarro butt about three inches long. I lit it on the side of the box; it wasn't too bad after the first couple of puffs. Rogers took a puff, just to be sociable, but made a face and gave it back.

"Were you in school when you got drafted?" she asked.

"Yeah. Just got a degree in physics. Was going after a teacher's certificate."

She nodded soberly. "I was in biology . . ."

"Figures." I ducked a handful of slush. "How far?"

"Six years, bachelor's and technical." She slid her boot along the ground, turning up a ridge of mud and slush the consistency of freezing ice milk. "Why the fuck did this have to happen?"

I shrugged. It didn't call for an answer, least of all the answer that the UNEF kept giving us. Intellectual and physical elite of the planet, going out to guard humanity against the Tauran menace. Soyashit. It was all just a big experiment. See whether we could goad the Taurans into ground action.

Awright blew the whistle two minutes early, as expected, but Rogers and I and the other two stringers got to sit for a minute while the epoxy and floor teams finished covering our stringer. It got cold fast, sitting there with our suits turned off, but we remained inactive on principle.

There really wasn't any sense in having us train in the cold. Typical army half-logic. Sure, it was going to be cold where we were going, but not ice-cold or snow-cold. Al-

most by definition, a portal planet remained within a degree
or two of absolute zero all the time—since collapsars don't
shine—and the first chill you felt would mean that you
were a dead man.

Twelve years before, when I was ten years old, they had
discovered the collapsar jump. Just fling an object at a collapsar with sufficient speed, and out it pops in some other
part of the galaxy. It didn't take long to figure out the for-
mula that predicted where it would come out: it travels
along the same "line" (actually an Einsteinian geodesic) it
would have followed if the collapsar hadn't been in the
way—until it reaches another collapsar field, whereupon it
reappears, repelled with the same speed at which it approached the original collapsar. Travel time between the
two collapsars . . . exactly zero.

It made a lot of work for mathematical physicists, who
had to redefine simultaneity, then tear down general relativity and build it back up again. And it made the politicians
very happy, because now they could send a shipload of
colonists to Fomalhaut for less than it had once cost to put
a brace of men on the moon. There were a lot of people
the politicians would love to see on Fomalhaut, imple-
menting a glorious adventure rather than stirring up trouble
at home.

The ships were always accompanied by an automated
probe that followed a couple of million miles behind. We
knew about the portal planets, little bits of flotsam that
whirled around the collapsars; the purpose of the drone was
to come back and tell us in the event that a ship had
smacked into a portal planet at .999 of the speed of light.

That particular catastrophe never happened, but one day
a drone limped back alone. Its data were analyzed, and it
turned out that the colonists' ship had been pursued by
another vessel and destroyed. This happened near Aldebaran, in the constellation Taurus, but since "Aldebaranian"
is a little hard to handle, they named the enemy "Tauran."

Colonizing vessels thenceforth went out protected by an
armed guard. Often the armed guard went out alone, and
finally the Colonization Group got shortened to UNEF,

United Nations Exploratory Force. Emphasis on the "force."

Then some bright lad in the General Assembly decided that we ought to field an army of footsoldiers to guard the portal planets of the nearer collapsars. This led to the Elite Conscription Act of 1996 and the most elitely conscripted army in the history of warfare.

So here we were, fifty men and fifty women, with IQs over 150 and bodies of unusual health and strength, slogging elitely through the mud and slush of central Missouri, reflecting on the usefulness of our skill in building bridges on worlds where the only fluid is an occasional standing pool of liquid helium.

3

About a month later, we left for our final training exercise, maneuvers on the planet Charon. Though nearing perihelion, it was still more than twice as far from the sun as Pluto.

The troopship was a converted "cattlewagon" made to carry two hundred colonists and assorted bushes and beasts. Don't think it was roomy, though, just because there were half that many of us. Most of the excess space was taken up with extra reaction mass and ordnance.

The whole trip took three weeks, accelerating at two gees halfway, decelerating the other half. Our top speed, as we roared by the orbit of Pluto, was around one-twentieth of the speed of light—not quite enough for relativity to rear its complicated head.

Three weeks of carrying around twice as much weight as normal . . . it's no picnic. We did some cautious exercises three times a day and remained horizontal as much as possible. Still, we got several broken bones and serious dislocations. The men had to wear special supporters to keep from littering the floor with loose organs. It was almost impossible to sleep; nightmares of choking and being crushed, rolling over periodically to prevent blood pooling and bedsores. One girl got so fatigued that she almost slept through the experience of having a rib push out into the open air.

I'd been in space several times before, so when we finally stopped decelerating and went into free fall, it was nothing but relief. But some people had never been out, except for our training on the moon, and succumbed to the sudden vertigo and disorientation. The rest of us cleaned up after them, floating through the quarters with sponges and inspirators to suck up the globules of partly-digested

10

"Concentrate, High-protein, Low-residue, Beef Flavor (Soya)."

We had a good view of Charon, coming down from orbit. There wasn't much to see, though. It was just a dim, off-white sphere with a few smudges on it. We landed about two hundred meters from the base. A pressurized crawler came out and mated with the ferry, so we didn't have to suit up. We clanked and squeaked up to the main building, a featureless box of grayish plastic.

Inside, the walls were the same drab color. The rest of the company was sitting at desks, chattering away. There was a seat next to Freeland.

"Jeff—feeling better?" He still looked a little pale.

"If the gods had meant for man to survive in free fall, they would have given him a cast iron glottis." He sighed heavily. "A little better. Dying for a smoke."

"Yeah."

"*You* seemed to take it all right. Went up in school, didn't you?"

"Senior thesis in vacuum welding, yeah. Three weeks in Earth orbit." I sat back and reached for my weed box for the thousandth time. It still wasn't there. The Life Support Unit didn't want to handle nicotine and THC.

"Training was bad enough," Jeff groused, "but *this* shit—"

"Tench-hut!" We stood up in a raggedy-ass fashion, by twos and threes. The door opened and a full major came in. I stiffened a little. He was the highest-ranking officer I'd ever seen. He had a row of ribbons stitched into his coveralls, including a purple strip meaning he'd been wounded in combat, fighting in the old American army. Must have been that Indochina thing, but it had fizzled out before I was born. He didn't look that old.

"Sit, sit." He made a patting motion with his hand. Then he put his hands on his hips and scanned the company, a small smile on his face. "Welcome to Charon. You picked a lovely day to land, the temperature outside is a summery eight point one five degrees Absolute. We expect little change for the next two centuries or so." Some of them laughed halfheartedly.

"Best you enjoy the tropical climate here at Miami Base; enjoy it while you can. We're on the center of sunside here, and most of your training will be on darkside. Over there, the temperature stays a chilly two point zero eight.

"You might as well regard all the training you got on Earth and the moon as just an elementary exercise, designed to give you a fair chance of surviving Charon. You'll have to go through your whole repertory here: tools, weapons, maneuvers. And you'll find that, at these temperatures, tools don't work the way they should; weapons don't want to fire. And people move v-e-r-y cautiously."

He studied the clipboard in his hand. "Right now, you have forty-nine women and forty-eight men. Two deaths on Earth, one psychiatric release. Having read an outline of your training program, I'm frankly surprised that so many of you pulled through.

"But you might as well know that I won't be displeased if as few as fifty of you, half, graduate from this final phase. And the only way not to graduate is to die. Here. The only way anybody gets back to Earth—including me—is after a combat tour.

"You will complete your training in one month. From here you go to Stargate collapsar, half a light year away. You will stay at the settlement on Stargate 1, the largest portal planet, until replacements arrive. Hopefully, that will be no more than a month; another group is due here as soon as you leave.

"When you leave Stargate, you will go to some strategically important collapsar, set up a military base there, and fight the enemy, if attacked. Otherwise, you will maintain the base until further orders.

"The last two weeks of your training will consist of constructing exactly that kind of a base, on darkside. There you will be totally isolated from Miami Base: no communication, no medical evacuation, no resupply. Sometime before the two weeks are up, your defense facilities will be evaluated in an attack by guided drones. They will be armed."

They had spent all that money on us just to kill us in training?

"All of the permanent personnel here on Charon are combat veterans. Thus, all of us are forty to fifty years of age. But I think we can keep up with you. Two of us will be with you at all times and will accompany you at least as far as Stargate. They are Captain Sherman Stott, your company commander, and Sergeant Octavio Cortez, your first sergeant. Gentlemen?"

Two men in the front row stood easily and turned to face us. Captain Stott was a little smaller than the major, but cut from the same mold: face hard and smooth as porcelain, cynical half-smile, a precise centimeter of beard framing a large chin, looking thirty at the most. He wore a large, gunpowder-type pistol on his hip.

Sergeant Cortez was another story, a horror story. His head was shaved and the wrong shape, flattened out on one side, where a large piece of skull had obviously been taken out. His face was very dark and seamed with wrinkles and scars. Half his left ear was missing, and his eyes were as expressive as buttons on a machine. He had a moustache-and-beard combination that looked like a skinny white caterpillar taking a lap around his mouth. On anybody else, his schoolboy smile might look pleasant, but he was about the ugliest, meanest-looking creature I'd ever seen. Still, if you didn't look at his head and considered the lower six feet or so, he could have posed as the "after" advertisement for a body-building spa. Neither Stott nor Cortez wore any ribbons. Cortez had a small pocket-laser suspended in a magnetic rig, sideways, under his left armpit. It had wooden grips that were worn smooth.

"Now, before I turn you over to the tender mercies of these two gentlemen, let me caution you again:

"Two months ago there was not a living soul on this planet, just some leftover equipment from the expedition of 1991. A working force of forty-five men struggled for a month to erect this base. Twenty-four of them, more than half, died in the construction of it. This is the most dangerous planet men have ever tried to live on, but the places you'll be going will be this bad and worse. Your cadre will try to keep you alive for the next month. Listen to them . . . and follow their example; all of them have survived here much longer than you'll have to. Captain?'' The captain stood up as the major went out the door.

"Tench-*hut*!" The last syllable was like an explosion and we all jerked to our feet.

"Now I'm only gonna say this *once* so you better listen," he growled. "We *are* in a combat situation here, and in a combat situation there is only *one* penalty for disobedience or insubordination." He jerked the pistol from his hip and held it by the barrel, like a club. "This is an Army model 1911 automatic *pistol*, caliber .45, and it is a primitive but effective weapon. The Sergeant and I are authorized to use our weapons to kill to enforce discipline. Don't make us do it because we will. We *will*." He put the pistol back. The holster snap made a loud crack in the dead quiet.

"Sergeant Cortez and I between us have killed more people than are sitting in this room. Both of us fought in Vietnam on the American side and both of us joined the United Nations International Guard more than ten years ago. I took a break in grade from major for the privilege of commanding this company, and First Sergeant Cortez took a break from sub-major, because we are both *combat* soldiers and this is the first *combat* situation since 1987.

"Keep in mind what I've said while the First Sergeant instructs you more specifically in what your duties will be under this command. Take over, Sergeant." He turned on his heel and strode out of the room. The expression on his face hadn't changed one millimeter during the whole harangue.

The First Sergeant moved like a heavy machine with lots of ball bearings. When the door hissed shut, he swiveled ponderously to face us and said, "At ease, siddown," in a surprisingly gentle voice. He sat on a table in the front of the room. It creaked, but held.

"Now the captain talks scary and I look scary, but we both mean well. You'll be working pretty closely with me, so you better get used to this thing I've got hanging in front of my brain. You probably won't see the captain much, except on maneuvers."

He touched the flat part of his head. "And speaking of brains, I still have just about all of mine, in spite of Chinese efforts to the contrary. All of us old vets who mustered into UNEF had to pass the same criteria that got you drafted by the Elite Conscription Act. So I suspect all of you are smart and tough—but just keep in mind that the captain and I are smart and tough *and* experienced.''

He flipped through the roster without really looking at it. ''Now, as the captain said, there'll be only one kind of disciplinary action on maneuvers. Capital punishment. But normally *we* won't have to kill you for disobeying; Charon'll save us the trouble.

''Back in the billeting area, it'll be another story. We don't much care what you do inside. Grab ass all day and fuck all night, makes no difference. . . . But once you suit up and go outside, you've gotta have discipline that would shame a Centurian. There will be situations where one stupid act could kill us all.

''Anyhow, the first thing we've gotta do is get you fitted to your fighting suits. The armorer's waiting at your billet; he'll take you one at a time. Let's go.''

4

"Now I know you got lectured back on Earth on what a fighting suit can do." The armorer was a small man, partially bald, with no insignia of rank on his coveralls. Sergeant Cortez had told us to call him "sir," since he was a lieutenant.

"But I'd like to reinforce a couple of points, maybe add some things your instructors Earthside weren't clear about or couldn't know. Your First Sergeant was kind enough to consent to being my visual aid. Sergeant?"

Cortez slipped out of his coveralls and came up to the little raised platform where a fighting suit was standing, popped open like a man-shaped clam. He backed into it and slipped his arms into the rigid sleeves. There was a click and the thing swung shut with a sigh. It was bright green with CORTEZ stenciled in white letters on the helmet.

"Camouflage, Sergeant." The green faded to white, then dirty gray. "This is good camouflage for Charon and most of your portal planets," said Cortez, as if from a deep well. "But there are several other combinations available." The gray dappled and brightened to a combination of greens and browns: "Jungle." Then smoothed out to a hard light ochre: "Desert." Dark brown, darker, to a deep flat black: "Night or space."

"Very good, Sergeant. To my knowledge, this is the only feature of the suit that was perfected after your training. The control is around your left wrist and is admittedly awkward. But once you find the right combination, it's easy to lock in.

"Now, you didn't get much in-suit training Earthside. We didn't want you to get used to using the thing in a friendly environment. The fighting suit is the deadliest personal weapon ever built, and with no weapon is it easier

16

for the user to kill himself through carelessness. Turn around, Sergeant.

"Case in point." He tapped a large square protuberance between the shoulders. "Exhaust fins. As you know, the suit tries to keep you at a comfortable temperature no matter what the weather's like outside. The material of the suit is as near to a perfect insulator as we could get, consistent with mechanical demands. Therefore, these fins get *hot*—especially hot, compared to darkside temperatures—as they bleed off the body's heat.

"All you have to do is lean up against a boulder of frozen gas; there's lots of it around. The gas will sublime off faster than it can escape from the fins; in escaping, it will push against the surrounding 'ice' and fracture it . . . and in about one-hundredth of a second, you have the equivalent of a hand grenade going off right below your neck. You'll never feel a thing.

"Variations on this theme have killed eleven people in the past two months. And they were just building a bunch of huts.

"I assume you know how easily the waldo capabilities can kill you or your companions. Anybody want to shake hands with the sergeant?" He paused, then stepped over and clasped his glove. "He's had lots of practice. Until *you* have, be extremely careful. You might scratch an itch and wind up breaking your back. Remember, semi-logarithmic response: two pounds' pressure exerts five pounds' force; three pounds' gives ten; four pounds', twenty-three; five pounds', forty-seven. Most of you can muster up a grip of well over a hundred pounds. Theoretically, you could rip a steel girder in two with that, amplified. Actually, you'd destroy the material of your gloves and, at least on Charon, die very quickly. It'd be a race between decompression and flash-freezing. You'd die no matter which won.

"The leg waldos are also dangerous, even though the amplification is less extreme. Until you're really skilled, don't try to run, or jump. You're likely to trip, and that means you're likely to die."

"Charon's gravity is three-fourths of Earth normal, so it's not too bad. But on a really small world, like Luna,

you could take a running jump and not come down for
twenty minutes, just keep sailing over the horizon. Maybe
bash into a mountain at eighty meters per second. On a
small asteroid, it'd be no trick at all to run up to escape
velocity and be off on an informal tour of intergalactic
space. It's a slow way to travel.

"Tomorrow morning, we'll start teaching you how to
stay alive inside this infernal machine. The rest of the afternoon and evening, I'll call you one at a time to be fitted.
That's all, Sergeant."

Cortez went to the door and turned the stopcock that let
air into the airlock. A bank of infrared lamps went on to
keep air from freezing inside it. When the pressures were
equalized, he shut the stopcock, unclamped the door and
stepped in, clamping it shut behind him. A pump hummed
for about a minute, evacuating the airlock; then he stepped
out and sealed the outside door.

It was pretty much like the ones on Luna.

"First I want Private Omar Almizar. The rest of you can
go find your bunks. I'll call you over the squawker."

"Alphabetical order, sir?"

"Yep. About ten minutes apiece. If your name begins
with Z, you might as well get sacked."

That was Rogers. She probably was thinking about getting sacked.

5

The sun was a hard white point directly overhead. It was a lot brighter than I had expected it to be; since we were eighty AUs out, it was only one 6400th as bright as it is on Earth. Still, it was putting out about as much light as a powerful streetlamp.

"This is considerably more light than you'll have on a portal planet." Captain Stott's voice crackled in our collective ear. "Be glad that you'll be able to watch your step."

We were lined up, single-file, on the permaplast sidewalk that connected the billet and the supply hut. We'd practiced walking inside, all morning, and this wasn't any different except for the exotic scenery. Though the light was rather dim, you could see all the way to the horizon quite clearly, with no atmosphere in the way. A black cliff that looked too regular to be natural stretched from one horizon to the other, passing within a kilometer of us. The ground was obsidian-black, mottled with patches of white or bluish ice. Next to the supply hut was a small mountain of snow in a bin marked OXYGEN.

The suit was fairly comfortable, but it gave you the odd feeling of simultaneously being a marionette and a puppeteer. You apply the impulse to move your leg and the suit picks it up and magnifies it and moves your leg *for* you.

"Today we're only going to walk around the company area, and nobody will *leave* the company area." The captain wasn't wearing his .45—unless he carried it as a good luck charm, under his suit—but he had a laser-finger like the rest of us. And his was probably hooked up.

Keeping an interval of at least two meters between each person, we stepped off the permaplast and followed the captain over smooth rock. We walked carefully for about an hour, spiraling out, and finally stopped at the far edge of the perimeter.

"Now everybody pay close attention. I'm going out to that blue slab of ice"—it was a big one, about twenty meters away—"and show you something that you'd better know if you want to stay alive."

He walked out in a dozen confident steps. "First I have to heat up a rock—filters down." I squeezed the stud under my armpit and the filter slid into place over my image converter. The captain pointed his finger at a black rock the size of a basketball, and gave it a short burst. The glare rolled a long shadow of the captain over us and beyond. The rock shattered into a pile of hazy splinters.

"It doesn't take long for these to cool down." He stopped and picked up a piece. "This one is probably twenty or twenty-five degrees. Watch." He tossed the "warm" rock onto the ice slab. It skittered around in a crazy pattern and shot off the side. He tossed another one, and it did the same.

"As you know, you are not quite *perfectly* insulated. These rocks are about the temperature of the soles of your boots. If you try to stand on a slab of hydrogen, the same thing will happen to you. Except that the rock is *already* dead.

"The reason for this behavior is that the rock makes a slick interface with the ice—a little puddle of liquid hydrogen—and rides a few molecules above the liquid on a cushion of hydrogen vapor. This makes the rock or *you* a frictionless bearing as far as the ice is concerned, and you *can't* stand up without any friction under your boots.

"After you have lived in your suit for a month or so you *should* be able to survive falling down, but right *now* you just don't know enough. Watch."

The captain flexed and hopped up onto the slab. His feet shot out from under him and he twisted around in midair, landing on hands and knees. He slipped off and stood on the ground.

"The idea is to keep your exhaust fins from making contact with the frozen gas. Compared to the ice they are as hot as a blast furnace, and contact with any weight behind it will result in an explosion."

After that demonstration, we walked around for another hour or so and returned to the billet. Once through the air-lock, we had to mill around for a while, letting the suits get up to something like room temperature. Somebody came up and touched helmets with me.

"William?" She had MCCOY stenciled above her face-plate.

"Hi, Sean. Anything special?"

"I just wondered if you had anyone to sleep with to-night."

That's right; I'd forgotten. There wasn't any sleeping roster here. Everybody chose his own partner. "Sure, I mean, uh, no . . . no, I haven't asked anybody. Sure, if you want to. . . ."

"Thanks, William. See you later." I watched her walk away and thought that if anybody could make a fighting suit look sexy, it'd be Sean. But even she couldn't.

Cortez decided we were warm enough and led us to the suit room, where we backed the things into place and hooked them up to the charging plates. (Each suit had a little chunk of plutonium that would power it for several years, but we were supposed to run on fuel cells as much as possible.) After a lot of shuffling around, everybody finally got plugged in and we were allowed to unsuit—ninety-seven naked chickens squirming out of bright green eggs. It was *cold*—the air, the floor and especially the suits—and we made a pretty disorderly exit toward the lockers.

I slipped on tunic, trousers and sandals and was still cold. I took my cup and joined the line for soya. Everybody was jumping up and down to keep warm.

"How c-cold, do you think, it is, M-Mandella?" That was McCoy.

"I don't, even want, to think, about it." I stopped jumping and rubbed myself as briskly as possible, while holding a cup in one hand. "At least as cold as Missouri was."

"Ung . . . wish they'd, get some, fucken, heat in, this place." It always affects the small women more than any-

body else. McCoy was the littlest one in the company, a
waspwaist doll barely five feet high.

"They've got the airco going. It can't be long now."

"I wish I, was a big, slab of, meat like, you."

I was glad she wasn't.

6

We had our first casualty on the third day, learning how to dig holes.

With such large amounts of energy stored in a soldier's weapons, it wouldn't be practical for him to hack out a hole in the frozen ground with the conventional pick and shovel. Still, you can launch grenades all day and get nothing but shallow depressions—so the usual method is to bore a hole in the ground with the hand laser, drop a timed charge in after it's cooled down and, ideally, fill the hole with stuff. Of course, there's not much loose rock on Charon, unless you've already blown a hole nearby.

The only difficult thing about the procedure is in getting away. To be safe, we were told, you've got to either be behind something really solid, or be at least a hundred meters away. You've got about three minutes after setting the charge, but you can't just sprint away. Not safely, not on Charon.

The accident happened when we were making a really deep hole, the kind you want for a large underground bunker. For this, we had to blow a hole, then climb down to the bottom of the crater and repeat the procedure again and again until the hole was deep enough. Inside the crater we used charges with a five-minute delay, but it hardly seemed enough time—you really had to go it slow, picking your way up the crater's edge.

Just about everybody had blown a double hole; everybody but me and three others. I guess we were the only ones paying really close attention when Bovanovitch got into trouble. All of us were a good two hundred meters away. With my image converter turned up to about forty power, I watched her disappear over the rim of the crater. After that, I could only listen in on her conversation with Cortez.

"I'm on the bottom, Sergeant." Normal radio procedure was suspended for maneuvers like this; nobody but the trainee and Cortez was allowed to broadcast.

"Okay, move to the center and clear out the rubble. Take your time. No rush until you pull the pin."

"Sure, Sergeant." We could hear small echoes of rocks clattering, sound conduction through her boots. She didn't say anything for several minutes.

"Found bottom." She sounded a little out of breath.

"Ice or rock?"

"Oh, it's rock, Sergeant. The greenish stuff."

"Use a low setting, then. One point two, dispersion four."

"God darn it, Sergeant, that'll take forever."

"Yeah, but that stuff's got hydrated crystals in it—heat it up too fast and you might make it fracture. And we'd just have to leave you there, girl. Dead and bloody."

"Okay, one point two dee four." The inside edge of the crater flickered red with reflected laser light.

"When you get about half a meter deep, squeeze it up to dee two."

"Roger." It took her exactly seventeen minutes, three of them at dispersion two. I could imagine how tired her shooting arm was.

"Now rest for a few minutes. When the bottom of the hole stops glowing, arm the charge and drop it in. Then *walk* out, understand? You'll have plenty of time."

"I understand, Sergeant. Walk out." She sounded nervous. Well, you don't often have to tiptoe away from a twenty-microton tachyon bomb. We listened to her breathing for a few minutes.

"Here goes." Faint slithering sound, the bomb sliding down.

"Slow and easy now. You've got five minutes."

"Y-yeah. Five." Her footsteps started out slow and regular. Then, after she started climbing the side, the sounds were less regular, maybe a little frantic. And with four minutes to go—

"Shit!" A loud scraping noise, then clatters and bumps. "Shit-shit."

"What's wrong, private?"

"Oh, shit." Silence. "Shit!"

"Private, you don't wanna get shot, you *tell me what's wrong!*"

"I . . . shit, I'm stuck. Fucken rockslide . . . shit. . . . DO SOMETHING! I can't move, shit I can't move I, I—"

"Shut up! How deep?"

"Can't move my, shit, my fucken legs. HELP ME—"

"Then goddammit use your arms—push! You can move a ton with each hand." Three minutes.

She stopped cussing and started to mumble, in Russian, I guess, a low monotone. She was panting, and you could hear rocks tumbling away.

"I'm free." Two minutes.

"Go as fast as you can." Cortez's voice was flat, emotionless.

At ninety seconds she appeared, crawling over the rim. "Run, girl. . . . You better run." She ran five or six steps and fell, skidded a few meters and got back up, running; fell again, got up again—

It looked as though she was going pretty fast, but she had only covered about thirty meters when Cortez said, "All right, Bovanovitch, get down on your stomach and lie still." Ten seconds, but she didn't hear or she wanted to get just a little more distance, and she kept running, careless leaping strides, and at the high point of one leap there was a flash and a rumble, and something big hit her below the neck, and her headless body spun off end over end through space, trailing a red-black spiral of flash-frozen blood that settled gracefully to the ground, a path of crystal powder that nobody disturbed while we gathered rocks to cover the juiceless thing at the end of it.

That night Cortez didn't lecture us, didn't even show up for night-chop. We were all very polite to each other and nobody was afraid to talk about it.

I sacked with Rogers—everybody sacked with a good friend—but all she wanted to do was cry, and she cried so long and so hard that she got me doing it, too.

"Fire team *A*—move out!" The twelve of us advanced in a ragged line toward the simulated bunker. It was about a kilometer away, across a carefully prepared obstacle course. We could move pretty fast, since all of the ice had been cleared from the field, but even with ten days' experience we weren't ready to do more than an easy jog.

I carried a grenade launcher loaded with tenth-microton practice grenades. Everybody had their laser-fingers set at a point oh eight dee one, not much more than a flashlight. This was a *simulated* attack—the bunker and its robot defender cost too much to use once and be thrown away.

"Team *B*, follow. Team leaders, take over."

We approached a clump of boulders at about the halfway mark, and Potter, my team leader, said, "Stop and cover." We clustered behind the rocks and waited for Team *B*.

Barely visible in their blackened suits, the dozen men and women whispered by us. As soon as they were clear, they jogged left, out of our line of sight.

"Fire!" Red circles of light danced a half-klick downrange, where the bunker was just visible. Five hundred meters was the limit for these practice grenades; but I might luck out, so I lined the launcher up on the image of the bunker, held it at a forty-five degree angle and popped off a salvo of three.

Return fire from the bunker started before my grenades even landed. Its automatic lasers were no more powerful than the ones we were using, but a direct hit would deactivate your image converter, leaving you blind. It was setting down a random field of fire, not even coming close to the boulders we were hiding behind.

Three magnesium-bright flashes blinked simultaneously about thirty meters short of the bunker. "Mandella! I thought you were supposed to be good with that thing."

"Damn it, Potter—it only throws half a klick. Once we get closer, I'll lay 'em right on top, every time."

"Sure you will." I didn't say anything. She wouldn't be team leader forever. Besides, she hadn't been such a bad girl before the power went to her head.

Since the grenadier is the assistant team leader, I was slaved into Potter's radio and could hear *B* team talk to her.

"Potter, this is Freeman. Losses?"

"Potter here—no, looks like they were concentrating on you."

"Yeah, we lost three. Right now we're in a depression about eighty, a hundred meters down from you. We can give cover whenever you're ready."

"Okay, start." Soft click: "*A* team, follow me." She slid out from behind the rock and turned on the faint pink beacon beneath her powerpack. I turned on mine and moved out to run alongside of her, and the rest of the team fanned out in a trailing wedge. Nobody fired while *A* team laid down a cover for us.

All I could hear was Potter's breathing and the soft *crunch-crunch* of my boots. Couldn't see much of anything, so I tongued the image converter up to a log two intensification. That made the image kind of blurry but adequately bright. Looked like the bunker had *B* team pretty well pinned down; they were getting quite a roasting. All of their return fire was laser. They must have lost their grenadier.

"Potter, this is Mandella. Shouldn't we take some of the heat off *B* team?"

"Soon as I can find us good enough cover. Is that all right with you? Private?" She'd been promoted to corporal for the duration of the exercise.

We angled to the right and lay down behind a slab of rock. Most of the others found cover nearby, but a few had to hug the ground.

"Freeman, this is Potter."

"Potter, this is Smithy. Freeman's out; Samuels is out. We only have five men left. Give us some cover so we can get—"

"Roger, Smithy." *Click.* "Open up, *A* team. The *B*'s are really hurtin'."

I peeked out over the edge of the rock. My rangefinder said that the bunker was about three hundred fifty meters away, still pretty far. I aimed a smidgeon high and popped three, then down a couple of degrees, three more. The first ones overshot by about twenty meters; then the second salvo flared up directly in front of the bunker. I tried to hold on that angle and popped fifteen, the rest of the magazine, in the same direction.

I should have ducked down behind the rock to reload, but I wanted to see where the fifteen would land, so I kept my eyes on the bunker while I reached back to unclip another magazine—

When the laser hit my image converter, there was a red glare so intense it seemed to go right through my eyes and bounce off the back of my skull. It must have been only a few milliseconds before the converter overloaded and went blind, but the bright green afterimage hurt my eyes for several minutes.

Since I was officially "dead," my radio automatically cut off, and I had to remain where I was until the mock battle was over. With no sensory input besides the feel of my own skin (and it ached where the image converter had shone on it) and the ringing in my ears, it seemed like an awfully long time. Finally, a helmet clanked against mine.

"You okay, Mandella?" Potter's voice.

"Sorry, I died of boredom twenty minutes ago."

"Stand up and take my hand." I did so and we shuffled back to the billet. It must have taken over an hour. She didn't say anything more, all the way back—it's a pretty awkward way to communicate—but after we'd cycled through the airlock and warmed up, she helped me undo my suit. I got ready for a mild tongue-lashing, but when the suit popped open, before I could even get my eyes adjusted to the light, she grabbed me around the neck and planted a wet kiss on my mouth.

"Nice shooting, Mandella."

"Huh?"

"Didn't you see? Of course not. . . . The last salvo before you got hit—four direct hits. The bunker decided it was knocked out, and all we had to do was walk the rest of the way.''

"Great." I scratched my face under the eyes, and some dry skin flaked off. She giggled.

"You should see yourself. You look like—"

"All personnel, report to the assembly area." That was the captain's voice. Bad news, usually.

She handed me a tunic and sandals. "Let's go." The assembly area-chop hall was just down the corridor. There was a row of roll-call buttons at the door; I pressed the one beside my name. Four of the names were covered with black tape. That was good, only four. We hadn't lost anybody during today's maneuvers.

The captain was sitting on the raised dais, which at least meant we didn't have to go through the tench-hut bullshit. The place filled up in less than a minute; a soft chime indicated the roll was complete.

Captain Stott didn't stand up. "You did *fairly* well today. Nobody killed, and I expected some to be. In that respect you exceeded my expectations but in *every* other respect you did a poor job.

"I am glad you're taking good care of yourselves, because each of you represents an investment of over a million dollars and one-fourth of a human life.

"But in this simulated battle against a *very* stupid robot enemy, thirty-seven of you managed to walk into laser fire and be killed in a *sim*ulated way, and since dead people require no food *you* will require no food, for the next three days. Each person who was a casualty in this battle will be allowed only two liters of water and a vitamin ration each day."

We knew enough not to groan or anything, but there were some pretty disgusted looks, especially on the faces that had singed eyebrows and a pink rectangle of sunburn framing their eyes.

"Mandella."

"Sir?"

"You are far and away the worst-burned casualty. Was your image converter set on normal?"

Oh, shit. "No, sir. Log two."

"I see. Who was your team leader for the exercises?"

"Acting Corporal Potter, sir."

"Private Potter, did you order him to use image intensification?"

"Sir, I . . . I don't remember."

"You don't. Well, as a memory exercise you may join the dead people. Is that satisfactory?"

"Yes, sir."

"Good. Dead people get one last meal tonight and go on no rations starting tomorrow. Are there any questions?" He must have been kidding. "All right. Dismissed."

I selected the meal that looked as if it had the most calories and took my tray over to sit by Potter.

"That was a quixotic damn thing to do. But thanks."

"Nothing. I've been wanting to lose a few pounds anyway." I couldn't see where she was carrying any extra.

"I know a good exercise," I said. She smiled without looking up from her tray. "Have anybody for tonight?"

"Kind of thought I'd ask Jeff. . . ."

"Better hurry, then. He's lusting after Maejima." Well, that was mostly true. Everybody did.

"I don't know. Maybe we ought to save our strength. That third day . . ."

"Come on." I scratched the back of her hand lightly with a fingernail. "We haven't sacked since Missouri. Maybe I've learned something new."

"Maybe you have." She tilted her head up at me in a sly way. "Okay."

Actually, she was the one with the new trick. The French corkscrew, she called it. She wouldn't tell me who taught it to her though. I'd like to shake his hand. Once I got my strength back.

8

The two weeks' training around Miami Base eventually cost us eleven lives. Twelve, if you count Dahlquist. I guess having to spend the rest of your life on Charon with a hand and both legs missing is close enough to dying.

Foster was crushed in a landslide and Freeland had a suit malfunction that froze him solid before we could carry him inside. Most of the other deaders were people I didn't know all that well. But they all hurt. And they seemed to make us more scared rather than more cautious.

Now darkside. A flyer brought us over in groups of twenty and set us down beside a pile of building materials thoughtfully immersed in a pool of helium II.

We used grapples to haul the stuff out of the pool. It's not safe to go wading, since the stuff crawls all over you and it's hard to tell what's underneath; you could walk out onto a slab of hydrogen and be out of luck.

I'd suggested that we try to boil away the pool with our lasers, but ten minutes of concentrated fire didn't drop the helium level appreciably. It didn't boil, either; helium II is a "superfluid," so what evaporation there was had to take place evenly, all over the surface. No hot spots, so no bubbling.

We weren't supposed to use lights, to "avoid detection." There was plenty of starlight with your image converter cranked up to log three or four, but each stage of amplification meant some loss of detail. By log four the landscape looked like a crude monochrome painting, and you couldn't read the names on people's helmets unless they were right in front of you.

The landscape wasn't all that interesting, anyhow. There were half a dozen medium-sized meteor craters (all with exactly the same level of helium II in them) and the suggestion of some puny mountains just over the horizon. The

uneven ground was the consistency of frozen spiderwebs;
every time you put your foot down, you'd sink half an inch
with a squeaking crunch. It could get on your nerves.

It took most of a day to pull all the stuff out of the pool.
We took shifts napping, which you could do either standing
up, sitting or lying on your stomach. I didn't do well in
any of those positions, so I was anxious to get the bunker
built and pressurized.

We couldn't build the thing underground—it'd just fill
up with helium II—so the first thing to do was to build an
insulating platform, a permaplast-vacuum sandwich three
layers thick.

I was an acting corporal, with a crew of ten people. We
were carrying the permaplast layers to the building site—
two people can carry one easily—when one of "my" men
slipped and fell on his back.

"Damn it, Singer, watch your step." We'd had a couple
of deaders that way.

"Sorry, Corporal. I'm bushed. Just got my feet tangled
up."

"Yeah, just watch it." He got back up all right, and he
and his partner placed the sheet and went back to get another.

I kept my eye on Singer. In a few minutes he was practically staggering, not easy to do in that suit of cybernetic
armor.

"Singer! After you set the plank, I want to see you."

"OK." He labored through the task and mooched over.

"Let me check your readout." I opened the door on his
chest to expose the medical monitor. His temperature was
two degrees high; blood pressure and heart rate both ele-
vated. Not up to the red line, though.

"You sick or something?"

"Hell, Mandella, I feel OK, just tired. Since I fell I been
a little dizzy."

I chinned the medic's combination. "Doc, this is Mandella. You wanna come over here for a minute?"

"Sure, where are you?" I waved and he walked over
from poolside.

"What's the problem?" I showed him Singer's readout.

He knew what all the other little dials and things meant, so it took him a while. "As far as I can tell, Mandella . . . he's just hot."

"Hell, I coulda told you that," said Singer.

"Maybe you better have the armorer take a look at his suit." We had two people who'd taken a crash course in suit maintenance; they were our "armorers."

I chinned Sanchez and asked him to come over with his tool kit.

"Be a couple of minutes, Corporal. Carryin' a plank."

"Well, put it down and get on over here." I was getting an uneasy feeling. Waiting for him, the medic and I looked over Singer's suit.

"Uh-oh," Doc Jones said. "Look at this." I went around to the back and looked where he was pointing. Two of the fins on the heat exchanger were bent out of shape.

"What's wrong?" Singer asked.

"You fell on your heat exchanger, right?"

"Sure, Corporal—that's it. It must not be working right."

"I don't think it's working at *all*," said Doc.

Sanchez came over with his diagnostic kit and we told him what had happened. He looked at the heat exchanger, then plugged a couple of jacks into it and got a digital readout from a little monitor in his kit. I didn't know what it was measuring, but it came out zero to eight decimal places.

Heard a soft click, Sanchez chinning my private frequency. "Corporal, this guy's a deader."

"What? Can't you fix the goddamn thing?"

"Maybe . . . maybe I could, if I could take it apart. But there's no way—"

"Hey! Sanchez?" Singer was talking on the general freak. "Find out what's wrong?" He was panting.

Click. "Keep your pants on, man, we're working on it." *Click*. "He won't last long enough for us to get the bunker pressurized. And I can't work on the heat exchanger from outside of the suit."

"You've got a spare suit, haven't you?"

"Two of 'em, the fit-anybody kind. But there's no place ... say ..."

"Right. Go get one of the suits warmed up." I chinned the general freak. "Listen, Singer, we've gotta get you out of that thing. Sanchez has a spare suit, but to make the switch, we're gonna have to build a house around you. Understand?"

"Huh-uh."

"Look, we'll make a box with you inside, and hook it up to the life-support unit. That way you can breathe while you make the switch."

"Soun's pretty compis ... compil ... cated t'me."

"Look, just come along—"

"I'll be all right, man, jus' lemme res'. . . ."

I grabbed his arm and led him to the building site. He was really weaving. Doc took his other arm, and between us, we kept him from falling over.

"Corporal Ho, this is Corporal Mandella." Ho was in charge of the life-support unit.

"Go away, Mandella, I'm, busy."

"You're going to be busier." I outlined the problem to her. While her group hurried to adapt the LSU—for this purpose, it need only be an air hose and heater—I got my crew to bring around six slabs of permaplast, so we could build a big box around Singer and the extra suit. It would look like a huge coffin, a meter square and six meters long.

We set the suit down on the slab that would be the floor of the coffin. "OK, Singer, let's go."

No answer.

"Singer, let's go."

No answer.

"Singer!" He was just standing there. Doc Jones checked his readout.

"He's out, man, unconscious."

My mind raced. There might just be room for another person in the box. "Give me a hand here." I took Singer's shoulders and Doc took his feet, and we carefully laid him out at the feet of the empty suit.

Then I lay down myself, above the suit. "OK, close 'er up."

"Look, Mandella, if anybody goes in there, it oughta be me."

"Fuck you, Doc. *My* job. My man." That sounded all wrong. William Mandella, boy hero.

They stood a slab up on edge—it had two openings for the LSU input and exhaust—and proceeded to weld it to the bottom plank with a narrow laser beam. On Earth, we'd just use glue, but here the only fluid was helium, which has lots of interesting properties, but is definitely not sticky.

After about ten minutes we were completely walled up. I could feel the LSU humming. I switched on my suit light—the first time since we landed on darkside—and the glare made purple blotches dance in front of my eyes.

"Mandella, this is Ho. Stay in your suit at least two or three minutes. We're putting hot air in, but it's coming back just this side of liquid." I watched the purple fade for a while.

"OK, it's still cold, but you can make it." I popped my suit. It wouldn't open all the way, but I didn't have too much trouble getting out. The suit was still cold enough to take some skin off my fingers and butt as I wiggled out.

I had to crawl feet-first down the coffin to get to Singer. It got darker fast, moving away from my light. When I popped his suit a rush of hot stink hit me in the face. In the dim light his skin was dark red and splotchy. His breathing was very shallow and I could see his heart palpitating.

First I unhooked the relief tubes—an unpleasant business—then the biosensors; and then I had the problem of getting his arms out of their sleeves.

It's pretty easy to do for yourself. You twist this way and turn that way and the arm pops out. Doing it from the outside is a different matter: I had to twist his arm and then reach under and move the suit's arm to match—it takes muscle to move a suit around from the outside.

Once I had one arm out it was pretty easy; I just crawled forward, putting my feet on the suit's shoulders, and pulled on his free arm. He slid out of the suit like an oyster slipping out of its shell.

I popped the spare suit and after a lot of pulling and

pushing, managed to get his legs in. Hooked up the biosensors and the front relief tube. He'd have to do the other
one himself; it's too complicated. For the nth time I was
glad not to have been born female; they have to have two
of those damned plumber's friends, instead of just one and
a simple hose.

I left his arms out of the sleeves. The suit would be
useless for any kind of work, anyhow; waldos have to be
tailored to the individual.

His eyelids fluttered. "Man . . . della. Where . . . the
fuck . . ."

I explained, slowly, and he seemed to get most of it.
"Now I'm gonna close you up and go get into my suit. I'll
have the crew cut the end off this thing and I'll haul you
out. Got it?"

He nodded. Strange to see that—when you nod or shrug
inside a suit, it doesn't communicate anything.

I crawled into my suit, hooked up the attachments and
chinned the general freak. "Doc, I think he's gonna be OK.
Get us out of here now."

"Will do." Ho's voice. The LSU hum was replaced by
a chatter, then a throb. Evacuating the box to prevent an
explosion.

One corner of the seam grew red, then white, and a bright
crimson beam lanced through, not a foot away from my
head. I scrunched back as far as I could. The beam slid up
the seam and around three corners, back to where it started.
The end of the box fell away slowly, trailing filaments of
melted 'plast.

"Wait for the stuff to harden, Mandella."

"Sanchez, I'm not that stupid."

"Here you go." Somebody tossed a line to me. That
would be smarter than dragging him out by myself. I
threaded a long bight under his arms and tied it behind his
neck. Then I scrambled out to help them pull, which was
silly—they had a dozen people already lined up to haul.

Singer got out all right and was actually sitting up while
Doc Jones checked his readout. People were asking me

about it and congratulating me, when suddenly Ho said "Look!" and pointed toward the horizon.

It was a black ship, coming in fast. I just had time to think it wasn't fair, they weren't supposed to attack until the last few days, and then the ship was right on top of us.

9

We all flopped to the ground instinctively, but the ship didn't attack. It blasted braking rockets and dropped to land on skids. Then it skied around to come to a rest beside the building site.

Everybody had it figured out and was standing around sheepishly when the two suited figures stepped out of the ship.

A familiar voice crackled over the general freak. "Every *one* of you saw us coming in and not *one* of you responded with laser fire. It wouldn't have done any good but it would have indicated a certain amount of fighting spirit. You have a week or less before the real thing and since the sergeant and *I* will be here *I* will insist that you show a little more will to live. Acting Sergeant Potter."

"Here, sir."

"Get me a detail of twelve people to unload cargo. We brought a hundred small robot drones for *target* practice so that you might have at least a fighting chance when a live target comes over.

"Move *now*. We only have thirty minutes before the ship returns to Miami."

I checked, and it was actually more like forty minutes.

Having the captain and sergeant there didn't really make much difference. We were still on our own; they were just observing.

Once we got the floor down, it only took one day to complete the bunker. It was a gray oblong, featureless except for the airlock blister and four windows. On top was a swivel-mounted gigawatt laser. The operator—you couldn't call him a "gunner"—sat in a chair holding dead-man switches in both hands. The laser wouldn't fire as long as he was holding one of those switches. If he let go, it would automatically aim for any moving aerial object and

fire at will. Primary detection and aiming was by means of
a kilometer-high antenna mounted beside the bunker.

It was the only arrangement that could really be expected
to work, with the horizon so close and human reflexes so
slow. You couldn't have the thing fully automatic, because
in theory, friendly ships might also approach.

The aiming computer could choose among up to twelve
targets appearing simultaneously (firing at the largest ones
first). And it would get all twelve in the space of half a
second.

The installation was partly protected from enemy fire by
an efficient ablative layer that covered everything except
the human operator. But then, they *were* dead-man
switches. One man above guarding eighty inside. The
army's good at that kind of arithmetic.

Once the bunker was finished, half of us stayed inside at
all times—feeling very much like targets—taking turns operating the laser, while the other half went on maneuvers.

About four klicks from the base was a large "lake" of
frozen hydrogen; one of our most important maneuvers was
to learn how to get around on the treacherous stuff.

It wasn't too difficult. You couldn't stand up on it, so
you had to belly down and sled.

If you had somebody to push you from the edge, getting
started was no problem. Otherwise, you had to scrabble
with your hands and feet, pushing down as hard as was
practical, until you started moving, in a series of little
jumps. Once started, you'd keep going until you ran out of
ice. You could steer a little bit by digging in, hand and
foot, on the appropriate side, but you couldn't slow to a
stop that way. So it was a good idea not to go too fast and
wind up positioned in such a way that your helmet didn't
absorb the shock of stopping.

We went through all the things we'd done on the Miami
side: weapons practice, demolition, attack patterns. We also
launched drones at irregular intervals, toward the bunker.
Thus, ten or fifteen times a day, the operators got to dem-
onstrate their skill in letting go of the handles as soon as
the proximity light went on.

I had four hours of that, like everybody else. I was nervous until the first "attack," when I saw how little there was to it. The light went on, I let go, the gun aimed, and when the drone peeped over the horizon—*zzt!* Nice touch of color, the molten metal spraying through space. Otherwise not too exciting.

So none of us were worried about the upcoming "graduation exercise," thinking it would be just more of the same.

Miami Base attacked on the thirteenth day with two simultaneous missiles streaking over opposite sides of the horizon at some forty kilometers per second. The laser vaporized the first one with no trouble, but the second got within eight klicks of the bunker before it was hit.

We were coming back from maneuvers, about a klick away from the bunker. I wouldn't have seen it happen if I hadn't been looking directly at the bunker the moment of the attack.

The second missile sent a shower of molten debris straight toward the bunker. Eleven pieces hit, and, as we later reconstructed it, this is what happened:

The first casualty was Maejima, so well-loved Maejima, inside the bunker, who was hit in the back and the head and died instantly. With the drop in pressure, the LSU went into high gear. Friedman was standing in front of the main airco outlet and was blown into the opposite wall hard enough to knock him unconscious; he died of decompression before the others could get him to his suit.

Everybody else managed to stagger through the gale and get into their suits, but Garcia's suit had been holed and didn't do him any good.

By the time we got there, they had turned off the LSU and were welding up the holes in the wall. One man was trying to scrape up the unrecognizable mess that had been Maejima. I could hear him sobbing and retching. They had already taken Garcia and Friedman outside for burial. The captain took over the repair detail from Potter. Sergeant Cortez led the sobbing man over to a corner and came back to work on cleaning up Maejima's remains, alone. He didn't order anybody to help and nobody volunteered.

10

As a graduation exercise, we were unceremoniously stuffed into a ship—*Earth's Hope*, the same one we rode to Charon—and bundled off to Stargate at a little more than one gee.

The trip seemed endless, about six months subjective time, and boring, but not as hard on the carcass as going to Charon had been. Captain Stott made us review our training orally, day by day, and we did exercises every day until we were worn to a collective frazzle.

Stargate 1 was like Charon's darkside, only more so. The base on Stargate 1 was smaller than Miami Base—only a little bigger than the one we constructed on darkside—and we were due to lay over a week to help expand the facilities. The crew there was very glad to see us, especially the two females, who looked a little worn around the edges.

We all crowded into the small dining hall, where Submajor Williamson, the man in charge of Stargate 1, gave us some disconcerting news:

"Everybody get comfortable. Get off the tables, though, there's plenty of floor.

"I have some idea of what you just went through, training on Charon. I won't say it's all been wasted. But where you're headed, things will be quite different. Warmer."

He paused to let that soak in.

"Aleph Aurigae, the first collapsar ever detected, revolves around the normal star Epsilon Aurigae in a twenty-seven year orbit. The enemy has a base of operations, not on a regular portal planet of Aleph, but on a planet in orbit around Epsilon. We don't know much about the planet, just that it goes around Epsilon once every 745 days, is about three-fourths the size of Earth, and has an albedo of 0.8, meaning it's probably covered with clouds. We can't say precisely how hot it will be, but judging from its distance from Epsilon, it's probably rather hotter than Earth. Of course, we don't know whether you'll be working . . . fighting on lightside or darkside, equator or poles. It's highly unlikely that the atmosphere will be breathable—at any rate, you'll stay inside your suits.

"Now you know exactly as much about where you're going as I do. Questions?"

"Sir," Stein drawled, "now we know where we're goin' . . . anybody know what we're goin' to do when we get there?"

Williamson shrugged. "That's up to your captain—and your sergeant, and the captain of *Earth's Hope*, and *Hope*'s logistic computer. We just don't have enough data yet to project a course of action for you. It may be a long and bloody battle; it may be just a case of walking in to pick up the pieces. Conceivably, the Taurans might want to make a peace offer,"—Cortez snorted—"in which case you would simply be part of our muscle, our bargaining power." He looked at Cortez mildly. "No one can say for sure."

The orgy that night was amusing, but it was like trying to sleep in the middle of a raucous beach party. The only area big enough to sleep all of us was the dining hall; they draped a few bedsheets here and there for privacy, then unleashed Stargate's eighteen sex-starved men on our women, compliant and promiscuous by military custom (and law), but desiring nothing so much as sleep on solid ground.

The eighteen men acted as if they were compelled to try as many permutations as possible, and their performance was impressive (in a strictly quantitative sense, that is). Those of us who were keeping count led a cheering section for some of the more gifted members. I think that's the right word.

The next morning—and every other morning we were on Stargate 1—we staggered out of bed and into our suits, to go outside and work on the "new wing." Eventually, Stargate would be tactical and logistic headquarters for the war, with thousands of permanent personnel, guarded by half-a-dozen heavy cruisers in *Hope*'s class. When we started, it was two shacks and twenty people; when we left, it was four shacks and twenty people. The work was hardly work at all, compared to darkside, since we had plenty of light and got sixteen hours inside for every eight hours' work. And no drone attack for a final exam.

When we shuttled back up to the *Hope*, nobody was too happy about leaving (though some of the more popular females declared it'd be good to get some rest). Stargate was the last easy, safe assignment we'd have before taking up arms against the Taurans. And as Williamson had pointed out the first day, there was no way of predicting what *that* would be like.

Most of us didn't feel too enthusiastic about making a collapsar jump, either. We'd been assured that we wouldn't even feel it happen, just free fall all the way.

I wasn't convinced. As a physics student, I'd had the usual courses in general relativity and theories of gravitation. We only had a little direct data at that time—Stargate was discovered when I was in grade school—but the mathematical model seemed clear enough.

The collapsar Stargate was a perfect sphere about three kilometers in radius. It was suspended forever in a state of gravitational collapse that should have meant its surface was dropping toward its center at nearly the speed of light. Relativity propped it up, at least gave it the illusion of being there . . . the way all reality becomes illusory and observer-oriented when you study general relativity. Or Buddhism. Or get drafted.

At any rate, there would be a theoretical point in space-time when one end of our ship was just above the surface of the collapsar, and the other end was a kilometer away (in our frame of reference). In any sane universe, this would set up tidal stresses and tear the ship apart, and we would be just another million kilograms of degenerate matter on the theoretical surface, rushing headlong to nowhere for the rest of eternity or dropping to the center in the next trillionth of a second. You pays your money and you takes your frame of reference.

But they were right. We blasted away from Stargate 1,

made a few course corrections and then just dropped, for about an hour.

Then a bell rang and we sank into our cushions under a steady two gravities of deceleration. We were in enemy territory.

11

We'd been decelerating at two gravities for almost nine days when the battle began. Lying on our couches being miserable, all we felt were two soft bumps, missiles being released. Some eight hours later, the squawkbox crackled: "Attention, all crew. This is the captain." Quinsana, the pilot, was only a lieutenant, but was allowed to call himself captain aboard the vessel, where he outranked all of us, even Captain Stott. "You grunts in the cargo hold can listen, too.

"We just engaged the enemy with two fifty-gigaton tachyon missiles and have destroyed both the enemy vessel and another object which it had launched approximately three microseconds before.

"The enemy has been trying to overtake us for the past 179 hours, ship time. At the time of the engagement, the enemy was moving at a little over half the speed of light, relative to Aleph, and was only about thirty AU's from *Earth's Hope*. It was moving at .47c relative to us, and thus we would have been coincident in space-time"— rammed!—"in a little more than nine hours. The missiles were launched at 0719 ship's time, and destroyed the enemy at 1540, both tachyon bombs detonating within a thousand klicks of the enemy objects."

The two missiles were a type whose propulsion system was itself only a barely-controlled tachyon bomb. They accelerated at a constant rate of 100 gees, and were traveling at a relativistic speed by the time the nearby mass of the enemy ship detonated them.

"We expect no further interference from enemy vessels. Our velocity with respect to Aleph will be zero in another five hours; we will then begin the journey back. The return will take twenty-seven days." General moans and dejected cussing. Everybody knew all that already, of course; but we didn't care to be reminded of it.

So after another month of logy calisthenics and drill, at a constant two gravities, we got our first look at the planet we were going to attack. Invaders from outer space, yes sir.

It was a blinding white crescent waiting for us two AU's out from Epsilon. The captain had pinned down the location of the enemy base from fifty AU's out, and we had jockeyed in on a wide arc, keeping the bulk of the planet between them and us. That didn't mean we were sneaking up on them—quite the contrary; they launched three abortive attacks—but it put us in a stronger defensive position. Until we had to go to the surface, that is. Then only the ship and its Star Fleet crew would be reasonably safe.

Since the planet rotated rather slowly—once every ten and one-half days—a "stationary" orbit for the ship had to be 150,000 klicks out. This made the people in the ship feel quite secure, with 6,000 miles of rock and 90,000 miles of space between them and the enemy. But it meant a whole second's time lag in communication between us on the ground and the ship's battle computer. A person could get awful dead while that neutrino pulse crawled up and back.

Our vague orders were to attack the base and gain control, while damaging a minimum of enemy equipment. We were to take at least one enemy alive. We were under no circumstances to allow ourselves to be taken alive, however. And the decision wasn't up to us; one special pulse from the battle computer, and that speck of plutonium in your power plant would fiss with all of .01% efficiency, and you'd be nothing but a rapidly expanding, very hot plasma.

They strapped us into six scoutships—one platoon of twelve people in each—and we blasted away from *Earth's Hope* at eight gees. Each scoutship was supposed to follow its own carefully random path to our rendezvous point, 108 klicks from the base. Fourteen drone ships were launched at the same time, to confound the enemy's anti-spacecraft system.

The landing went off almost perfectly. One ship suffered

minor damage, a near miss boiling away some of the ablative material on one side of the hull, but it'd still be able to make it and return, keeping its speed down while in the atmosphere.

We zigged and zagged and wound up first ship at the rendezvous point. There was only one trouble. It was under four kilometers of water.

I could almost hear that machine, 90,000 miles away, grinding its mental gears, adding this new bit of data. We proceeded just as if we were landing on solid ground: braking rockets, falling, skids out, hit the water, skip, hit the water, skip, hit the water, sink.

It would have made sense to go ahead and land on the bottom—we were streamlined, after all, and water just another fluid—but the hull wasn't strong enough to hold up a four kilometer column of water. Sergeant Cortez was in the scoutship with us.

"Sarge, tell that computer to *do* something! We're gonna get—"

"Oh, shut up, Mandella. Trust in th' lord." "Lord" was definitely lower-case when Cortez said it.

There was a loud bubbly sigh, then another, and a slight increase in pressure on my back that meant the ship was rising. "Flotation bags?" Cortez didn't deign to answer, or didn't know.

That was it. We rose to within ten or fifteen meters of the surface and stopped, suspended there. Through the port I could see the surface above, shimmering like a mirror of hammered silver. I wondered what it would be like to be a fish and have a definite roof over your world.

I watched another ship splash in. It made a great cloud of bubbles and turbulence, then fell—slightly tail-first—for a short distance before large bags popped out under each delta wing. Then it bobbed up to about our level and stayed.

"This is Captain Stott. Now listen carefully. There is a beach some twenty-eight klicks from your present position, in the direction of the enemy. You will be proceeding to this beach by scoutship and from there will mount your assault on the Tauran position." That was *some* improvement; we'd only have to walk eighty klicks.

We deflated the bags, blasted to the surface and flew in a slow, spread-out formation to the beach. It took several minutes. As the ship scraped to a halt, I could hear pumps humming, making the cabin pressure equal to the air pressure outside. Before it had quite stopped moving, the escape slot beside my couch slid open. I rolled out onto the wing of the craft and jumped to the ground. Ten seconds to find cover—I sprinted across loose gravel to the "treeline," a twisty bramble of tall sparse bluish-green shrubs. I dove into the briar patch and turned to watch the ships leave. The drones that were left rose slowly to about a hundred meters, then took off in all directions with a bone-jarring roar. The real scoutships slid slowly back into the water. Maybe that was a good idea.

It wasn't a terribly attractive world but certainly would be easier to get around in than the cryogenic nightmare we were trained for. The sky was a uniform dull silver brightness that merged with the mist over the ocean so completely it was impossible to tell where water ended and air began. Small wavelets licked at the black gravel shore, much too slow and graceful in the three-quarters Earth-normal gravity. Even from fifty meters away, the rattle of billions of pebbles rolling with the tide was loud in my ears.

The air temperature was 79 degrees Centigrade, not quite hot enough for the sea to boil, even though the air pressure was low compared to Earth's. Wisps of steam drifted quickly upward from the line where water met land. I wondered how a lone man would survive exposed here without a suit. Would the heat or the low oxygen (partial pressure one-eighth Earth normal) kill him first? Or was there some deadly microorganism that would beat them both . . . ?

"This is Cortez. Everybody come over and assemble on me." He was standing on the beach a little to the left of me, waving his hand in a circle over his head. I walked toward him through the shrubs. They were brittle, unsubstantial, seemed paradoxically dried-out in the steamy air. They wouldn't offer much in the way of cover.

"We'll be advancing on a heading .05 radians east of north. I want Platoon One to take point. Two and Three follow about twenty meters behind, to the left and right.

Seven, command platoon, is in the middle, twenty meters behind Two and Three. Five and Six, bring up the rear, in a semicircular closed flank. Everybody straight?'' Sure, we could do that "arrowhead" maneuver in our sleep. "OK, let's move out.''

I was in Platoon Seven, the "command group.'' Captain Stott put me there not because I was expected to give any commands, but because of my training in physics.

The command group was supposedly the safest place, buffered by six platoons: people were assigned to it because there was some tactical reason for them to survive at least a little longer than the rest. Cortez was there to give orders. Chavez was there to correct suit malfunctions. The senior medic, Doc Wilson (the only medic who actually had an M.D.), was there, and so was Theodopolis, the radio engineer, our link with the captain, who had elected to stay in orbit.

The rest of us were assigned to the command group by dint of special training or aptitude that wouldn't normally be considered of a "tactical" nature. Facing a totally unknown enemy, there was no way of telling what might prove important. Thus I was there because I was the closest the company had to a physicist. Rogers was biology. Tate was chemistry. Ho could crank out a perfect score on the Rhine extrasensory perception test, every time. Bohrs was a polyglot, able to speak twenty-one languages fluently, idiomatically. Petrov's talent was that he had tested out to have not one molecule of xenophobia in his psyche. Keating was a skilled acrobat. Debby Hollister—"Lucky" Hollister—showed a remarkable aptitude for making money, and also had a consistently high Rhine potential.

12

When we first set out, we were using the "jungle" camouflage combination on our suits. But what passed for jungle in these anemic tropics was too sparse; we looked like a band of conspicuous harlequins trooping through the woods. Cortez had us switch to black, but that was just as bad, as the light of Epsilon came evenly from all parts of the sky, and there were no shadows except ours. We finally settled on the dun-colored desert camouflage.

The nature of the countryside changed slowly as we walked north, away from the sea. The thorned stalks—I guess you could call them trees—came in fewer numbers but were bigger around and less brittle; at the base of each was a tangled mass of vine with the same bluegreen color, which spread out in a flattened cone some ten meters in diameter. There was a delicate green flower the size of a man's head near the top of each tree.

Grass began to grow some five klicks from the sea. It seemed to respect the trees' "property rights," leaving a strip of bare earth around each cone of vine. At the edge of such a clearing, it would grow as timid bluegreen stubble, then, moving away from the tree, would get thicker and taller until it reached shoulderhigh in some places, where the separation between two trees was unusually large. The grass was a lighter, greener shade than the trees and vines. We changed the color of our suits to the bright green we had used for maximum visibility on Charon. Keeping to the thickest part of the grass, we were fairly inconspicuous.

We covered over twenty klicks each day, buoyant after months under two gees. Until the second day, the only form of animal life we saw was a kind of black worm, fingersized, with hundreds of cilium legs like the bristles of a brush. Rogers said that there obviously had to be some larger creature around, or there would be no reason for the trees to have thorns. So we were doubly on guard, expecting trouble both from the Taurans and the unidentified "large creature."

Potter's second platoon was on point; the general freak was reserved for her, since her platoon would likely be the first to spot any trouble.

"Sarge, this is Potter," we all heard. "Movement ahead."

"Get down, then!"

"We are. Don't think they see us."

"First platoon, go up to the right of point. Keep down. Fourth, get up to the left. Tell me when you get in position. Sixth platoon, stay back and guard the rear. Fifth and third, close with the command group."

Two dozen people whispered out of the grass to join us. Cortez must have heard from the fourth platoon.

"Good. How about you, first? . . . OK, fine. How many are there?"

"Eight we can see." Potter's voice.

"Good. When I give the word, open fire. Shoot to kill."

"Sarge, . . . they're just animals."

"Potter—if you've known all this time what a Tauran looks like, you should've told us. Shoot to kill."

"But we need . . ."

"We need a prisoner, but we don't need to escort him forty klicks to his home base and keep an eye on him while we fight. Clear?"

"Yes. Sergeant."

"OK. Seventh, all you brains and weirds, we're going up and watch. Fifth and third, come along to guard."

We crawled through the meter-high grass to where the second platoon had stretched out in a firing line.

"I don't see anything," Cortez said.

"Ahead and just to the left. Dark green."

They were only a shade darker than the grass. But after you saw the first one, you could see them all, moving slowly around some thirty meters ahead.

"Fire!" Cortez fired first; then twelve streaks of crimson leaped out and the grass wilted black, disappeared, and the creatures convulsed and died trying to scatter.

"Hold fire, hold it!" Cortez stood up. "We want to have something left—second platoon, follow me." He strode out toward the smoldering corpses, laser-finger pointed out front, obscene divining rod pulling him toward the carnage .... I felt my gorge rising and knew that all the lurid training tapes, all the horrible deaths in training accidents, hadn't prepared me for this sudden reality ... that I had a magic wand that I could point at a life and make it a smoking piece of half-raw meat; I wasn't a soldier nor ever wanted to be one nor ever would want—

"OK, seventh, come on up." While we were walking toward them, one of the creatures moved, a tiny shudder, and Cortez flicked the beam of his laser over it with an almost negligent gesture. It made a hand-deep gash across the creature's middle. It died, like the others, without emitting a sound.

They were not quite as tall as humans, but wider in girth. They were covered with dark green, almost black, fur— white curls where the laser had singed. They appeared to have three legs and an arm. The only ornament to their shaggy heads was a mouth, wet black orifice filled with flat black teeth. They were thoroughly repulsive, but their worst feature was not a difference from human beings, but a similarity. . . . Whenever the laser had opened a body cavity, milk-white glistening veined globes and coils of organs spilled out, and their blood was dark clotting red.

"Rogers, take a look. Taurans or not?"

Rogers knelt by one of the disemboweled creatures and opened a flat plastic box, filled with glittering dissecting tools. She selected a scalpel. "One way we might be able to find out." Doc Wilson watched over her shoulder as she methodically slit the membrane covering several organs.

"Here." She held up a blackish fibrous mass between two fingers, a parody of daintiness through all that armor.

"So?"

"It's grass, Sergeant. If the Taurans eat the grass and breathe the air, they certainly found a planet remarkably like their home." She tossed it away. "They're animals, Sergeant, just fucken animals."

"I don't know," Doc Wilson said. "Just because they walk around on all fours, threes maybe, and eat grass . . ."

"Well, let's check out the brain." She found one that had been hit in the head and scraped the superficial black char from the wound. "Look at that."

It was almost solid bone. She tugged and ruffled the hair all over the head of another one. "What the hell does it use for sensory organs? No eyes, or ears, or . . ." She stood up.

"Nothing in that fucken head but a mouth and ten centimeters of skull. To protect nothing, not a fucken thing."

"If I could shrug, I'd shrug," the doctor said. "It doesn't prove anything—a brain doesn't have to look like a mushy walnut and it doesn't have to be in the head. Maybe that skull isn't bone, maybe *that's* the brain, some crystal lattice . . ."

"Yeah, but the fucken stomach's in the right place, and if those aren't intestines I'll eat—"

"Look," Cortez said, "this is real interesting, but all we need to know is whether that thing's dangerous, then we've gotta move on; we don't have all—"

"They aren't dangerous," Rogers began. "They don't—"

"Medic! DOC!" Somebody back at the firing line was waving his arms. Doc sprinted back to him, the rest of us following.

"What's wrong?" He had reached back and unclipped his medical kit on the run.

"It's Ho. She's out."

Doc swung open the door on Ho's biomedical monitor. He didn't have to look far. "She's dead."

"Dead?" Cortez said. "What the hell—"

"Just a minute." Doc plugged a jack into the monitor and fiddled with some dials on his kit. "Everybody's biomed readout is stored for twelve hours. I'm running it backwards, should be able to—there!"

"What?"

"Four and a half minutes ago—must have been when you opened fire—Jesus!"

"Well?"

"Massive cerebral hemorrhage. No . . ." He watched the

dials. "No . . . warning, no indication of anything out of the ordinary; blood pressure up, pulse up, but normal under the circumstances . . . nothing to . . . indicate—" He reached down and popped her suit. Her fine oriental features were distorted in a horrible grimace, both gums showing. Sticky fluid ran from under her collapsed eyelids, and a trickle of blood still dripped from each ear. Doc Wilson closed the suit back up.

"I've never seen anything like it. It's as if a bomb went off in her skull."

"Oh fuck," Rogers said, "she was Rhine-sensitive, wasn't she."

"That's right," Cortez sounded thoughtful. "All right, everybody listen up. Platoon leaders, check your platoons and see if anybody's missing, or hurt. Anybody else in seventh?"

"I . . . I've got a splitting headache, Sarge," Lucky said.

Four others had bad headaches. One of them affirmed that he was slightly Rhine-sensitive. The others didn't know.

"Cortez, I think it's obvious," Doc Wilson said, "that we should give these . . . monsters wide berth, especially shouldn't harm any more of them. Not with five people susceptible to whatever apparently killed Ho."

"Of course, God damn it, I don't need anybody to tell me that. We'd better get moving. I just filled the captain in on what happened; he agrees that we'd better get as far away from here as we can, before we stop for the night.

"Let's get back in formation and continue on the same bearing. Fifth platoon, take over point; second, come back to the rear. Everybody else, same as before."

"What about Ho?" Lucky asked.

"She'll be taken care of. From the ship."

After we'd gone half a klick, there was a flash and rolling thunder. Where Ho had been came a wispy luminous mushroom cloud boiling up to disappear against the gray sky.

13

We stopped for the "night"—actually, the sun wouldn't set for another seventy hours—atop a slight rise some ten klicks from where we had killed the aliens. But they weren't aliens, I had to remind myself—*we* were.

Two platoons deployed in a ring around the rest of us, and we flopped down exhausted. Everybody was allowed four hours' sleep and had two hours' guard duty.

Potter came over and sat next to me. I chinned her frequency.

"Hi, Marygay."

"Oh, William," her voice over the radio was hoarse and cracking. "God, it's so horrible."

"It's over now—"

"I killed one of them, the first instant, I shot it right in the, in the . . ."

I put my hand on her knee. The contact had a plastic click and I jerked it back, visions of machines embracing, copulating. "Don't feel singled out, Marygay; whatever guilt there is, is . . . belongs evenly to all of us, . . . but a triple portion for Cor—"

"You privates quit jawin' and get some sleep. You both pull guard in two hours."

"OK, Sarge." Her voice was so sad and tired I couldn't bear it. I felt if I could only touch her, I could drain off the sadness like ground wire draining current, but we were each trapped in our own plastic world—

"G'night, William."

"Night." It's almost impossible to get sexually excited inside a suit, with the relief tube and all the silver chloride sensors poking you, but somehow this was my body's response to the emotional impotence, maybe remembering more pleasant sleeps with Marygay, maybe feeling that in the midst of all this death, personal death could be very

55

soon, cranking up the procreative derrick for one last try
. . . lovely thoughts like this. I fell asleep and dreamed that
I was a machine, mimicking the functions of life, creaking
and clanking my clumsy way through a world, people too
polite to say anything but giggling behind my back, and
the little man who sat inside my head pulling the levers
and clutches and watching the dials, he was hopelessly mad
and was storing up hurts for the day—

"Mandella—wake up, goddammit, your shift!"

I shuffled over to my place on the perimeter to watch for
god knows what . . . but I was so weary I couldn't keep my
eyes open. Finally I tongued a stimtab, knowing I'd pay
for it later.

For over an hour I sat there, scanning my sector left,
right, near, far, the scene never changing, not even a breath
of wind to stir the grass.

Then suddenly the grass parted and one of the three-
legged creatures was right in front of me. I raised my finger
but didn't squeeze.

"Movement!"

"Movement!"

"Jesus Chri—there's one right—"

"HOLD YOUR FIRE! F' shit's sake don't shoot!"

"Movement."

"Movement." I looked left and right, and as far as I
could see, every perimeter guard had one of the blind,
dumb creatures standing right in front of him.

Maybe the drug I'd taken to stay awake made me more
sensitive to whatever they did. My scalp crawled and I felt
a formless *thing* in my mind, the feeling you get when
somebody has said something and you didn't quite hear it,
want to respond, but the opportunity to ask him to repeat
it is gone.

The creature sat back on its haunches, leaning forward
on the one front leg. Big green bear with a withered arm.
Its power threaded through my mind, spiderwebs, echo of
night terrors, trying to communicate, trying to destroy me,
I couldn't know.

"All right, everybody on the perimeter, fall back, slow.

Don't make any quick gestures. . . . Anybody got a headache or anything?''

"Sergeant, this is Hollister." Lucky.

"They're trying to say something . . . I can almost . . .
no, just . . .''

"All I can get is that they think we're, think we're . . .
well, *funny*. They're not afraid.''

"You mean the one in front of you isn't—''

"No, the feeling comes from all of them, they're all
thinking the same thing. Don't ask me how I know, I just
do.''

"Maybe they thought it was funny, what they did to
Ho.''

"Maybe. I don't feel they're dangerous. Just curious
about us.''

"Sergeant, this is Bohrs.''

"Yeah.''

"The Taurans've been here at least a year—maybe
they've learned how to communicate with these . . . over-
grown teddy bears. They might be spying on us, might be
sending back—''

"I don't think they'd show themselves if that were the
case," Lucky said. "They can obviously hide from us
pretty well when they want to.''

"Anyhow," Cortez said, "if they're spies, the damage
has been done. Don't think it'd be smart to take any action
against them. I know you'd all like to see 'em dead for
what they did to Ho, so would I, but we'd better be careful.''

I didn't want to see them dead, but I'd just as soon not
have seen them in any condition. I was walking backwards
slowly, toward the middle of camp. The creature didn't
seem disposed to follow. Maybe he just knew we were
surrounded. He was pulling up grass with his arm and
munching.

"OK, all of you platoon leaders, wake everybody up, get
a roll count. Let me know if anybody's been hurt. Tell your
people we're moving out in one minute.''

I don't know what Cortez had expected, but of course
the creatures followed right along. They didn't keep us sur-

rounded; just had twenty or thirty following us all the time. Not the same ones, either. Individuals would saunter away, and new ones would join the parade. It was pretty obvious that *they* weren't going to tire out.

We were each allowed one stimtab. Without it, no one could have marched an hour. A second pill would have been welcome after the edge started to wear off, but the mathematics of the situation forbade it; we were still thirty klicks from the enemy base, fifteen hours' marching at the least. And though you could stay awake and energetic for a hundred hours on the tabs, aberrations of judgment and perception snowballed after the second one, until *in extremis* the most bizarre hallucinations would be taken at face value, and a person could fidget for hours deciding whether to have breakfast.

Under artificial stimulation, the company traveled with great energy for the first six hours, was slowing by the seventh, and ground to an exhausted halt after nine hours and nineteen kilometers. The teddy bears had never lost sight of us and, according to Lucky, had never stopped "broadcasting." Cortez's decision was that we would stop for seven hours, each platoon taking one hour of perimeter guard. I was never so glad to have been in the seventh platoon, as we stood guard the last shift and thus were able to get six hours of uninterrupted sleep.

In the few moments I lay awake after finally lying down, the thought came to me that the next time I closed my eyes could well be the last. And partly because of the drug hangover, mostly because of the past day's horrors, I found that I really didn't give a shit.

14

Our first contact with the Taurans came during my shift.

The teddy bears were still there when I woke up and replaced Doc Jones on guard. They'd gone back to their original formation, one in front of each guard position. The one who was waiting for me seemed a little larger than normal, but otherwise looked just like all the others. All the grass had been cropped where he was sitting, so he occasionally made forays to the left or right. But he always returned to sit right in front of me, you would say *staring* if he had had anything to stare with.

We had been facing each other for about fifteen minutes when Cortez's voice rumbled:

"Awright everybody, wake up and get hid!"

I followed instinct and flopped to the ground and rolled into a tall stand of grass.

"Enemy vessel overhead." His voice was almost laconic.

Strictly speaking, it wasn't really overhead, but rather passing somewhat east of us. It was moving slowly, maybe a hundred klicks per hour, and looked like a broomstick surrounded by a dirty soap bubble. The creature riding it was a little more human-looking than the teddy bears, but still no prize. I cranked my image amplifier up to forty log two for a closer look.

He had two arms and two legs, but his waist was so small you could encompass it with both hands. Under the tiny waist was a large horseshoe-shaped pelvic structure nearly a meter wide, from which dangled two long skinny legs with no apparent knee joint. Above that waist his body swelled out again, to a chest no smaller than the huge pelvis. His arms looked surprisingly human, except that they were too long and undermuscled. There were too many fingers on his hands. Shoulderless, neckless. His head was a

59

nightmarish growth that swelled like a goiter from his massive chest. Two eyes that looked like clusters of fish eggs, a bundle of tassles instead of a nose, and a rigidly open hole that might have been a mouth sitting low down where his adam's apple should have been. Evidently the soap bubble contained an amenable environment, as he was wearing absolutely nothing except his ridged hide, that looked like skin submerged too long in hot water, then dyed a pale orange. "He" had no external genitalia, but nothing that might hint of mammary glands. So we opted for the male pronoun by default.

Obviously, he either didn't see us or thought we were part of the herd of teddy bears. He never looked back at us, but just continued in the same direction we were headed, .05 rad east of north.

"Might as well go back to sleep now, if you can sleep after looking at *that* thing. We move out at 0435." Forty minutes.

Because of the planet's opaque cloud cover, there had been no way to tell, from space, what the enemy base looked like or how big it was. We only knew its position, the same way we knew the position the scoutships were supposed to land on. So it too could easily have been underwater, or underground.

But some of the drones were reconnaissance ships as well as decoys: and in their mock attacks on the base, one managed to get close enough to take a picture. Captain Stott beamed down a diagram of the place to Cortez—the only one with a visor in his suit—when we were five klicks from the base's "radio" position. We stopped and he called all the platoon leaders in with the seventh platoon to confer. Two teddy bears loped in, too. We tried to ignore them.

"OK, the captain sent down some pictures of our objective. I'm going to draw a map; you platoon leaders copy." They took pads and styli out of their leg pockets, while Cortez unrolled a large plastic mat. He gave it a shake to randomize any residual charge, and turned on his stylus.

"Now, we're coming from this direction." He put an arrow at the bottom of the sheet. "First thing we'll hit is this row of huts, probably billets or bunkers, but who the hell knows. . . . Our initial objective is to destroy these buildings—the whole base is on a flat plain; there's no way we could really sneak by them.''

"Potter here. Why can't we jump over them?"

"Yeah, we could do that, and wind up completely surrounded, cut to ribbons. We take the buildings.

"After we do that . . . all I can say is that we'll have to think on our feet. From the aerial reconnaissance, we can figure out the function of only a couple of buildings—and that stinks. We might wind up wasting a lot of time demolishing the equivalent of an enlisted-men's bar, ignoring a huge logistic computer because it looks like . . . a garbage dump or something.''

"Mandella here," I said. "Isn't there a spaceport of some kind—seems to me we ought to . . .''

"I'll *get* to that, damn it. There's a ring of these huts all around the camp, so we've got to break through somewhere. This place'll be closest, less chance of giving away our position before we attack.

"There's nothing in the whole place that actually looks like a weapon. That doesn't mean anything, though; you could hide a gigawatt laser in each of those huts.

"Now, about five hundred meters from the huts, in the middle of the base, we'll come to this big flower-shaped structure." Cortez drew a large symmetrical shape that looked like the outline of a flower with seven petals. "What the hell this is, your guess is as good as mine. There's only one of them, though, so we don't damage it any more than we have to. Which means . . . we blast it to splinters if I think it's dangerous.

"Now, as far as your spaceport, Mandella, is concerned—there just isn't one. Nothing.

"That cruiser the *Hope* caulked had probably been left in orbit, like ours has to be. If they have any equivalent of a scoutship, or drone missiles, they're either not kept here or they're well hidden.''

"Bohrs here. Then what did they attack with, while we were coming down from orbit?"

"I wish we knew, Private.

"Obviously, we don't have any way of estimating their

numbers, not directly. Recon pictures failed to show a single Tauran on the grounds of the base. Meaning nothing, because it *is* an alien environment. Indirectly, though . . . we count the number of broomsticks, those flying things.

"There are fifty-one huts, and each has at most one broomstick. Four don't have any parked outside, but we located three at various other parts of the base. Maybe this indicates that there are fifty-one Taurans, one of whom was outside the base when the picture was taken."

"Keating here. Or fifty-one officers."

"That's right—maybe fifty thousand infantrymen stacked in one of these buildings. No way to tell. Maybe ten Taurans, each with five broomsticks, to use according to his mood.

"We've got one thing in our favor, and that's communications. They evidently use a frequency modulation of megahertz electromagnetic radiation."

"Radio!"

"That's right, whoever you are. Identify yourself when you speak. So it's quite possible that they can't detect our phased-neutrino communications. Also, just prior to the attack, the *Hope* is going to deliver a nice dirty fission bomb; detonate it in the upper atmosphere right over the base. That'll restrict them to line-of-sight communications for some time; even those will be full of static."

"Why don't . . . Tate here . . . why don't they just drop the bomb right in their laps. Save us a lot of—"

"That doesn't even deserve an answer, Private. But the answer is, they might. And you better hope they don't. If they caulk the base, it'll be for the safety of the *Hope. After* we've attacked, and probably before we're far enough away for it to make much difference.

"We keep that from happening by doing a good job. We have to reduce the base to where it can no longer function; at the same time, leave as much intact as possible. And take one prisoner."

"Potter here. You mean, at least one prisoner."

"I mean what I say. One only. Potter . . . you're relieved of your platoon. Send Chavez up."

"All right, Sergeant." The relief in her voice was unmistakable.

Cortez continued with his map and instructions. There was one other building whose function was pretty obvious; it had a large steerable dish antenna on top. We were to destroy it as soon as the grenadiers got in range.

The attack plan was very loose. Our signal to begin would be the flash of the fission bomb. At the same time, several drones would converge on the base, so we could see what their antispacecraft defenses were. We would try to reduce the effectiveness of those defenses without destroying them completely.

Immediately after the bomb and the drones, the grenadiers would vaporize a line of seven huts. Everybody would break through the hole into the base . . . and what would happen after that was anybody's guess.

Ideally, we'd sweep from that end of the base to the other, destroying certain targets, caulking all but one Tauran. But that was unlikely to happen, as it depended on the Taurans' offering very little resistance.

On the other hand, if the Taurans showed obvious superiority from the beginning, Cortez would give the order to scatter. Everybody had a different compass bearing for retreat—we'd blossom out in all directions, the survivors to rendezvous in a valley some forty klicks east of the base. Then we'd see about a return engagement, after the *Hope* softened the base up a bit.

"One last thing," Cortez rasped. "Maybe some of you feel the way Potter evidently does, maybe some of your men feel that way . . . that we ought to go easy, not make this so much of a bloodbath. Mercy is a luxury, a weakness we can't afford to indulge in at this stage of the war. *All* we know about the enemy is that they have killed seven hundred and ninety-eight humans. They haven't shown any restraint in attacking our cruisers, and it'd be foolish to expect any this time, this first ground action.

"*They* are responsible for the lives of all of your comrades who died in training, and for Ho, and for all the others who are surely going to die today. I can't *understand* anybody who wants to spare them. But that doesn't make any difference. You have your orders and, what the hell, you might as well know, all of you have a post-hypnotic suggestion that I will trigger by a phrase, just before the battle. It will make your job easier.''

"Sergeant . . ."

"Shut up. We're short on time; get back to your platoons and brief them. We move out in five minutes.''

The platoon leaders returned to their men, leaving Cortez and ten of us—plus three teddy bears, milling around, getting in the way.

15

We took the last five klicks very carefully, sticking to the highest grass, running across occasional clearings. When we were 500 meters from where the base was supposed to be, Cortez took the third platoon forward to scout, while the rest of us laid low.

Cortez's voice came over the general freak: "Looks pretty much like we expected. Advance in a file, crawling. When you get to the third platoon, follow your squad leader to the left or right."

We did that and wound up with a string of eighty-three people in a line roughly perpendicular to the direction of attack. We were pretty well hidden, except for the dozen or so teddy bears that mooched along the line, munching grass.

There was no sign of life inside the base. All of the buildings were windowless and a uniform shiny white. The huts that were our first objective were large featureless half-buried eggs some sixty meters apart. Cortez assigned one to each grenadier.

We were broken into three fire teams: team A consisted of platoons two, four, and six; team B was one, three, and five; the command platoon was team C.

"Less than a minute now—filters down!—when I say 'fire,' grenadiers, take out your targets. God help you if you miss."

There was a sound like a giant's belch, and a stream of five or six iridescent bubbles floated up from the flower-shaped building. They rose with increasing speed until they were almost out of sight, then shot off to the south, over our heads. The ground was suddenly bright, and for the first time in a long time, I saw my shadow, a long one pointed north. The bomb had gone off prematurely. I just had time to think that it didn't make too much difference;

it'd still make alphabet soup out of their communications—

"Drones!" A ship came screaming in just about tree level, and a bubble was in the air to meet it. When they contacted, the bubble popped and the drone exploded into a million tiny fragments. Another one came from the opposite side and suffered the same fate.

"FIRE!" Seven bright glares of 500-microton grenades and a sustained concussion that surely would have killed an unprotected man.

"Filters up." Gray haze of smoke and dust. Clods of dirt falling with a sound like heavy raindrops.

"Listen up:

> *'Scots, wha hae wi' Wallace bled;*
> *Scots, wham Bruce has aften led,*
> *Welcome to your gory bed,*
> *Or to victory!' "*

I hardly heard him for trying to keep track of what was going on in my skull. I knew it was just post-hypnotic suggestion, even remembered the session in Missouri when they'd implanted it, but that didn't make it any less compelling. My mind reeled under the strong pseudo-memories: shaggy hulks that were Taurans (not at all what we now knew they looked like) boarding a colonists' vessel, eating babies while mothers watched in screaming terror (the colonists never took babies; they wouldn't stand the acceleration), then raping the women to death with huge veined purple members (ridiculous that they would feel desire for humans), holding the men down while they plucked flesh from their living bodies and gobbled it (as if they could assimilate the alien protein) . . . a hundred grisly details as sharply remembered as the events of a minute ago, ridiculously overdone and logically absurd. But while my conscious mind was rejecting the silliness, somewhere much deeper, down in that sleeping animal where we keep our real motives and morals, something was thirsting for alien blood, secure in the conviction that the noblest thing a man could do would be to die killing one of those horrible monsters. . . .

I knew it was all purest soyashit, and I hated the men who had taken such obscene liberties with my mind, but I could even *hear* my teeth grinding, feel my cheeks frozen in a spastic grin, blood-lust ... A teddy bear walked in front of me, looking dazed. I started to raise my laser-finger, but somebody beat me to it and the creature's head exploded in a cloud of gray splinters and blood.

Lucky groaned, half-whining, "Dirty ... filthy fucken bastards." Lasers flared and crisscrossed, and all of the teddy bears fell dead.

"*Watch* it, goddammit," Cortez screamed. "*Aim* those fuckin things—they aren't toys!

"Team *A*, move out—into the craters to cover *B*."

Somebody was laughing and sobbing. "What the fuck is wrong with *you*, Petrov?" Strange to hear Cortez cussing.

I twisted around and saw Petrov, behind and to my left, lying in a shallow hole, digging frantically with both hands, crying and gurgling.

"Fuck," Cortez said. "Team *B*! Ten meters past the craters, get down in a line. Team *C*—into the craters with *A*."

I scrambled up and covered the hundred meters in twelve amplified strides. The craters were practically large enough to hide a scoutship, some ten meters in diameter. I jumped to the opposite side of the hole and landed next to a fellow named Chin. He didn't even look around when I landed, just kept scanning the base for signs of life.

"Team *A*—ten meters, past team *B*, down in line." Just as he finished, the building in front of us burped, and a salvo of the bubbles fanned out toward our lines. Most people saw it coming and got down, but Chin was just getting up to make his rush and stepped right into one.

It grazed the top of his helmet and disappeared with a faint pop. He took one step backwards and toppled over the edge of the crater, trailing an arc of blood and brains. Lifeless, spreadeagled, he slid halfway to the bottom, shoveling dirt into the perfectly symmetrical hole where the bubble had chewed indiscriminately through plastic, hair, skin, bone, and brain.

"Everybody hold it. Platoon leaders, casualty report ... check ... check, check ... check, check, check ... check.

We have three deaders. Wouldn't be *any* if you'd have kept low. So everybody grab dirt when you hear that thing go off. Team *A*, complete the rush.''

They completed the maneuver without incident. "OK. Team *C*, rush to where *B* . . . hold it! Down!''

Everybody was already hugging the ground. The bubbles slid by in a smooth arc about two meters off the ground. They went serenely over our heads and, except for one that made toothpicks out of a tree, disappeared in the distance.

"*B*, rush past *A* ten meters. *C*, take over *B*'s place. You *B* grenadiers, see if you can reach the Flower.''

Two grenades tore up the ground thirty or forty meters from the structure. In a good imitation of panic, it started belching out a continuous stream of bubbles—still, none coming lower than two meters off the ground. We kept hunched down and continued to advance.

Suddenly, a seam appeared in the building and widened to the size of a large door. Taurans came swarming out.

"Grenadiers, hold your fire. *B* team, laser fire to the left and right—keep'm bunched up. *A* and *C*, rush down the center.''

One Tauran died trying to run through a laser beam. The others stayed where they were.

In a suit, it's pretty awkward to run and keep your head down at the same time. You have to go from side to side, like a skater getting started; otherwise you'll be airborne. At least one person, somebody in *A* team, bounced too high and suffered the same fate as Chin.

I was feeling pretty fenced-in and trapped, with a wall of laser fire on each side and a low ceiling that meant death to touch. But in spite of myself, I felt happy, euphoric, finally getting the chance to kill some of those villainous baby-eaters. Knowing it was soyashit.

They weren't fighting back, except for the rather ineffective bubbles (obviously not designed as an anti-personnel weapon), and they didn't retreat back into the building, either. They milled around, about a hundred of them, and watched us get closer. A couple of grenades would caulk them all, but I guess Cortez was thinking about the prisoner.

"OK, when I say 'go,' we're going to flank 'em. *B* team will hold fire . . . Second and fourth platoons to the right, sixth and seventh to the left. *B* team will move forward in line to box them in.

"Go!" We peeled off to the left. As soon as the lasers stopped, the Taurans bolted, running in a group on a collision course with our flank.

"*A* team, down and fire! Don't shoot until you're sure of your aim—if you miss you might hit a friendly. And fer Chris' sake save me one!"

It was a horrifying sight, that herd of monsters bearing down on us. They were running in great leaps—the bubbles avoiding them—and they all looked like the one we saw earlier, riding the broomstick; naked except for an almost transparent sphere around their whole bodies, that moved along with them. The right flank started firing, picking off individuals in the rear of the pack.

Suddenly a laser flared through the Taurans from the other side, somebody missing his mark. There was a horrible scream, and I looked down the line to see someone—I think it was Perry—writhing on the ground, right hand over the smoldering stump of his arm, seared off just below the elbow. Blood sprayed through his fingers, and the suit, its camouflage circuits scrambled, flickered black-white-jungle-desert-green-gray. I don't know how long I stared—long enough for the medic to run over and start giving aid—but when I looked up the Taurans were almost on top of me.

My first shot was wild and high, but it grazed the top of the leading Tauran's protective bubble. The bubble disappeared and the monster stumbled and fell to the ground, jerking spasmodically. Foam gushed out of his mouth-hole, first white, then streaked red. With one last jerk he became rigid and twisted backwards, almost to the shape of a horseshoe. His long scream, a high-pitched whistle, stopped just as his comrades trampled over him. I hated myself for smiling.

It was slaughter, even though our flank was outnumbered five to one. They kept coming without faltering, even when they had to climb over the drift of bodies and parts of bodies that piled up high, parallel to our flank. The ground between us was slick red with Tauran blood—all God's children got hemoglobin—and like the teddy bears, their guts looked pretty much like guts to my untrained eye. My helmet reverberated with hysterical laughter while we slashed them to gory chunks, and I almost didn't hear Cortez:

"Hold your fire—I said HOLD IT, goddammit! *Catch* a couple of the bastards, they won't hurt you."

I stopped shooting and eventually so did everybody else. When the next Tauran jumped over the smoking pile of meat in front of me, I dove to try to tackle him around those spindly legs.

It was like hugging a big, slippery balloon. When I tried to drag him down, he popped out of my arms and kept running.

We managed to stop one of them by the simple expedient of piling half-a-dozen people on top of him. By that time the others had run through our line and were headed for the row of large cylindrical tanks that Cortez had said were probably for storage. A little door had opened in the base of each one.

"We've *got* our prisoner," Cortez shouted. *"Kill!"*

They were fifty meters away and running hard, difficult targets. Lasers slashed around them, bobbing high and low. One fell, sliced in two, but the others, about ten of them, kept going and were almost to the doors when the grenadiers started firing.

They were still loaded with 500-mike bombs, but a near miss wasn't enough—the concussion would just send them flying, unhurt in their bubbles.

"The buildings! Get the fucken buildings!" The grenadiers raised their aim and let fly, but the bombs only seemed to scorch the white outside of the structures until, by chance, one landed in a door. That split the building just as if it had a seam; the two halves popped away and a cloud of machinery flew into the air, accompanied by a huge pale flame that rolled up and disappeared in an instant. Then the others all concentrated on the doors, except for potshots at some of the Taurans, not so much to get them as to blow them away before they could get inside. They seemed awfully eager.

All this time, we were trying to get the Taurans with laser fire, while they weaved and bounced around trying to get into the structures. We moved in as close to them as we could without putting ourselves in danger from the grenade blasts, yet too far away for good aim.

Still, we were getting them one by one and managed to destroy four of the seven buildings. Then, when there were only two aliens left, a nearby grenade blast flung one of them to within a few meters of a door. He dove in and several grenadiers fired salvos after him, but they all fell short or detonated harmlessly on the side. Bombs were falling all around, making an awful racket, but the sound was suddenly drowned out by a great sigh, like a giant's intake of breath, and where the building had been was a thick cylindrical cloud of smoke, solid-looking, dwindling away into the stratosphere, straight as if laid down by a ruler. The other Tauran had been right at the base of the cylinder; I could see pieces of him flying. A second later, a shock wave hit us and I rolled helplessly, pinwheeling, to smash into the pile of Tauran bodies and roll beyond.

I picked myself up and panicked for a second when I saw there was blood all over my suit—when I realized it was only alien blood, I relaxed but felt unclean.

"*Catch* the bastard! Catch him!" In the confusion, the Tauran had gotten free and was running for the grass. One platoon was chasing after him, losing ground, but then all of *B* team ran over and cut him off. I jogged over to join in the fun.

There were four people on top of him, and a ring around them of about fifty people, watching the struggle.

"Spread out, dammit! There might be a thousand more of them waiting to get us in one place." We dispersed, grumbling. By unspoken agreement we were all sure that there were no more live Taurans on the face of the planet.

Cortez was walking toward the prisoner while I backed away. Suddenly the four men collapsed in a pile on top of the creature . . . Even from my distance I could see the foam spouting from his mouth-hole. His bubble had popped. Suicide.

"Damn!" Cortez was right there. "Get off that bastard."
The four men got off and Cortez used his laser to slice the
monster into a dozen quivering chunks. Heart-warming
sight.

"That's all right, though, we'll find another one—everybody! Back in the arrowhead formation. Combat assault,
on the Flower."

Well, we assaulted the Flower, which had evidently run
out of ammunition (it was still belching, but no bubbles),
and it was empty. We scurried up ramps and through cor-
ridors, fingers at the ready, like kids playing soldier. There
was nobody home.

The same lack of response at the antenna installation, the
"Salami," and twenty other major buildings, as well as the
forty-four perimeter huts still intact. So we had "captured"
dozens of buildings, mostly of incomprehensible purpose,
but failed in our main mission, capturing a Tauran for the
xenologists to experiment with. Oh well, they could have
all the bits and pieces they'd ever want. That was something.

After we'd combed every last square centimeter of the
base, a scoutship came in with the real exploration crew,
the scientists. Cortez said, "All right, snap out of it," and
the hypnotic compulsion fell away.

At first it was pretty grim. A lot of the people, like Lucky
and Marygay, almost went crazy with the memories of
bloody murder multiplied a hundred times. Cortez ordered
everybody to take a sed-tab, two for the ones most upset.
I took two without being specifically ordered to do so.

Because it *was* murder, unadorned butchery—once we
had the anti-spacecraft weapon doped out, we hadn't been
in any danger. The Taurans hadn't seemed to have any
conception of person-to-person fighting. We had just
herded them up and slaughtered them, the first encounter
between mankind and another intelligent species. Maybe it
was the second encounter, counting the teddy bears. What
might have happened if we had sat down and tried to communicate? But they got the same treatment.

I spent a long time after that telling myself over and over

that it hadn't been *me* who so gleefully carved up those frightened, stampeding creatures. Back in the twentieth century, they had established to everybody's satisfaction that "I was just following orders" was an inadequate excuse for inhuman conduct . . . but what can you do when the orders come from deep down in that puppet master of the unconscious?

Worst of all was the feeling that perhaps my actions weren't all that inhuman. Ancestors only a few generations back would have done the same thing, even to their fellow men, without any hypnotic conditioning.

I was disgusted with the human race, disgusted with the army and horrified at the prospect of living with myself for another century or so. . . . Well, there was always brain-wipe.

A ship with a lone Tauran survivor had escaped and had gotten away clean, the bulk of the planet shielding it from *Earth's Hope* while it dropped into Aleph's collapsar field. Escaped home, I guessed, wherever that was, to report what twenty men with hand-weapons could do to a hundred fleeing on foot, unarmed.

I suspected that the next time humans met Taurans in ground combat, we would be more evenly matched. And I was right.

SERGEANT
MANDELLA
2007–2024 A.D.

1

I was scared enough.

Sub-major Stott was pacing back and forth behind the small podium in the assembly room/chop hall/gymnasium of the *Anniversary*. We had just made our final collapsar jump, from Tet-38 to Yod-4. We were decelerating at 1½ gravities and our velocity relative to that collapsar was a respectable .90c. We were being chased.

"I wish you people would relax for a while and just trust the ship's computer. The Tauran vessel at any rate will not be within strike range for another two weeks. Mandella!"

He was always very careful to call me "Sergeant" Mandella in front of the company. But everybody at this particular briefing was either a sergeant or a corporal: squad leaders. "Yes, sir."

"You're responsible for the psychological as well as the physical well-being of the men and women in your squad. Assuming that you are aware that there is a morale problem aboard this vessel, what have you done about it?"

"As far as my squad is concerned, sir?"

"Of course."

"We talk it out, sir."

"And have you arrived at any cogent conclusion?"

"Meaning no disrespect, sir, I think the major problem is obvious. My people have been cooped up in this ship for fourteen—"

"Ridiculous! Every one of us has been adequately conditioned against the pressures of living in close quarters *and* the enlisted people have the privilege of confraternity." That was a delicate way of putting it. "Officers must remain celibate, and yet *we* have no morale problem."

If he thought his officers were celibate, he should sit down and have a long talk with Lieutenant Harmony. Maybe he just meant line officers, though. That would be

77

just him and Cortez. Probably 50 percent right. Cortez was awfully friendly with Corporal Kamehameha.

"Sir, perhaps it was the detoxification back at Stargate; maybe—"

"No. The therapists only worked to erase the hate conditioning—everybody knows how *I* feel about that—and they may be misguided but they are skilled.

"Corporal Potter." He always called her by her rank to remind her why she hadn't been promoted as high as the rest of us. Too soft. "Have you 'talked it out' with your people, too?"

"We've discussed it, sir."

The sub-major could "glare mildly" at people. He glared mildly at Marygay until she elaborated.

"I don't believe it's the fault of the conditioning. My people are impatient, just tired of doing the same thing day after day."

"They're anxious for combat, then?" No sarcasm in his voice.

"They want to get off the ship, sir."

"They *will* get off the ship," he said, allowing himself a microscopic smile. "And then they'll probably be just as impatient to get back on."

It went back and forth like that for a long while. Nobody wanted to come right out and say that their squad was scared: scared of the Tauran cruiser closing on us, scared of the landing on the portal planet. Sub-major Stott had a bad record of dealing with people who admitted fear.

I fingered the fresh T/O they had given us. It looked like this:

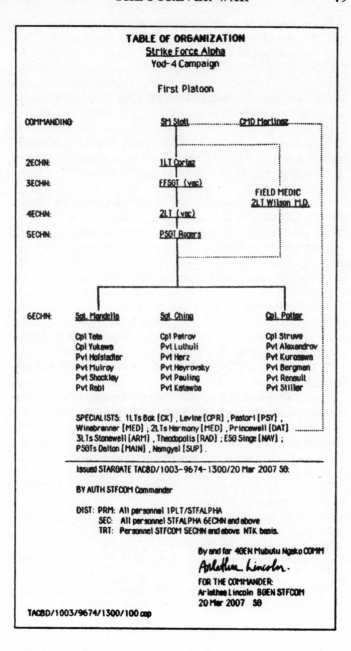

TABLE OF ORGANIZATION
<u>Strike Force Alpha</u>
Yod-4 Campaign

First Platoon

COMMANDING	<u>SM Stott</u>	<u>CMD Martinez</u>
2ECHN:	<u>1LT Cortez</u>	
3ECHN:	<u>FFSGT (vac)</u>	FIELD MEDIC
		<u>2LT Wilson M.D.</u>
4ECHN:	<u>2LT (vac)</u>	
5ECHN:	<u>PSGT Rogers</u>	

6ECHN:	<u>Sgt. Mandella</u>	<u>Sgt. Ching</u>	<u>Cpl. Potter</u>
	Cpl Tate	Cpl Petrov	Cpl Struve
	Cpl Yukawa	Pvt Luthuli	Pvt Alexandrov
	Pvt Hofstadter	Pvt Herz	Pvt Kurosawa
	Pvt Mulroy	Pvt Heyrovsky	Pvt Bergman
	Pvt Shockley	Pvt Pauling	Pvt Renault
	Pvt Rabi	Pvt Katawba	Pvt Stiller

SPECIALISTS: 1LTs Bok [CK] , Levine [CPR] , Pastori [PSY] ,
Winebrenner [MED] ; 2LTs Harmony [MED] , Princewell [DAT]
3LTs Stonewall [ARM] , Theodopolis [RAD] ; ESG Singe [NAV] ;
PSGTs Dalton [MAIN] , Namgyal [SUP] .

Issued STARGATE TACBD/1003-9674-1300/20 Mar 2007 SG:

BY AUTH STFCOM Commander

DIST: PRM: All personnel 1PLT/STFALPHA
      SEC: All personnel STFALPHA 6ECHN and above
      TRT: Personnel STFCOM 5ECHN and above NTK basis.

By and for 4GEN Mubutu Ngako COMM

Arlothea Lincoln.

FOR THE COMMANDER:
Arlothea Lincoln BGEN STFCOM
20 Mar 2007   SG

TACBD/1003/9674/1300/100 cap

I knew most of the people from the raid on Aleph, the first face-to-face contact between humans and Taurans. The only new people in my platoon were Luthuli and Heyrovsky. In the company as a whole (excuse me, the "strike force"), we had twenty replacements for the nineteen people we lost from the Aleph raid: one amputation, four deaders, fourteen psychotics.

I couldn't get over the "20 Mar 2007" at the bottom of the T/O. I'd been in the army ten years, though it felt like less than two. Time dilation, of course; even with the collapsar jumps, traveling from star to star eats up the calendar.

After this raid, I would probably be eligible for retirement, with full pay. If I lived through the raid, and if they didn't change the rules on us. Me a twenty-year man, and only twenty-five years old.

Stott was summing up when there was a knock on the door, a single loud rap. "Enter," he said.

An ensign I knew vaguely walked in casually and handed Stott a slip of paper, without saying a word. He stood there while Stott read it, slumping with just the right degree of insolence. Technically, Stott was out of his chain of command; everybody in the navy disliked him anyhow.

Stott handed the paper back to the ensign and looked through him.

"You will alert your squads that preliminary evasive maneuvers will commence at 2010, fifty-eight minutes from now." He hadn't looked at his watch. "All personnel will be in acceleration shells by 2000. Tench . . . hut!"

We rose and, without enthusiasm, chorused, "Fuck you, sir." Idiotic custom.

Stott strode out of the room and the ensign followed, smirking.

I turned my ring to my assistant squad leader's position and talked into it: "Tate, this is Mandella." Everyone else in the room was doing the same.

A tinny voice came out of the ring. "Tate here. What's up?"

"Get ahold of the men and tell them we have to be in the shells by 2000. Evasive maneuvers."

"Crap. They told us it would be days."

"I guess something new came up. Or maybe the Commodore has a bright idea."

"The Commodore can stuff it. You up in the lounge?"

"Yeah."

"Bring me back a cup when you come, okay? Little sugar?"

"Roger. Be down in about half an hour."

"Thanks. I'll get on it."

There was a general movement toward the coffee machine. I got in line behind Corporal Potter.

"What do you think, Marygay?"

"Maybe the Commodore just wants us to try out the shells once more."

"Before the real thing."

"Maybe." She picked up a cup and blew into it. She looked worried. "Or maybe the Taurans had a ship way out, waiting for us. I've wondered why they don't do it. We do, at Stargate."

"Stargate's a different thing. It takes seven cruisers, moving all the time, to cover all the possible exit angles. We can't afford to do it for more than one collapsar, and neither could they."

She didn't say anything while she filled her cup. "Maybe we've stumbled on their version of Stargate. Or maybe they have more ships than we do by now."

I filled and sugared two cups, sealed one. "No way to tell." We walked back to a table, careful with the cups in the high gravity.

"Maybe Singhe knows something," she said.

"Maybe he does. But I'd have to get him through Rogers and Cortez. Cortez would jump down my throat if I tried to bother him now."

"Oh, I can get him directly. We . . ." She dimpled a little bit. "We've been friends."

I sipped some scalding coffee and tried to sound nonchalant. "So that's where you've been disappearing to."

"You disapprove?" she said, looking innocent.

"Well . . . damn it, no, of course not. But—but he's an officer! A *navy* officer!"

"He's attached to us and that makes him part army."
She twisted her ring and said, "Directory." To me: "What
about you and Little Miss Harmony?"

"That's not the same thing." She was whispering a directory code into the ring.

"Yes, it is. You just wanted to do it with an officer.
Pervert." The ring bleated twice. Busy. "How was she?"

"Adequate." I was recovering.

"Besides, Ensign Singhe is a perfect gentleman. And not
the least bit jealous."

"Neither am I," I said. "If he ever hurts you, tell me
and I'll break his ass."

She looked at me across her cup. "If Lieutenant Harmony ever hurts you, tell me and I'll break *her* ass."

"It's a deal." We shook on it solemnly.

2

The acceleration shells were something new, installed while we rested and resupplied at Stargate. They enabled us to use the ship at closer to its theoretical efficiency, the tachyon drive boosting it to as much as 25 gravities.

Tate was waiting for me in the shell area. The rest of the squad was milling around, talking. I gave him his coffee.

"Thanks. Find out anything?"

"Afraid not. Except the swabbies don't seem to be scared, and it's their show. Probably just another practice run."

He slurped some coffee. "What the hell. It's all the same to us, anyhow. Just sit there and get squeezed half to death. God, I hate those things."

"Maybe they'll eventually make us obsolete, and we can go home."

"Sure thing." The medic came by and gave me my shot.

I waited until 1950 and hollered to the squad, "Let's go. Strip down and zip up."

The shell is like a flexible spacesuit; at least the fittings on the inside are pretty similar. But instead of a life support package, there's a hose going into the top of the helmet and two coming out of the heels, as well as two relief tubes per suit. They're crammed in shoulder-to-shoulder on light acceleration couches; getting to your shell is like picking your way through a giant plate of olive drab spaghetti.

When the lights in my helmet showed that everybody was suited up, I pushed the button that flooded the room. No way to see, of course, but I could imagine the pale blue solution—ethylene glycol and something else—foaming up around and over us. The suit material, cool and dry, collapsed in to touch my skin at every point. I knew that my internal body pressure was increasing rapidly to match the increasing fluid pressure outside. That's what the shot was

83

for; keep your cells from getting squished between the devil and the deep blue sea. You could still feel it, though. By the time my meter said "2" (external pressure equivalent to a column of water two nautical miles deep), I felt that I was at the same time being crushed and bloated. By 2005 it was at 2.7 and holding steady. When the maneuvers began at 2010, you couldn't feel the difference. I thought I saw the needle fluctuate a tiny bit, though.

The major drawback to the system is that, of course, anybody caught outside of his shell when the *Anniversary* hit 25 G's would be just so much strawberry jam. So the guiding and the fighting have to be done by the ship's tactical computer—which does most of it anyway, but it's nice to have a human overseer.

Another small problem is that if the ship gets damaged and the pressure drops, you'll explode like a dropped melon. If it's the internal pressure, you get crushed to death in a microsecond.

And it takes ten minutes, more or less, to get depressurized and another two or three to get untangled and dressed. So it's not exactly something you can hop out of and come up fighting.

The accelerating was over at 2038. A green light went on and I chinned the button to depressurize.

Marygay and I were getting dressed outside.

"How'd that happen?" I pointed to an angry purple welt that ran from the bottom of her right breast to her hipbone.

"That's the second time," she said, mad. "The first one was on my back—I think that shell doesn't fit right, gets creases."

"Maybe you've lost weight."

"Wise guy." Our caloric intake had been rigorously monitored ever since we left Stargate the first time. You can't use a fighting suit unless it fits you like a second skin.

A wall speaker drowned out the rest of her comment. "Attention all personnel. Attention. All army personnel echelon six and above and all navy personnel echelon four and above will report to the briefing room at 2130."

It repeated the message twice. I went off to lie down for

a few minutes while Marygay showed her bruise to the medic and the armorer. I didn't feel a bit jealous.

The Commodore began the briefing. "There's not much to tell, and what there is is not good news.

"Six days ago, the Tauran vessel that is pursuing us released a drone missile. Its initial acceleration was on the order of 80 gravities.

"After blasting for approximately a day, its acceleration suddenly jumped to 148 gravities." Collective gasp.

"Yesterday, it jumped to 203 gravities. I shouldn't need to remind anyone here that this is twice the accelerative capability of the enemy's drones in our last encounter.

"We launched a salvo of drones, four of them, intersecting what the computer predicted to be the four most probable future trajectories of the enemy drone. One of them paid off, while we were doing evasive maneuvers. We contacted and destroyed the Tauran weapon about ten million kilometers from here."

That was practically next door. "The only encouraging thing we learned from the encounter was from spectral analysis of the blast. It was no more powerful an explosion than ones we have observed in the past, so at least their progress in propulsion hasn't been matched by progress in explosives.

"This is the first manifestation of a very important effect that has heretofore been of interest only to theorists. Tell me, soldier." He pointed at Negulesco. "How long has it been since we first fought the Taurans, at Aleph?"

"That depends on your frame of reference, Commodore," she answered dutifully. "To me, it's been about eight months."

"Exactly. You've lost about nine years, though, to time dilation, while we maneuvered between collapsar jumps. In an engineering sense, as we haven't done any important research and development aboard ship . . . that enemy vessel comes from our future!" He paused to let that sink in.

"As the war progresses, this can only become more and more pronounced. The Taurans don't have any cure for relativity, of course, so it will be to our benefit as often as to theirs.

"For the present, though, it is *we* who are operating with a handicap. As the Tauran pursuit vessel draws closer, this handicap will become more severe. They can simply out-shoot us.

"We're going to have to do some fancy dodging. When we get within five hundred million kilometers of the enemy ship, everybody gets in his shell and we just have to trust the logistic computer. It will put us through a rapid series of random changes in direction and velocity.

"I'll be blunt. As long as they have one more drone than we, they can finish us off. They haven't launched any more since that first one. Perhaps they are holding their fire . . . or maybe they only had one. In that case, it's we who have them.

"At any rate, all personnel will be required to be in their shells with no more than ten minutes' notice. When we get within a thousand million kilometers of the enemy, you are to stand *by* your shells. By the time we are within five hundred million kilometers, you will be in them, and all shell compounds flooded and pressurized. We cannot wait for anyone.

"That's all I have to say. Sub-major?"

"I'll speak to my people later, Commodore. Thank you."

"Dismissed." And none of this "fuck you, sir" non-sense. The navy thought that was just a little beneath their dignity. We stood at attention—all except Stott—until he had left the room. Then some other swabbie said "dismissed" again, and we left.

My squad had clean-up detail, so I told everybody who was to do what, put Tate in charge, and left. Went up to the NCO room for some company and maybe some infor-mation.

There wasn't much happening but idle speculation, so I took Rogers and went off to bed. Marygay had disappeared again, hopefully trying to wheedle something out of Singhe.

3

We had our promised get-together with the sub-major the next morning, when he more or less repeated what the commodore had said, in infantry terms and in his staccato monotone. He emphasized the fact that all we knew about the Tauran ground forces was that if their naval capability was improved, it was likely they would be able to handle us better than last time.

But that brings up an interesting point. Eight months or nine years before, we'd had a tremendous advantage: they had seemed not quite to understand what was going on. As belligerent as they had been in space, we'd expected them to be real Huns on the ground. Instead, they practically lined themselves up for slaughter. One escaped and presumably described the idea of old-fashioned in-fighting to his fellows.

But that, of course, didn't mean that the word had necessarily gotten to this particular bunch, the Taurans guarding Yod-4. The only way we know of to communicate faster than the speed of light is to physically carry a message through successive collapsar jumps. And there was no way of telling how many jumps there were between Yod-4 and the Tauran home base—so these might be just as passive as the last bunch, or might have been practicing infantry tactics for most of a decade. We would find out when we got there.

The armorer and I were helping my squad pull maintenance on their fighting suits when we passed the thousand million kilometer mark and had to go up to the shells.

We had about five hours to kill before we had to get into our cocoons. I played a game of chess with Rabi and lost. Then Rogers led the platoon in some vigorous calisthenics, probably for no other reason than to get their minds off the prospect of having to lie half-crushed in the shells for at least four hours. The longest we'd gone before was half that.

Ten minutes before the five hundred million kilometer mark, we squad leaders took over and supervised buttoning everybody up. In eight minutes we were zipped and flooded and at the mercy of—or safe in the arms of—the logistic computer.

While I was lying there being squeezed, a silly thought took hold of my brain and went round and round like a charge in a superconductor: according to military formalism, the conduct of war divides neatly into two categories, tactics and logistics. Logistics has to do with moving troops and feeding them and just about everything except the actual fighting, which is tactics. And now we're fighting, but we don't have a *tactical* computer to guide us through attack and defense, just a huge, super-efficient pacifistic cybernetic grocery clerk of a logistic, mark that word, *logistic* computer.

The other side of my brain, perhaps not quite as pinched, would argue that it doesn't matter what name you give to a computer, it's a pile of memory crystals, logic banks, nuts and bolts . . . If you program it to be Ghengis Khan, it is a tactical computer, even if its usual function is to monitor the stock market or control sewage conversion.

But the other voice was obdurate and said by that kind of reasoning, a man is only a hank of hair and a piece of bone and some stringy meat; and no matter what kind of a man he is, if you teach him well, you can take a Zen monk and turn him into a slavering bloodthirsty warrior.

Then what the hell are you, we, am I, answered the other side. A peace-loving, vacuum-welding specialist *cum* physics teacher snatched up by the Elite Conscription Act and reprogrammed to be a killing machine. You, I have killed and liked it.

But that was hypnotism, motivational conditioning, I argued back at myself. They don't do that anymore.

And the only reason, I said, they don't do it is that they think you'll kill better without it. That's logic.

Speaking of logic, the original question was, why do they

send a logistic computer to do a man's job? Or something like that . . . and we were off again.

The light blinked green and I chinned the switch automatically. The pressure was down to 1.3 before I realized that it meant we were alive, we had won the first skirmish.

I was only partly right.

4

I was belting on my tunic when my ring tingled and I held it up to listen. It was Rogers.

"Mandella, go check squad bay *3*. Something went wrong; Dalton had to depressurize it from Control."

Bay *3*—that was Marygay's squad! I rushed down the corridor in bare feet and got there just as they opened the door from inside the pressure chamber and began straggling out.

The first out was Bergman. I grabbed his arm. "What the hell is going on, Bergman?"

"Huh?" He peered at me, still dazed, as everyone is when they come out of the chamber. "Oh, s'you. Mandella. I dunno. Whad'ya mean?"

I squinted in through the door, still holding on to him. "You were late, man, you depressurized late. What happened?"

He shook his head, trying to clear it. "Late? Whad' late. Uh, how late?"

I looked at my watch for the first time. "Not too—" Jesus Christ. "Uh, we zipped in at 0520, didn't we?"

"Yeah, I think that's it."

Still no Marygay among the dim figures picking their way through the ranked couches and jumbled tubing. "Um, you were only a couple of minutes late . . . but we were only supposed to be under for four hours, maybe less. It's 1050."

"Um." He shook his head again. I let go of him and stood back to let Stiller and Demy through the door.

"Everybody's late, then," Bergman said. "So we aren't in any trouble."

"Uh—" Non sequiturs. "Right, right—Hey, Stiller! You seen—"

From inside: "Medic! MEDIC!"

Somebody who wasn't Marygay was coming out. I pushed her roughly out of my way and dove through the door, landed on somebody else and clambered over to where Struve, Marygay's assistant, was standing over a pod and talking very loud and fast into his ring.

"—and blood God yes we need—"

It was Marygay still lying in her suit she was

"—got the word from Dalton—"

covered every square inch of her with a uniform bright sheen of blood

"—when she didn't come out—"

it started as an angry welt up by her collarbone and was just a welt as it traveled between her breasts until it passed the sternum's support

"—I came over and popped the—"

and opened up into a cut that got deeper as it ran down over her belly and where it stopped

"—yeah, she's still—"

a few centimeters above the pubis a membraned loop of gut was protruding . . .

"—OK, left hip. Mandella—"

She was still alive, her heart palpitating, but her blood-streaked head lolled limply, eyes rolled back to white slits, bubbles of red froth appearing and popping at the corner of her mouth each time she exhaled shallowly.

"—tattooed on her left hip. Mandella! Snap out of it! Reach under her and find out what her blood—"

"TYPE O RH NEGATIVE GOD damn . . . it. Sorry—Oh negative." Hadn't I seen that tattoo ten thousand times?

Struve passed this information on and I suddenly remembered the first-aid kit on my belt, snapped it off and fumbled through it.

Stop the bleeding—protect the wound—treat for shock, that's what the book said. Forgot one, forgot one . . . *clear air passages.*

She was breathing, if that's what they meant. How do you stop the bleeding or protect the wound with one measly pressure bandage when the wound is nearly a meter long? Treat for shock, that I could do. I fished out the green ampoule, laid it against her arm and pushed the button.

Then I laid the sterile side of the bandage gently on top of the exposed intestine and passed the elastic strip under the small of her back, adjusted it for nearly zero tension and fastened it.

"Anything else you can do?" Struve asked.

I stood back and felt helpless. "I don't know. Can you think of anything?"

"I'm no more of a medic than you are." Looking up at the door, he kneaded a fist, biceps straining. "Where the hell are they? You have morph-plex in that kit?"

"Yeah, but somebody told me not to use it for internal—"

"William?"

Her eyes were open and she was trying to lift her head. I rushed over and held her. "It'll be all right, Marygay. The medic's coming."

"What . . . all right? I'm thirsty. Water."

"No, honey, you can't have any water. Not for a while, anyhow." Not if she was headed for surgery.

"Why is all the blood?" she said in a small voice. Her head rolled back. "Been a bad girl."

"It must have been the suit," I said rapidly. "Remember earlier, the creases?"

She shook her head. "Suit?" She turned suddenly paler and retched weakly. "Water . . . William, please."

Authoritative voice behind me: "Get a sponge or a cloth soaked in water." I looked around and saw Doc Wilson with two stretcher bearers.

"First half-liter femoral," he said to no one in particular as he carefully peeked under the pressure bandage. "Follow that relief tube down a couple of meters and pinch it off. Find out if she's passed any blood."

One of the medics ran a ten-centimeter needle into Marygay's thigh and started giving her whole blood from a plastic bag.

"Sorry I'm late," Doc Wilson said tiredly. "Business is booming. What'd you say about the suit?"

"She had two minor injuries before. Suit doesn't fit quite right, creases up under pressure."

He nodded absently, checking her blood pressure. "You, anybody, give—" Somebody handed him a paper towel dripping water. "Uh, give her any medication?"

"One ampoule of No-shock."

He wadded the paper towel up loosely and put it in Marygay's hand. "What's her name?" I told him.

"Marygay, we can't give you a drink of water but you can suck on this. Now I'm going to shine a bright light in your eye." While he was looking through her pupil with a metal tube, he said, "Temperature?" and one of the medics read a number from a digital readout box and withdrew a probe. "Passed blood?"

"Yes. Some."

He put his hand lightly on the pressure bandage. "Marygay, can you roll over a little on your right side?"

"Yes," she said slowly, and put her elbow down for leverage. "No," she said and started crying.

"Now, now," he said absently and pushed up on her hip just enough to be able to see her back. "Only the one wound," he muttered. "Hell of a lot of blood."

He pressed the side of his ring twice and shook it by his ear. "Anybody up in the shop?"

"Harrison, unless he's on a call."

A woman walked up, and at first I didn't recognize her, pale and disheveled, bloodstained tunic. It was Estelle Harmony.

Doc Wilson looked up. "Any new customers, Doctor Harmony?"

"No," she said dully. "The maintenance man was a double traumatic amputation. Only lived a few minutes. We're keeping him running for transplants."

"All those others?"

"Explosive decompression." She sniffed. "Anything I can do here?"

"Yeah, just a minute." He tried his ring again. "God damn it. You don't know where Harrison is?"

"No . . . well, maybe, he might be in Surgery *B* if there was trouble with the cadaver maintenance. Think I set it up all right, though."

"Yeah, well, hell you know how . . ."

"Mark!" said the medic with the blood bag.

"One more half-liter femoral," Doc Wilson said. "Es-

telle, you mind taking over for one of the medics here,
prepare this gal for surgery?''

''No, keep me busy.''

''Good—Hopkins, go up to the shop and bring down a
roller and a liter, uh, two liters isotonic fluorocarb with the
primary spectrum. If they're Merck they'll say 'abdominal
spectrum.' '' He found a part of his sleeve with no blood
on it and wiped his forehead. ''If you find Harrison, send
him over to surgery *A* and have him set up the anesthetic
sequence for abdominal.''

''And bring her up to *A*?''

''Right. If you can't find Harrison, get somebody—'' he
stabbed a finger in my direction, ''—this guy, to roll the
patient up to *A*; you run ahead and start the sequence.''

He picked up his bag and looked through it. ''We could
start the sequence here,'' he muttered. ''But hell, not with
paramethadone—Marygay? How do you feel?''

She was still crying. ''I'm . . . hurt.''

''I know,'' he said gently. He thought for a second and
said to Estelle, ''No way to tell really how much blood she
lost. She may have been passing it under pressure. Also
there's some pooling in the abdominal cavity. Since she's
still alive I don't think she could've bled under pressure for
very long. Hope no brain damage yet.''

He touched the digital readout attached to Marygay's
arm. ''Monitor the blood pressure, and if you think it's
indicated, give her five cc's vasoconstrictor. I've gotta go
scrub down.''

He closed his bag. ''You have any vasoconstrictor besides the pneumatic ampoule?''

Estelle checked her own bag. ''No, just the emergency
pneumatic . . . uh . . . yes, I've got controlled dosage on the
'dilator, though.''

''OK, if you have to use the 'constrictor and her pressure
goes up too fast—''

''I'll give her vasodilator two cc's at a time.''

''Check. Hell of a way to run things, but . . . well. If
you're not too tired, I'd like you to stand by me upstairs.''

''Sure.'' Doc Wilson nodded and left.

Estelle began sponging Marygay's belly with isopropyl

alcohol. It smelled cold and clean. "Somebody gave her No-shock?"

"Yes," I said, "about ten minutes ago."

"Ah. That's why the Doc was worried—no, you did the right thing. But No-shock's got some vasoconstrictor. Five cc's more might run up an overdose." She continued silently scrubbing, her eyes coming up every few seconds to check the blood pressure monitor.

"William?" It was the first time she'd shown any sign of knowing me. "This wom—, uh, Marygay, she's your lover? Your regular lover?"

"That's right."

"She's very pretty." A remarkable observation, her body torn and caked with crusting blood, her face smeared where I had tried to wipe away the tears. I suppose a doctor or a woman or a lover can look beneath that and see beauty.

"Yes, she is." She had stopped crying and had her eyes squeezed shut, sucking the last bit of moisture from the paper wad.

"Can she have some more water?"

"OK, same as before. Not too much."

I went out to the locker alcove and into the head for a paper towel. Now that the fumes from the pressurizing fluid had cleared, I could smell the air. It smelled wrong. Light machine oil and burnt metal, like the smell of a metalworking shop. I wondered whether they had overloaded the airco. That had happened once before, after the first time we'd used the acceleration chambers.

Marygay took the water without opening her eyes.

"Do you plan to stay together when you get back to Earth?"

"Probably," I said. "*If* we get back to Earth. Still one more battle."

"There won't be any more battles," she said flatly. "You mean you haven't heard?"

"What?"

"Don't you know the ship was hit?"

"Hit!" Then how could any of us be alive?

"That's right." She went back to her scrubbing. "Four squad bays. Also the armor bay. There isn't a fighting suit left on the ship . . . and we can't fight in our underwear.''

"What—squad bays, what happened to the people?"

"No survivors."

Thirty people. "Who was it?"

"All of the third platoon. First squad of the second platoon."

Al-Sadat, Busia, Maxwell, Negulesco. "My God."

"Thirty deaders, and they don't have the slightest notion of what caused it. Don't know but that it may happen again any minute."

"It wasn't a drone?"

"No, we got all of their drones. Got the enemy vessel, too. Nothing showed up on any of the sensors, just *blam!* and a third of the ship was torn to hell. We were lucky it wasn't the drive or the life support system." I was hardly hearing her. Penworth, LaBatt, Smithers. Christine and Frida. All dead. I was numb.

She took a blade-type razor and a tube of gel out of her bag. "Be a gentleman and look the other way," she said. "Oh, here." She soaked a square of gauze in alcohol and handed it to me. "Be useful. Do her face."

I started and, without opening her eyes, Marygay said, "That feels good. What are you doing?"

"Being a gentleman. And useful, too—"

"All personnel, attention, all personnel." There wasn't a squawk-box in the pressure chamber, but I could hear it clearly through the door to the locker alcove. "All personnel echelon 6 and above, unless directly involved in medical or maintenance emergencies, report immediately to the assembly area."

"I've got to go, Marygay."

She didn't say anything. I didn't know whether she had heard the announcement.

"Estelle," I addressed her directly, gentleman be damned. "Will you—"

"Yes. I'll let you know as soon as we can tell."

"Well."

"It's going to be all right." But her expression was grim

and worried. "Now get going," she said, softly.

By the time I picked my way out into the corridor, the 'box was repeating the message for the fourth time. There was a new smell in the air, that I didn't want to identify.

5

Halfway to the assembly area I realized what a mess I was, and ducked into the head by the NCO lounge. Corporal Kamehameha was hurriedly brushing her hair.

"William! What happened to you?"

"Nothing." I turned on a tap and looked at myself in the mirror. Dried blood smeared all over my face and tunic. "It was Marygay, Corporal Potter, her suit . . . well, evidently it got a crease, uh . . ."

"Dead?"

"No, just badly, uh, she's going into surgery—"

"Don't use hot water. You'll just set the stain."

"Oh. Right." I used the hot to wash my face and hand, dabbed at the tunic with cold. "Your squad's just two bays down from Al's isn't it?"

"Yes."

"Did you see what happened?"

"No. Yes. Not *when* it happened." For the first time I noticed that she was crying, big tears rolling down her cheeks and off her chin. Her voice was even, controlled. She pulled at her hair savagely. "It's a mess."

I stepped over and put my hand on her shoulder. "DON'T touch me!" she flared and knocked my hand off with the brush. "Sorry. Let's go."

At the door to the head she touched me lightly on the arm. "William . . ." She looked at me defiantly. "I'm just glad it wasn't me. You understand? That's the only way you can look at it."

I understood, but I didn't know that I believed her.

"I can sum it up very briefly," the commodore said in a tight voice, "if only because we know so little.

"Some ten seconds after we destroyed the enemy vessel, two objects, very small objects, struck the *Anniversary*

98

amidships. By inference, since they were not detected and we know the limits of our detection apparatus, we know that they were moving in excess of nine-tenths of the speed of light. That is to say, more precisely, their velocity vector *normal* to the axis of the *Anniversary* was greater than nine-tenths of the speed of light. They slipped in behind the repeller fields.''

When the *Anniversary* is moving at relativistic speeds, it is designed to generate two powerful electromagnetic fields, one centered about five thousand kilometers from the ship and the other about ten thousand klicks away, both in line with the direction of motion of the ship. These fields are maintained by a ''ramjet'' effect, energy picked up from interstellar gas as we mosey along.

Anything big enough to worry about hitting (that is, anything big enough to see with a strong magnifying glass) goes through the first field and comes out with a very strong negative charge all over its surface. As it enters the second field, it's repelled away from the path of the ship. If the object is too big to be pushed around this way, we can sense it at a greater distance and maneuver out of its way.

''I shouldn't have to emphasize how formidable a weapon this is. When the *Anniversary* was struck, our rate of speed with respect to the enemy was such that we traveled our own length every ten-thousandth of a second. Further, we were jerking around erratically with a constantly changing and purely random lateral acceleration. Thus the objects that struck us must have been guided, not aimed. And the guidance system was self-contained, since there were no Taurans alive at the time they struck us. All of this in a package no larger than a small pebble.

''Most of you are too young to remember the term *future shock*. Back in the seventies, some people felt that technological progress was so rapid that people, normal people, couldn't cope with it; that they wouldn't have time to get used to the present before the future was upon them. A man named Toffler coined the term *future shock* to describe this situation.'' The commodore could get pretty academic.

''We're caught up in a physical situation that resembles this scholarly concept. The result has been disaster. Tragedy. And, as we discussed in our last meeting, there is no way to counter it. Relativity traps us in the enemy's past; relativity brings them from our future. We can only hope that next time, the situation will be reversed. And all we can do to help bring that about is try to get back to Stargate, and then to Earth, where specialists may be able to deduce something, some sort of counterweapon, from the nature of the damage.

"Now we could attack the Tauran's portal planet from space and perhaps destroy the base without using you infantry. But I think there would be a very great risk involved. We might be ... shot down by whatever hit us today, and never return to Stargate with what I consider to be vital information. We could send a drone with a message detailing our assumptions about this new enemy weapon ... but that might be inadequate. And the Force would be that much further behind, technologically.

"Accordingly, we have set a course that will take us around Yod-4, keeping the collapsar as much as possible between us and the Tauran base. We will avoid contact with the enemy and return to Stargate as quickly as possible."

Incredibly, the commodore sat down and kneaded his temples. "All of you are at least squad or section leaders. Most of you have good combat records. And I hope that some of you will be rejoining the Force after your two years are up. Those of you who do will probably be made lieutenants, and face your first real command.

"It is to these people I would like to speak for a few moments, not as your ... as one of your commanders, but just as a senior officer and advisor.

"One cannot make command decisions simply by assessing the tactical situation and going ahead with whatever course of action will do the most harm to the enemy with a minimum of death and damage to your own men and materiel. Modern warfare has become very complex, especially during the last century. Wars are won not by a simple series of battles won, but by a complex interrelationship among military victory, economic pressures, logistic maneuvering, access to the enemy's information, political postures—dozens, literally dozens of factors."

I was hearing this, but the only thing that was getting through to my brain was that a third of our friends' lives had been snuffed out less than an hour before, and he was sitting up there giving us a lecture on military theory.

"So sometimes you have to throw away a battle in order to help win the war. This is exactly what we are going to do.

"This was not an easy decision. In fact, it was probably the hardest decision of my military career. Because, on the surface at least, it may look like cowardice.

"The logistic computer calculates that we have about a 62 percent chance of success, should we attempt to destroy the enemy base. Unfortunately, we would have only a 30 percent chance of survival—as some of the scenarios leading to success involve ramming the portal planet with the *Anniversary* at light speed." Jesus Christ.

"I hope none of you ever has to face such a decision. When we get back to Stargate, I will in all probability be court-martialed for cowardice under fire. But I honestly believe that the information that may be gained from analysis of the damage to the *Anniversary* is more important than the destruction of this one Tauran base." He sat up straight. "More important than one soldier's career."

I had to stifle an impulse to laugh. Surely "cowardice" had nothing to do with his decision. Surely he had nothing so primitive and unmilitary as a will to live.

The maintenance crew managed to patch up the huge rip in the side of the *Anniversary* and to repressurize that section. We spent the rest of the day cleaning up the area; without, of course, disturbing any of the precious evidence for which the commodore was willing to sacrifice his career.

The hardest part was jettisoning the bodies. It wasn't so bad except for the ones whose suits had burst.

I went to Estelle's cabin the next day, as soon as she was off duty.

"It wouldn't serve any good purpose for you to see her now." Estelle sipped her drink, a mixture of ethyl alcohol, citric acid and water, with a drop of some ester that approximated the aroma of orange rind.

"Is she out of danger?"

"Not for a couple of weeks. Let me explain." She set down her drink and rested her chin on interlaced fingers. "This sort of injury would be fairly routine under normal circumstances. Having replaced the lost blood, we'd simply sprinkle some magic powder into her abdominal cavity and paste her back up. Have her hobbling around in a couple of days.

"But there are complications. Nobody's ever been injured in a pressure suit before. So far, nothing really unusual has cropped up. But we want to monitor her innards very closely for the next few days.

"Also, we were very concerned about peritonitis. You know what peritonitis is?"

"Yes." Well, vaguely.

"Because a part of her intestine had ruptured under pressure. We didn't want to settle for normal prophylaxis because a lot of the, uh, contamination had impacted on the peritoneum under pressure. To play it safe, we completely sterilized the whole shebang, the abdominal cavity and her entire digestive system from the duodenum south. Then, of course, we had to replace all of her normal intestinal flora, now dead, with a commercially prepared culture. Still standard procedure, but not normally called for unless the damage is more severe."

"I see." And it was making me a little queasy. Doctors don't seem to realize that most of us are perfectly content not having to visualize ourselves as animated bags of skin filled with obscene glop.

"This in itself is enough reason not to see her for a couple of days. The changeover of intestinal flora has a pretty violent effect on the digestive system—not dangerous, since she's under constant observation. But tiring and, well, embarrassing.

"With all of this, she would be completely out of danger if this were a normal clinical situation. But we're decelerating at a constant 1-½ gees, and her internal organs have gone through a lot of jumbling around. You might as well know that if we do any blasting, anything over about two gees, she's going to die."

"But . . . but we're *bound* to go over two on the final approach! What—"

"I know, I know. But that won't be for a couple of weeks. Hopefully, she will have mended by then.

"William, face it. It's a miracle she survived to get into surgery. So there's a big chance she won't make it back to Earth. It's sad; she's a special person, *the* special person to you, maybe. But we've had so much death . . . you ought to be getting used to it, come to terms with it."

I took a long pull at my drink, identical to hers except for the citric acid. "You're getting pretty hard-boiled."

"Maybe . . . no. Just realistic. I have a feeling we're headed for a lot more death and sorrow."

"Not me. As soon as we get to Stargate, I'm a civilian."

"Don't be so sure." The old familiar argument. "Those clowns who signed us up for two years can just as easily make it four or—"

"Or six or twenty or the duration. But they won't. It would be mutiny."

"I don't know. If they could condition us to kill on cue, they can condition us to do almost anything. Re-enlist."

That was a chiller.

Later on we tried to make love, but both of us had too much to think about.

I got to see Marygay for the first time about a week later. She was wan, had lost a lot of weight and seemed very confused. Doc Wilson assured me that it was just the medication; they hadn't seen any evidence of brain damage.

She was still in bed, still being fed through a tube. I began to get very nervous about the calendar. Every day there seemed to be some improvement, but if she was still in bed when we hit that collapsar push, she wouldn't have a chance. I couldn't get any encouragement from Doc Wilson or Estelle; they said it depended on Marygay's resilience.

The day before the push, they transferred her from bed to Estelle's acceleration couch in the infirmary. She was lucid and was taking food orally, but she still couldn't move under her own power, not at 1-½ gees.

I went to see her. "Heard about the course change? We have to go through Aleph-9 to get back to Tet-38. Four more months on this damn hulk. But another six years' combat pay when we get back to Earth."

"That's good."

"Ah, just think of the great things we'll—"

"William."

I let it trail off. Never could lie.

"Don't try to jolly me. Tell me about vacuum welding, about your childhood, anything. Just don't bullshit me about getting back to Earth." She turned her face to the wall.

"I heard the doctors talking out in the corridor, one morning when they thought I was asleep. But it just confirmed what I already knew, the way everybody'd been moping around.

"So tell me, you were born in New Mexico in 1975. What then? Did you stay in New Mexico? Were you bright in school? Have any friends, or were you too bright like me? How old were you when you first got sacked?"

We talked in this vein for a while, uncomfortable. An idea came to me while we were rambling, and when I left Marygay I went straight to Dr. Wilson.

"We're giving her a fifty-fifty chance, but that's pretty arbitrary. None of the published data on this sort of thing really fits."

"But it is safe to say that her chances of survival are better, the less acceleration she has to endure."

"Certainly. For what it's worth. The commodore's going to take it as gently as possible, but that'll still be four or five gees. Three might even be too much; we won't know until it's over."

I nodded impatiently. "Yes, but I think there's a way to expose her to less acceleration than the rest of us."

"If you've developed an acceleration shield," he said smiling, "you better hurry and file a patent. You could sell it for a considerable—"

"No, Doc, it wouldn't be worth much under normal conditions; our shells work better and they evolved from the same principles."

"Explain away."

"We put Marygay into a shell and flood—"

"Wait, wait. Absolutely not. A poorly-fitting shell was what caused this in the first place. And this time, she'd have to use somebody else's."

"I know, Doc, let me explain. It doesn't have to fit her exactly as long as the life support hookups can function. The shell won't be pressurized on the inside; it won't have to be because she won't be subjected to those thousands of kilograms-per-square-centimeter pressure from the fluid outside."

"I'm not sure I follow."

"It's just an adaptation of—you've studied physics, haven't you?"

"A little bit, in medical school. My worst courses, after Latin."

"Do you remember the principle of equivalence?"

"I remember there was something by that name. Something to do with relativity, right?"

"Uh-huh. It means that . . . there's no difference being in a gravitational field and being in an equivalent accelerated frame of—it means that when the *Anniversary* is blasting five gees, the effect on us is the same as if it were sitting on its tail on a big planet, on one with five gees' surface gravity."

"Seems obvious."

"Maybe it is. It means that there's no experiment you could perform on the ship that could tell you whether you were blasting or just sitting on a big planet."

"Sure there is. You could turn off the engines, and if—"

"Or you could look outside, sure; I mean isolated, physics-lab type experiments."

"All right. I'll accept that. So?"

"You know Archimedes' Law?"

"Sure, the fake crown—that's what always got me about physics, they make a big to-do about obvious things, and when it gets to the rough parts—"

"Archimedes' Law says that when you immerse something in a fluid, it's buoyed up by a force equal to the weight of the fluid it displaces."

"That's reasonable."

"And that holds, no matter what kind of gravitation or acceleration you're in—In a ship blasting at five gees, the water displaced, if it's water, weighs five times as much as regular water, at one gee."

"Sure."

"So if you float somebody in the middle of a tank of water, so that she's weightless, she'll still be weightless when the ship is doing five gees."

"Hold on, son. You had me going there, but it won't work."

"Why not?" I was tempted to tell him to stick to his pills and stethoscopes and let me handle the physics, but it was a good thing I didn't.

"What happens when you drop a wrench in a submarine?"

"Submarine?"

"That's right. They work by Archimedes'—"

"Ouch! You're right. Jesus. Hadn't thought it through."

"That wrench falls right to the floor just as if the submarine weren't weightless." He looked off into space, tapping a pencil on the desk. "What you describe is similar to the way we treat patients with severe skin damage, like burns, on Earth. But it doesn't give any support to the internal organs, the way the acceleration shells do, so it wouldn't do Marygay any good. . . ."

I stood up to go. "Sorry I wasted—"

"Hold on there, though, just a minute. We might be able to use your idea part-way."

"How do you mean?"

"I wasn't thinking it through, either. The way we normally use the shells is out of the question for Marygay, of course." I didn't like to think about it. Takes a lot of hypno-conditioning to lie there and have oxygenated fluorocarbon forced into every natural body orifice and one artificial one. I fingered the valve fitting imbedded above my hipbone.

"Yeah, that's obvious, it'd tear her—say . . . you mean, low pressure—"

"That's right. We wouldn't need thousands of atmospheres to protect her against five gees' straight-line acceleration; that's only for all the swerving and dodging—I'm going to call Maintenance. Get down to your squad bay; that's the one we'll use. Dalton'll meet you there."

Five minutes before injection into the collapsar field, and I started the flooding sequence. Marygay and I were the only ones in shells; my presence wasn't really vital since the flooding and emptying could be done by Control. But it was safer to have redundancy in the system and besides, I wanted to be there.

It wasn't nearly as bad as the normal routine; none of the crushing-bloating sensation. You were just suddenly filled with the plastic-smelling stuff (you never perceived the first moments, when it rushed in to replace the air in your lungs), and then there was a slight acceleration, and then you were breathing air again, waiting for the shell to pop; then unplugging and unzipping and climbing out—

Marygay's shell was empty. I walked over to it and saw blood.

"She hemorrhaged." Doc Wilson's voice echoed sepulchrally. I turned, eyes stinging, and saw him leaning in the door to the locker alcove. He was unaccountably, horribly, smiling.

"Which was expected. Doctor Harmony's taking care of it. She'll be just fine."

6

Marygay was walking in another week, "Confraternizing" in two, and pronounced completely healed in six.

Ten long months in space and it was army, army, army all the way. Calisthenics, meaningless work details, compulsory lectures—there was even talk that they were going to reinstate the sleeping roster we'd had in basic, but they never did, probably out of fear of mutiny. A random partner every night wouldn't have set too well with those of us who'd established more-or-less permanent pairs.

All this crap, this insistence on military discipline, bothered me mainly because I was afraid it meant they weren't going to let us out. Marygay said I was being paranoid; they only did it because there was no other way to maintain order for ten months.

Most of the talk, besides the usual bitching about the army, was speculation about how much Earth would have changed and what we would do when we got out. We'd be fairly rich: twenty-six years' salary all at once. Compound interest, too; the $500 we'd been paid for our first month in the army had grown to over $1500.

We arrived at Stargate in late 2023, Greenwich date.

The base had grown astonishingly in the nearly seventeen years we had been on the Yod-4 campaign. It was one building the size of Tycho City, housing nearly ten thousand. There were seventy-eight cruisers, the size of *Anniversary* or larger, involved in raids on Tauran-held portal planets. Another ten guarded Stargate itself, and two were in orbit waiting for their infantry and crew to be outprocessed. One other ship, the *Earth's Hope II*, had returned from fighting and had been waiting at Stargate for another cruiser to return.

108

They had lost two-thirds of their crew, and it was just not economical to send a cruiser back to Earth with only thirty-nine people aboard. Thirty-nine confirmed civilians.

We went planetside in two scoutships.

7

General Botsford (who had only been a full major the first time we met him, when Stargate was two huts and twenty-four graves) received us in an elegantly appointed seminar room. He was pacing back and forth at the end of the room, in front of a huge holographic operations chart.

"You know," he said, too loud, and then, more conversationally, "you know that we could disperse you into other strike forces and send you right out again. The Elite Conscription Act has been changed now, five years' subjective in service instead of two.

"And I don't see why some of you don't *want* to stay in! Another couple of years and compound interest would make you independently wealthy for life. Sure, you took heavy losses—but that was inevitable, you were the first. Things are going to be easier now. The fighting suits have been improved, we know more about the Taurans' tactics, our weapons are more effective . . . there's no need to be afraid."

He sat down at the head of the table and looked at nobody in particular.

"My own memories of combat are over a half-century old. To me it was exhilarating, strengthening. I must be a different kind of person than all of you."

Or have a very selective memory, I thought.

"But that's neither here nor there. I have one alternative to offer you, one that doesn't involve direct combat.

"We're very short of qualified instructors. The Force will offer any one of you a lieutenancy if you will accept a training position. It can be on Earth; on the Moon at double pay; on Charon at triple pay; or here at Stargate for quadruple pay. Furthermore, you don't have to make up your mind now. You're all getting a free trip back to Earth—I envy you, I haven't been back in fifteen years, will probably never go back—and you can get the feel of being a civilian again. If you don't like it, just walk into any UNEF installation and you'll walk out an officer. Your choice of assignment.

"Some of you are smiling. I think you ought to reserve judgment. Earth is not the same place you left."

He pulled a little card out of his tunic and looked at it, smiling. "Most of you have something on the order of four hundred thousand dollars coming to you, accumulated pay and interest. But Earth is on a war footing and, of course, it is the citizens of Earth who are supporting the war. Your income puts you in a ninety-two-percent income-tax bracket: thirty-two thousand might last you about three years if you're careful.

"Eventually you're going to have to get a job, and this is one job for which you are uniquely trained. There are not that many jobs available. The population of Earth is nearly nine billion, with five or six billion unemployed.

"Also keep in mind that your friends and sweethearts of two years ago are now going to be twenty-one years older than you. Many of your relatives will have passed away. I think you'll find it a very lonely world.

"But to tell you something about this world, I'm going to turn you over to Captain Siri, who just arrived from Earth. Captain?"

"Thank you, General." It looked as if there was something wrong with his skin, his face; and then I realized he was wearing powder and lipstick. His nails were smooth white almonds.

"I don't know where to begin." He sucked in his upper lip and looked at us, frowning. "Things have changed so very much since I was a boy.

"I'm twenty-three, so I was still in diapers when you people left for Aleph . . . to begin with, how many of you are homosexual?" Nobody. "That doesn't really surprise me. I am, of course. I guess about a third of everybody in Europe and America is.

"Most governments encourage homosexuality—the United Nations is neutral, leaves it up to the individual countries—they encourage homolife mainly because it's the one sure method of birth control.''

That seemed specious to me. Our method of birth control in the army is pretty foolproof: all men making a deposit in the sperm bank, and then vasectomy.

''As the General said, the population of the world is nine billion. It's more than doubled since you were drafted. And nearly two-thirds of those people get out of school only to go on relief.

''Speaking of school, how many years of public schooling did the government give you?''

He was looking at me, so I answered. ''Fourteen.''

He nodded. ''It's eighteen now. More, if you don't pass your examinations. And you're required by law to pass your exams before you're eligible for any job or Class One relief. And brother-boy, anything besides Class One is hard to live on. Yes?'' Hofstadter had his hand up.

''Sir, is it eighteen years public school in every country? Where do they find enough schools?''

''Oh, most people take the last five or six years at home or in a community center, via holoscreen. The UN has forty or fifty information channels, giving instruction twenty-four hours a day.

''But most of you won't have to concern yourselves with that. If you're in the Force, you're already too smart by half.''

He brushed hair from his eyes in a thoroughly feminine gesture, pouting a little. ''Let me do some history to you. I guess the first really important thing that happened after you left was the Ration War.

''That was 2007. A lot of things happened at once. Locust plague in North America, rice blight from Burma to the South China Sea, red tides all along the west coast of South America: suddenly there just wasn't enough food to go around. The UN stepped in and took over food distribution. Every man, woman, and child got a ration booklet, allowing thim to consume so many calories per month. If tha went over ther monthly allotment, tha just went hungry until the first of the next month.''

Some of the new people we'd picked up after Aleph used

"tha, ther, thim" instead of "he, his, him," for the collective pronoun. I wondered whether it had become universal.

"Of course, an illegal market developed, and soon there was great inequality in the amount of food people in various strata of society consumed. A vengeance group in Ecuador, the Imparciales, systematically began to assassinate people who appeared to be well-fed. The idea caught on pretty quickly, and in a few months there was a full-scale, undeclared class war going on all over the world. The United Nations managed to get things back under control in a year or so, by which time the population was down to four billion, crops were more or less recovered, and the food crisis was over. They kept the rationing, but it's never been really severe again.

"Incidentally, the General translated the money coming to you into dollars just for your own convenience. The world has only one currency now, calories. Your thirty-two thousand dollars comes to about three thousand million calories. Or three million K's, kilocalories.

"Ever since the Ration War, the UN has encouraged subsistence farming wherever it's practical. Food you grow yourself, of course, isn't rationed. . . . It got people out of the cities, onto UN farming reservations, which helped alleviate some urban problems. But subsistence farming seems to encourage large families, so the population of the world has more than doubled since the Ration War.

"Also, we no longer have the abundance of electrical power I remember from boyhood . . . probably a good deal less than you remember. There are only a few places in the world where you can have power all day and night. They keep saying it's a temporary situation, but it's been going on for over a decade."

He went on like that for a long time. Well, hell, it wasn't really surprising, much of it. We'd probably spent more time in the past two years talking about what home was going to be like than about anything else. Unfortunately, most of the bad things we'd prognosticated seemed to have come true, and not many of the good things.

The worst thing for me, I guess, was that they'd taken over most of the good parkland and subdivided it into little farms. If you wanted to find some wilderness, you had to go someplace where they couldn't possibly make a plant grow.

He said that the relations between people who chose homolife and the ones he called "breeders" were quite smooth, but I wondered. I never had much trouble accepting homosexuals myself, but then I'd never had to cope with such an abundance of them.

He also said, in answer to an impolite question, that his powder and paint had nothing to do with his sexual orientation. It was just stylish. I decided I'd be an anachronism and just wear my face.

I don't guess it should have surprised me that language had changed considerably in twenty years. My parents were always saying things were "cool," joints were "grass," and so on.

We had to wait several weeks before we could get a ride back to Earth. We'd be going back on the *Anniversary*, but first she had to be taken apart and put back together again.

Meanwhile, we were put in cozy little two-man billets and released from all military responsibilities. Most of us spent our days down at the library, trying to catch up on twenty-two years of current events. Evenings, we'd get together at the Flowing Bowl, an NCO club. The privates, of course, weren't supposed to be there, but we found that nobody argues with a person who has two of the fluorescent battle ribbons.

I was surprised that they served heroin fixes at the bar. The waiter said that you get a compensating shot to keep you from getting addicted to it. I got really stoned and tried one. Never again.

Sub-major Stott stayed at Stargate, where they were assembling a new Strike Force Alpha. The rest of us boarded the *Anniversary* and had a fairly pleasant six-month journey. Cortez didn't insist on everything being capital-M military, so it was a lot better than the trip from Yod-4.

8

I hadn't given it too much thought, but of course we were celebrities on Earth: the first vets home from the war. The Secretary General greeted us at Kennedy and we had a week-long whirl of banquets, receptions, interviews, and all that. It was enjoyable enough, and profitable—I made a million κ's from Time-Life/Fax—but we really saw little of Earth until after the novelty wore off and we were more or less allowed to go our own way.

I picked up the Washington monorail at Grand Central Station and headed home. My mother had met me at Kennedy, suddenly and sadly old, and told me my father was dead. Flyer accident. I was going to stay with her until I could get a job.

She was living in Columbia, a satellite of Washington. She had moved back into the city after the Ration War—having moved out in 1980—and then failing services and rising crime had forced her out again.

She was waiting for me at the monorail station. Beside her stood a blond giant in a heavy black vinyl uniform, with a big gunpowder pistol on his hip and spiked brass knuckles on his right hand.

"William, this is Carl, my bodyguard and very dear friend." Carl slipped off the knuckles long enough to shake hands with surprising gentleness. "Pleasameecha Misser Mandella."

We got into a groundcar that had "Jefferson" written on it in bright orange letters. I thought that was an odd thing to name a car, but then found out that it was the name of the high-rise Mother and Carl lived in. The groundcar was one of several that belonged to the community, and she paid 100κ per kilometer for the use of it.

I had to admit that Columbia was rather pretty: formal gardens and lots of trees and grass. Even the high-rises, roughly conical jumbles of granite with trees growing out at odd places, looked more like mountains than buildings. We drove into the base of one of these mountains, down a well-lit corridor to where a number of other cars were parked. Carl carried my solitary bag to the elevator and set it down.

"Miz Mandella, if is awright witcha, I gots to go pick up Miz Freeman in like five. She over West Branch."

"Sure, Carl, William can take care of me. He's a soldier, you know." That's right, I remember learning eight silent ways to kill a man. Maybe if things got really tight, I could get a job like Carl's.

"Righty-oh, yeah, you tol' me. Whassit like, man?"

"Mostly boring," I said automatically. "When you aren't bored, you're scared."

He nodded wisely. "Thass what I heard. Miz Mandella, I be 'vailable anytime after six. Righty-oh?"

"That's fine, Carl."

The elevator came and a tall skinny boy stepped out, an unlit joint dangling from his lips. Carl ran his fingers over the spikes on his knuckles, and the boy walked rapidly away.

"Gots ta watch out fer them riders. T'care a yerself, Miz Mandella."

We got on the elevator and Mother punched 47. "What's a rider?"

"Oh, they're just young toughs who ride up and down the elevators looking for defenseless people without bodyguards. They aren't too much of a problem here."

The forty-seventh floor was a huge mall filled with shops and offices. We went to a food store.

"Have you gotten your ration book yet, William?" I told her I hadn't, but the Force had given me travel tickets worth a hundred thousand "calories" and I'd used up only half of them.

It was a little confusing, but they'd explained it to us.

When the world went on a single currency, they'd tried to coordinate it with the food rationing in some way, hoping to eventually eliminate the ration books, so they'd made the new currency K'S, kilocalories, because that's the unit for measuring the energy equivalent of food. But a person who eats 2,000 kilocalories of steak a day obviously has to pay more than a person eating the same amount of bread. So they instituted a sliding "ration factor," so complicated that nobody could understand it. After a few weeks they were using the books again, but calling food kilocalories "calories" in an attempt to make things less confusing. Seemed to me they'd save a lot of trouble all around if they'd just call money dollars again, or rubles or sisterces or whatever . . . anything but kilocalories.

Food prices were astonishing, except for grains and legumes. I insisted on splurging on some good red meat: 1500 calories worth of ground beef, costing 1730K. The same amount of fakesteak, made from soy beans, would have cost 80K.

I also got a head of lettuce for 140K and a little bottle of olive oil for 175K. Mother said she had some vinegar. Started to buy some mushrooms but she said she had a neighbor who grew them and could trade something from her balcony garden.

At her apartment on the ninety-second floor, she apologized for the smallness of the place. It didn't seem so little to me, but then she'd never lived on a spaceship.

Even this high up, there were bars on the windows. The door had four separate locks, one of which didn't work because somebody had used a crowbar on it.

Mother went off to turn the ground beef into a meatloaf and I settled down with the evening 'fax. She pulled some carrots from her little garden and called the mushroom lady, whose son came over to make the trade. He had a riot gun slung under his arm.

"Mother, where's the rest of the Star?" I called into the kitchen.

"As far as I know, it's all there. What were you looking for?"

"Well . . . I found the classified section, but no 'Help Wanted.' "

She laughed. "Son, there hasn't been a 'Help Wanted' ad in ten years. The government takes care of jobs . . . well, most of them."

"Everybody works for the government?"

"No, that's not it." She came in, wiping her hands on a frayed towel. "The government, they tell us, handles the distribution of all natural resources. And there aren't many resources more valuable than empty jobs."

"Well, I'll go talk to them tomorrow."

"Don't bother, son. How much retirement pay you say you're getting from the Force?"

"Twenty thousand κ a month. Doesn't look like it'll go far."

"No, it won't. But your father's pension gave me less than half that, and they wouldn't give me a job. Jobs are assigned on a basis of need. And you've got to be living on rice and water before the Employment Board considers you needy."

"Well, hell, it's a bureaucracy—there must be somebody I can pay off, slip me into a good—"

"No. Sorry, that's one part of the UN that's absolutely incorruptible. The whole shebang is cybernetic, untouched by human souls. You can't—"

"But you said you *had* a job!"

"I was getting to that. If you want a job badly enough, you can go to a dealer and sometimes get a hand-me-down."

"Hand-me-down? Dealer?"

"Take my job as an example, son. A woman named Hailey Williams has a job in a hospital, running a machine that analyzes blood, a chromatography machine. She works six nights a week, for 12,000κ a week. She gets tired of working, so she contacts a dealer and lets him know that her job is available.

"Some time before this, I'd given the dealer his initial fee of 50,000κ to get on his list. He comes by and describes the job to me and I say fine, I'll take it. He knew I would and already has fake identification and a uniform. He distributes small bribes to the various supervisors who might know Miss Williams by sight.

"Miss Williams shows me how to run the machine and quits. She still gets the weekly 12,000κ credited to her account, but she pays me half. I pay the dealer ten percent

and wind up with 5400κ per week. This, added to the nine
grand I get monthly from your father's pension, makes me
quite comfortable.

"Then it gets complicated. Finding myself with plenty
of money and too little time, I contact the dealer again,
offering to sublet half my job. The next day a girl shows
up who also has 'Hailey Williams' identification. I show
her how to run the machine, and she takes over Monday-
Wednesday-Friday. Half of my real salary is 2700κ, so she
gets half that, 1350κ, and pays the dealer 135."

She got a pad and a stylus and did some figuring. "So
the real Hailey Williams gets 6000κ weekly for doing nothing. I work three days a week for 4050κ. My assistant
works three days for 1115κ. The dealer gets 100,000κ in
fees and 735κ per week. Lopsided, isn't it?"

"Hmm . . . I'll say. Quite illegal, too, I suppose."

"For the dealer. Everybody else might lose their job and
have to start over, if the Employment Board finds out. But
the dealer gets brainwiped."

"Guess I better find a dealer, while I can still afford the
fifty-grand bite." Actually, I still had over three million,
but planned to run through most of it in a short time. Hell,
I'd earned it.

I was getting ready to go the next morning when Mother
came in with a shoebox. Inside, there was a small pistol in
a clip-on holster.

"This belonged to your father," she explained. "Better
wear it if you're planning to go downtown without a bodyguard."

It was a gunpowder pistol with ridiculously thin bullets.
I hefted it in my hand. "Did Dad ever use it?"

"Several times . . . just to scare away riders and hitters,
though. He never actually shot anybody."

"You're probably right that I need a gun," I said, putting
it back. "But I'd have to have something with more heft
to it. Can I buy one legally?"

"Sure, there's a gun store down in the Mall. As long as
you don't have a police record, you can buy anything that

suits you." Good; I'd get a little pocket laser. I could hardly hit the wall with a gunpowder pistol.

"But . . . William, I'd feel a lot better if you'd hire a bodyguard, at least until you know your way around." We'd gone all around that last night. Being an official Trained Killer, I thought I was tougher than any clown I might hire for the job.

"I'll check into it, Mother. Don't worry—I'm not even going downtown today, just into Hyattsville."

"That's just as bad."

When the elevator came, it was already occupied. He looked at me blandly as I got in, a man a little older than me, clean-shaven and well dressed. He stepped back to let me at the row of buttons. I punched 47 and then, realizing his motive might not have been politeness, turned to see him struggling to get at a metal pipe stuck in his waistband. It had been hidden by his cape.

"Come on, fella," I said, reaching for a nonexistent weapon. "You wanna get caulked?"

He had the pipe free but let it hang loosely at his side. "Caulked?"

"Killed. Army term." I took one step toward him, trying to remember. Kick just under the knee, then either groin or kidney. I decided on the groin.

"No." He put the pipe back in his waistband. "I don't want to get 'caulked.' " The door opened at 47 and I backed out.

The gun shop was all bright white plastic and gleamy black metal. A little bald man bobbed over to wait on me. He had a pistol in a shoulder rig.

"And a fine morning to you, sir," he said and giggled. "What will it be today?"

"Lightweight pocket laser," I said. "Carbon dioxide."

He looked at me quizzically and then brightened. "Coming right up, sir." Giggle. "Special today, I throw in a handful of tachyon grenades."

"Fine." They'd be handy.

He looked at me expectantly. "So? What's the popper?"

"Huh?"

"The punch, man; you set me up, now knock me down. Laser." He giggled.

I was beginning to understand. "You mean I can't buy a laser."

"Of *course* not, sweetie," he said and sobered. "You didn't know that?"

"I've been out of the country for a long time."

"The world, you mean. You've been out of the world a long time." He put his left hand on a chubby hip in a gesture that incidentally made his gun easier to get. He scratched the center of his chest.

I stood very still. "That's right. I just got out of the Force."

His jaw dropped. "Hey, no bully-bull? You been out shootin' 'em up, out in space?"

"That's right."

"Hey, all that crap about you not gettin' older, there's nothin' to that, is there?"

"Oh, it's true. I was born in 1975."

"Well, god . . . damn. You're almost as old as I am." He giggled. "I thought that was just something the government made up."

"Anyhow . . . you say I can't buy a laser—"

"Oh, no. No no no. I run a legal shop here."

"What can I buy?"

"Oh, pistol, rifle, shotgun, knife, body armor . . . just no lasers or explosives or fully automatic weapons."

"Let me see a pistol. The biggest you have."

"Ah, I've got just the thing." He motioned me over to a display case and opened the back, taking out a huge revolver.

"Four-ten-gauge six-shooter." He cradled it in both hands. "Dinosaur-stopper. Authentic Old West styling. Slugs or flechettes."

"Flechettes?"

"Sure—uh, they're like a bunch of tiny darts. You shoot and they spread out in a pattern. Hard to miss that way."

Sounded like my speed. "Anyplace I can try it out?"

" 'Course, of course, we have a range in back. Let me get my assistant." He rang a bell and a boy came out to watch the store while we went in back. He picked up a red-and-green box of shotgun shells on the way.

The range was in two sections, a little anteroom with a plastic transparent door and a long corridor on the other side of the door with a table at one end and targets at the other. Behind the targets was a sheet of metal that evidently deflected the bullets down into a pool of water.

He loaded the pistol and set it on the table. "Please don't pick it up until the door's closed." He went into the anteroom, closed the door, and picked up a microphone. "Okay. First time, you better hold on to it with both hands." I did so, raising it up in line with the center target, a square of paper looking about the size of your thumbnail at arm's length. Doubted I'd even come near it. I pulled the trigger and it went back easily enough, but nothing happened.

"No, no," he said over the microphone with a tinny giggle. "Authentic Old West styling. You've got to pull the hammer back."

Sure, just like in the flicks. I hauled the hammer back, lined it up again, and squeezed the trigger.

The noise was so loud it made my face sting. The gun bucked up and almost hit me on the forehead. But the three center targets were gone: just tiny tatters of paper drifting in the air.

"I'll take it."

He sold me a hip holster, twenty shells, a chest-and-back shield, and a dagger in a boot sheath. I felt more heavily armed than I had in a fighting suit. But no waldos to help me cart it around.

The monorail had two guards for each car. I was beginning to feel that all my heavy artillery was superfluous, until I got off at the Hyattsville station.

Everyone who got off at Hyattsville was either heavily armed or had a bodyguard. The people loitering around the station were all armed. The police carried lasers.

I pushed a "cab call" button, and the readout told me mine would be No. 3856. I asked a policeman and he told me to wait for it down on the street; it would cruise around the block twice.

During the five minutes I waited, I twice heard staccato arguments of gunfire, both of them rather far away. I was glad I'd bought the shield.

Eventually the cab came. It swerved to the curb when I waved at it, the door sliding open as it stopped. Looked as if it worked the same way as the autocabs I remembered. The door stayed open while it checked the thumbprint to verify that I was the one who had called, then slammed shut. It was thick steel. The view through the windows was dim and distorted; probably thick bulletproof plastic. Not quite the same as I remembered.

I had to leaf through a grimy book to find the code for the address of the bar in Hyattsville where I was supposed to meet the dealer. I punched it out and sat back to watch the city go by.

This part of town was mostly residential: grayed-brick warrens built around the middle of the last century competing for space with more modern modular setups and, occasionally, individual houses behind tall brick or concrete walls with jagged broken glass and barbed wire at the top. A few people seemed to be going somewhere, walking very quickly down the sidewalks, hands on weapons. Most of the people I saw were either sitting in doorways, smoking, or loitering around shopfronts in groups of no fewer than six. Everything was dirty and cluttered. The gutters were clotted with garbage, and shoals of waste paper drifted with the wind of the light traffic.

It was understandable, though; street-sweeping was probably a very high-risk profession.

The cab pulled up in front of Tom & Jerry's Bar and Grill and let me out after I paid 430ᴋ. I stepped to the sidewalk with my hand on the shotgun-pistol, but there was nobody around. I hustled into the bar.

It was surprisingly clean on the inside, dimly lit and furnished in fake leather and fake pine. I went to the bar and got some fake bourbon and, presumably, real water for 120ᴋ. The water cost 20ᴋ. A waitress came over with a tray.

"Pop one, brother-boy?" The tray had a rack of old-fashioned hypodermic needles.

"Not today, thanks." If I was going to "pop one," I'd use an aerosol. The needles looked unsanitary and painful.

She set the dope down on the bar and eased onto the stool next to me. She sat with her chin cupped in her palm and stared at her reflection in the mirror behind the bar. "God. Tuesdays."

I mumbled something.

"You wanna go in back fer a quickie?"

I looked at her with what I hoped was a neutral expression. She was wearing only a short skirt of some gossamer material, and it plunged in a shallow V in the front, exposing her hipbones and a few bleached pubic hairs. I wondered what could possibly keep it up. She wasn't bad looking, could have been anywhere from her late twenties to her early forties. No telling what they could do with cosmetic surgery and makeup nowadays, though. Maybe she was older than my mother.

"Thanks anyhow."

"Not today?"

"That's right."

"I can get you a nice boy, if—"

"No. No thanks." What a world.

She pouted into the mirror, an expression that was probably older than *Homo sapiens*. "You don't like me."

"I like you fine. That's just not what I came here for."

"Well . . . different funs for different ones." She shrugged. "Hey, Jerry. Get me a short beer."

He brought it.

"Oh, damn, my purse is locked up. Mister, can you spare forty calories?" I had enough ration tickets to take care of a whole banquet. Tore off a fifty and gave it to the bartender.

"Jesus." She stared. "How'd you get a full book at the end of the month?"

I told her in as few words as possible who I was and how I managed to have so many calories. There had been two months' worth of books waiting in my mail, and I hadn't even used up the ones the Force had given me. She offered to buy a book from me for ten grand, but I didn't want to get involved in more than one illegal enterprise at a time.

Two men came in, one unarmed and the other with both a pistol and a riot gun. The bodyguard sat by the door and the other came over to me.

"Mr. Mandella?"

"That's right."

"Shall we take a booth?" He didn't offer his name.

He had a cup of coffee, and I sipped a mug of beer. "I don't keep any written records, but I have an excellent memory. Tell me what sort of a job you're interested in, what your qualifications are, what salary you'll accept, and so on."

I told him I'd prefer to wait for a job where I could use my physics—teaching or research, even engineering. I wouldn't need a job for two or three months, since I planned to travel and spend money for a while. Wanted at least 20,000K monthly, but how much I'd accept would depend on the nature of the job.

He didn't say a word until I'd finished. "Righty-oh. Now, I'm afraid . . . you'd have a hard time, getting a job in physics. Teaching is out; I can't supply jobs where the person is constantly exposed to the public. Research, well, your degree is almost a quarter of a century old. You'd have to go back to school, maybe five or six years."

"Might do that," I said.

"The one really marketable feature you have is your combat experience. I could probably place you in a supervisory job at a bodyguard agency for even more than twenty grand. You could make almost that much, being a bodyguard yourself."

"Thanks, but I wouldn't want to take chances for somebody else's hide."

"Righty-oh. Can't say I blame you." He finished his coffee in a long slurp. "Well, I've got to run, got a thousand things to do. I'll keep you in mind and talk to some people."

"Good. I'll see you in a few months."

"Righty-oh. Don't need to make an appointment. I come

in here every day at eleven for coffee. Just show up.''

I finished my beer and called a cab to take me home. I wanted to walk around the city, but Mother was right. I'd get a bodyguard first.

9

I came home and the phone was blinking pale blue. Didn't know what to do so I punched "Operator."

A pretty young girl's head materialized in the cube. "Jefferson operator," she said. "May I help you?"

"Yes . . . what does it mean when the cube is blinking blue?"

"Huh?"

"What does it mean when the phone—"

"Are you serious?" I was getting a little tired of this kind of thing.

"It's a long story. Honest, I don't know."

"When it blinks blue you're supposed to call the operator."

"Okay, here I am."

"No, not me, the *real* operator. Punch nine. Then punch zero."

I did that and an old harridan appeared. "Ob-a-ray-duh."

"This is William Mandella at 301-52-574-3975. I was supposed to call you."

"Juzza segun." She reached outside the field of view and typed something. "You godda call from 605-19-556-2027."

I scribbled it down on the pad by the phone. "Where's that?"

"Juzza segun. South Dakota."

"Thanks." I didn't know anybody in South Dakota.

A pleasant-looking old woman answered the phone. "Yes?"

"I had a call from this number . . . uh . . . I'm—"

"Oh. Sergeant Mandella! Just a second."

I watched the diagonal bar of the holding pattern for a second, then fifty or so more. Then a head came into focus.

Marygay. "William. I had a heck of a time finding you."

"Darling, me too. What are you doing in South Dakota?"

"My parents live here, in a little commune. That's why it took me so long to get to the phone." She held up two grimy hands. "Digging potatoes."

"But when I checked . . . the records said—the records in Tucson said your parents were both dead."

"No, they're just dropouts—you know about dropouts?—new name, new life. I got the word through a cousin."

"Well—well, how've you been? Like the country life?"

"That's one reason I've been wanting to get you. Willy, I'm bored. It's all very healthy and nice, but I want to do something dissipated and wicked. Naturally I thought of you."

"I'm flattered. Pick you up at eight?"

She checked a clock above the phone. "No, look, let's get a good night's sleep. Besides, I've got to get in the rest of the potatoes. Meet me at . . . the Ellis Island jetport at ten tomorrow morning. Mmm . . . Trans-World information desk."

"Okay. Make reservations for where?"

She shrugged. "Pick a place."

"London used to be pretty wicked."

"Sounds good. First class?"

"What else? I'll get us a suite on one of the dirigibles."

"Good. Decadent. How long shall I pack for?"

"We'll buy clothes along the way. Travel light. Just one stuffed wallet apiece."

She giggled. "Wonderful. Tomorrow at ten."

"Fine—uh . . . Marygay, do you have a gun?"

"It's that bad?"

"Here around Washington it is."

"Well, I'll get one. Dad has a couple over the fireplace. Guess they're left over from Tucson."

"We'll hope we won't need them."

"Willy, you know it'll just be for decoration. I couldn't even kill a Tauran."

"Of course." We just looked at each other for a second. "Tomorrow at ten, then."

"Right. Love you."

"Uh . . ."

She giggled again and hung up.

That was just too many things to think about all at once.

I got us two round-the-world dirigible tickets; unlimited stops as long as you kept going east. It took me a little over two hours to get to Ellis by autocab and monorail. I was early, but so was Marygay.

She was talking to the girl at the desk and didn't see me coming. Her outfit was really arresting, a tight coverall of plastic in a pattern of interlocking hands; as your angle of sight changed, various strategic hands became transparent. She had a ruddy sun-glow all over her body. I don't know whether the feeling that rushed over me was simple honest lust or something more complicated. I hurried up behind her.

Whispering: "What are we going to do for three hours?"

She turned and gave me a quick hug and thanked the girl at the desk, then grabbed my hand and pulled me along to a slidewalk.

"Um . . . where are we headed?"

"Don't ask questions, Sergeant. Just follow me."

We stepped onto a roundabout and transferred to an east-bound slidewalk.

"Do you want something to eat or drink?" she asked innocently.

I tried to leer. "Any alternatives?"

She laughed gaily. Several people stared. "Just a second . . . here!" We jumped off. It was a corridor marked "Roomettes." She handed me a key.

That damned plastic coverall was held on by static electricity. Since the roomette was nothing but a big waterbed, I almost broke my neck the first time it shocked me.

I recovered.

We were lying on our stomachs, looking through the one-way glass wall at the people rushing around down on the concourse. Marygay passed me a joint.

"William, have you used that thing yet?"

"What thing?"

"That hawg-leg. The pistol."

"Only shot it once, in the store where I bought it."

"Do you really think you could point it at someone and blow him apart?"

I took a shallow puff and passed it back. "Hadn't given it much thought, really. Until we talked last night."

"Well?"

"I . . . I don't really know. The only time I've killed was on Aleph, under hypnotic compulsion. But I don't think it would . . . bother me, not that much, not if the person was trying to kill me in the first place. Why should it?"

"Life," she said plaintively, "life is . . ."

"Life is a bunch of cells walking around with a common purpose. If that common purpose is to get my ass—"

"Oh, William. You sound like old Cortez."

"Cortez kept us alive."

"Not many of us," she snapped.

I rolled over and studied the ceiling tiles. She traced little designs on my chest, pushing the sweat around with her fingertip. "I'm sorry, William. I guess we're both just trying to adjust."

"That's okay. You're right, anyhow."

We talked for a long time. The only urban center Marygay had been to since our publicity rounds (which were very sheltered) was Sioux Falls. She had gone with her parents and the commune bodyguard. It sounded like a scaled-down version of Washington: the same problems, but not as acute.

We ticked off the things that bothered us: violence, high cost of living, too many people everywhere. I'd have added homolife, but Marygay said I just didn't appreciate the social dynamic that had led to it; it had been inevitable. The only thing she said she had against it was that it took so many of the prettiest men out of circulation.

And the main thing that was wrong was that everything seemed to have gotten just a little worse, or at best remained the same. You would have predicted that at least a few facets of everyday life would improve markedly in twenty-two years. Her father contended the War was behind it all: any person who showed a shred of talent was sucked up by UNEF; the very best fell to the Elite Conscription Act and wound up being cannon fodder.

It was hard not to agree with him. Wars in the past often accelerated social reform, provided technological benefits, even sparked artistic activity. This one, however, seemed tailor-made to provide none of these positive by-products. Such improvements as had been made on late-twentieth-century technology were—like tachyon bombs and warships two kilometers long—at best, interesting developments of things that only required the synergy of money and existing engineering techniques. Social reform? The world was technically under martial law. As for art, I'm not sure I know good from bad. But artists to some extent have to reflect the temper of the times. Paintings and sculpture were full of torture and dark brooding; movies seemed static and plotless; music was dominated by nostalgic revivals of earlier forms; architecture was mainly concerned with finding someplace to put everybody; literature was damn near incomprehensible. Most people seemed to spend most of their time trying to find ways to outwit the government, trying to scrounge a few extra K's or ration tickets without putting their lives in too much danger.

And in the past, people whose country was at war were constantly in contact with the war. The newspapers would be full of reports, veterans would return from the front; sometimes the front would move right into town, invaders marching down Main Street or bombs whistling through the night air—but always the sense of either working toward victory or at least delaying defeat. The enemy was a tangible thing, a propagandist's monster whom you could understand, whom you could hate.

But this war . . . the enemy was a curious organism only vaguely understood, more often the subject of cartoons than nightmares. The main effect of the war on the home front was economic, unemotional—more taxes but more jobs as well. After twenty-two years, only twenty-seven returned veterans; not enough to make a decent parade. The most important fact about the war to most people was that if it ended suddenly, Earth's economy would collapse.

*   *   *

You approached the dirigible by means of a small pro-
peller-driven aircraft that drifted up to match trajectories
and docked alongside. A clerk took our baggage and we
checked our weapons with the purser, then went outside.

Just about everybody on the flight was standing out on
the promenade deck, watching Manhattan creep toward the
horizon. It was an eerie sight. The day was very still, so
the bottom thirty or forty stories of the buildings were buried in smog. It looked like a city built on a cloud, a thun-
derhead floating. We watched it for a while and then went
inside to eat.

The meal was elegantly served and simple: filet of beef,
two vegetables, wine. Cheese and fruit and more wine for
dessert. No fiddling with ration tickets; a loophole in the
rationing laws implied that they were not required for meals
consumed en route, on intercontinental transport.

We spent a lazy, comfortable three days crossing the At-
lantic. The dirigibles had been a new thing when we first
left Earth, and now they had turned out to be one of the
few successful new financial ventures of the late twentieth
century . . . the company that built them had bought up a
few obsolete nuclear weapons; one bomb-sized hunk of
plutonium would keep the whole fleet in the air for years.
And, once launched, they never did come down. Floating
hotels, supplied and maintained by regular shuttles, they
were one last vestige of luxury in a world where nine billion people had something to eat, and almost nobody had
enough.

London was not as dismal from the air as New York
City had been; the air was clean even if the Thames was
poison. We packed our handbags, claimed our weapons,
and landed on a VTO pad atop the London Hilton. We
rented a couple of tricycles at the hotel and, maps in hand,
set off for Regent Street, planning on dinner at the vener-
able Cafe Royal.

The tricycles were little armored vehicles, stabilized gy-
roscopically so they couldn't be tipped over. Seemed overly
cautious for the part of London we traveled through, but I

supposed there were probably sections as rough as Washington.

I got a dish of marinated venison and Marygay got salmon; both very good but astoundingly expensive. At first I was a bit overawed by the huge room, filled with plush and mirrors and faded gilding, very quiet even with a dozen tables occupied, and we talked in whispers until we realized that was foolish.

Over coffee I asked Marygay what the deal was with her parents.

"Oh, it happens often enough," she said. "Dad got mixed up in some ration ticket thing. He'd gotten some black market tickets that turned out to be counterfeit. Cost him his job and he probably would have gone to jail, but while he was waiting for trial a bodysnatcher got him."

"Bodysnatcher?"

"That's right. All the commune organizations have them. They've got to get reliable farm labor, people who aren't eligible for relief . . . people who can't just lay down their tools and walk off when it gets rough. Almost everybody can get enough assistance to stay alive, though; everyone who isn't on the government's fecal roster."

"So he skipped out before his trial came up?"

She nodded. "It was a case of choosing between commune life, which he knew wasn't easy, and going on the dole after a few years' working on a prison farm; ex-convicts can't get legitimate jobs. They had to forfeit their condominium, which they'd put up for bail, but the government would've gotten that anyhow, once he was in jail.

"So the bodysnatcher offered him and Mother new identities, transportation to the commune, a cottage, and a plot of land. They took it."

"And what did the bodysnatcher get?"

"He himself probably didn't get anything. The commune got their ration tickets; they were allowed to keep their money, although they didn't have very much—"

"What happens if they get caught?"

"Not a chance." She laughed. "The communes provide over half the country's produce—they're really just an unofficial arm of the government. I'm sure the CBI knows

exactly where they are. . . . Dad grumbles that it's just a
fancy way of being in jail anyhow.''

"What a weird setup.''

"Well, it keeps the land farmed.'' She pushed her empty
dessert plate a symbolic centimeter away from her. "And
they're eating better than most people, better than they ever
had in the city. Mom knows a hundred ways to fix chicken
and potatoes.''

After dinner we went to a musical show. The hotel had
gotten us tickets to a "cultural translation'' of the old rock
opera *Hair*. The program explained that they had taken
some liberties with the original choreography, because back
in those days they didn't allow actual coition on stage. The
music was pleasantly old-fashioned, but neither of us was
quite old enough to work up any blurry-eyed nostalgia over
it. Still, it was much more enjoyable than the movies I'd
seen, and some of the physical feats performed were quite
inspiring. We slept late the next morning.

We dutifully watched the changing of the guard at Buck-
ingham Palace, walked through the British Museum, ate
fish and chips, ran up to Stratford-on-Avon and caught the
Old Vic doing an incomprehensible play about a mad king,
and didn't get into any trouble until the day before we were
to leave for Lisbon.

It was about 2 A.M. and we were tooling our tricycles
down a nearly deserted thoroughfare. Turned a corner and
there was a gang of boys beating the hell out of someone.
I screeched to the curb and leaped out of my vehicle, firing
the shotgun-pistol over their heads.

It was a girl they were attacking; it was rape. Most of
them scattered, but one pulled a pistol out of his coat and
I shot him. I remember trying to aim for his arm. The blast
hit his shoulder and ripped off his arm and what seemed to
be half of his chest; it flung him two meters to the side of
a building and he must have been dead before he hit the
ground.

The others ran, one of them shooting at me with a little
pistol as he went. I watched him trying to kill me for the
longest time before it occurred to me to shoot back. I sent

one blast way high and he dove into an alley and disappeared.

The girl looked dazedly around, saw the mutilated body of her attacker, and staggered to her feet and ran off screaming, naked from the waist down. I knew I should have tried to stop her, but I couldn't find my voice and my feet seemed nailed to the sidewalk. A tricycle door slammed and Marygay was beside me.

"What hap—" She gasped, seeing the dead man. "Wh-what was he doing?"

I just stood there stupefied. I'd certainly seen enough death these past two years, but this was a different thing . . . there was nothing noble in being crushed to death by the failure of some electronic component, or in having your suit fail and freeze you solid; or even dying in a shoot-out with the incomprehensible enemy . . . but death seemed natural in that setting. Not on a quaint little street in old-fashioned London, not for trying to steal what most people would give freely.

Marygay was pulling my arm. "We've got to get out of here. They'll *brainwipe* you!"

She was right. I turned and took one step and fell to the concrete. I looked down at the leg that had betrayed me and bright red blood was pulsing out of a small hole in my calf. Marygay tore a strip of cloth from her blouse and started to bind it. I remember thinking it wasn't a big enough wound to go into shock over, but my ears started to ring and I got lightheaded and everything went red and fuzzy. Before I went under, I heard a siren wailing in the distance.

Fortunately, the police also picked up the girl, who was wandering down the street a few blocks away. They compared her version of the thing with mine, both of us under hypnosis. They let me go with a stern admonition to leave law enforcement up to professional law enforcers.

I wanted to get out of the cities: just put a pack on my back and wander through the woods for a while, get my mind straightened out. So did Marygay. But we tried to make arrangements and found that the country was worse than the cities. Farms were practically armed camps, the areas between ruled by nomad gangs who survived by making lightning raids into villages and farms, murdering and plundering for a few minutes, and then fading back into the forest, before help could arrive.

Still, Britishers called their island "the most civilized country in Europe." From what we'd heard about France and Spain and Germany, especially Germany, they were probably right.

I talked it over with Marygay, and we decided to cut short our tour and go back to the States. We could finish the tour after we'd become acclimated to the twenty-first century. It was just too much foreignness to take in one dose.

The dirigible line refunded most of our money and we took a conventional suborbital flight back home. The high altitude made my leg throb, though it was nearly healed. They'd made great strides in the treatment of gunshot wounds, in the past twenty years. Lots of practice.

We split up at Ellis. Her description of commune life appealed to me more than the city; I made arrangements to join her after a week or so, and went back to Washington.

10

I rang the bell and a strange woman answered the door, opening it a couple of centimeters and peering through.

"Pardon me," I said, "isn't this Mrs. Mandella's residence?"

"Oh, you must be William!" She closed the door and unfastened the chains and opened it wide. "Beth, look who's here!"

My mother came into the living room from the kitchen, drying her hands on a towel. "Willy . . . what are you doing back so soon?"

"Well, it's—it's a long story."

"Sit down, sit down," the other woman said. "Let me get you a drink, don't start till I get back."

"Wait," my mother said. "I haven't even introduced you two. William, this is Rhonda Wilder. Rhonda, William."

"I've been so looking forward to meeting you," she said. "Beth has told me all about you—one cold beer, right?"

"Right." She was likable enough, a trim middle-aged woman. I wondered why I hadn't met her before. I asked my mother whether she was a neighbor.

"Uh . . . really more than that, William. She's been my roommate for a couple of years. That's why I had an extra room when you came home—a single person isn't allowed two bedrooms."

"But why—"

"I didn't tell you because I didn't want you to feel that you were putting her out of her room while you stayed here. And you weren't, actually; she has—"

"That's right." Rhonda came in with the beer. "I've got relatives in Pennsylvania, out in the country. I can stay with them any time."

137

"Thanks." I took the beer. "Actually, I won't be here long. I'm kind of en route to South Dakota. I could find another place to flop."

"Oh, no," Rhonda said. "I can take the couch." I was too old-fashioned male-chauv to allow that; we discussed it for a minute and I wound up with the couch.

I filled Rhonda in on who Marygay was and told them about our disturbing experiences in England, how we came back to get our bearings. I had expected my mother to be horrified that I had killed a man, but she accepted it without comment. Rhonda clucked a little bit about our being out in a city after midnight, especially without a bodyguard.

We talked on these and other topics until late at night, when Mother called her bodyguard and went off to work.

Something had been nagging at me all night, the way Mother and Rhonda acted toward each other. I decided to bring it out into the open, once Mother was gone.

"Rhonda—" I settled down in the chair across from her. I didn't know exactly how to put it. "What, uh, what exactly is your relationship with my mother?"

She took a long drink. "Good friends." She stared at me with a mixture of defiance and resignation. "Very good friends. Sometimes lovers."

I felt very hollow and lost. My mother?

"Listen," she continued. "You had better stop trying to live in the nineties. This may not be the best of all possible worlds, but you're stuck with it."

She crossed and took my hand, almost kneeling in front of me. Her voice was softer. "William . . . look, I'm only two years older than you are—that is, I was born two years before—what I mean is, I can understand how you feel. B—your mother understands too. It, our . . . relationship, wouldn't be a secret to anybody else. It's perfectly normal. A lot has changed, these twenty years. You've got to change too."

I didn't say anything.

She stood up and said firmly, "You think, because your mother is sixty, she's outgrown her need for love? She needs it more than you do. Even now. Especially now."

Accusation in her eyes. "Especially now with you com-

ing back from the dead past. Reminding her of how old
she is. How—old I am, twenty years younger.'' Her voice
quavered and cracked, and she ran to her room.

I wrote Mother a note saying that Marygay had called;
an emergency had come up and I had to go immediately to
South Dakota. I called a bodyguard and left.

A whining, ozone-leaking, battered old bus let me out at
the intersection of a bad road and a worse one. It had taken
me an hour to go the 2000 kilometers to Sioux Falls, two
hours to get a chopper to Geddes, 150 kilometers away,
and three hours waiting and jouncing on the dilapidated bus
to go the last 12 kilometers to Freehold, an organization of
communes where the Potters had their acreage. I wondered
if the progression was going to continue and I would be
four hours walking down this dirt road to the farm.

It was a half-hour before I even came to a building. My
bag was getting intolerably heavy and the bulky pistol was
chafing my hip. I walked up a stone path to the door of a
simple plastic dome and pulled a string that caused a bell
to tinkle inside. A peephole darkened.

''Who is it?'' Voice muffled by thick wood.

''Stranger asking directions.''

''Ask.'' I couldn't tell whether it was a woman or a
child.

''I'm looking for the Potters' farm.''

''Just a second.'' Footsteps went away and came back.
''Down the road one point nine klicks. Lots of potatoes and
green beans on your right. You'll probably smell the chickens.''

''Thanks.''

''If you want a drink we got a pump out back. Can't let
you in without my husband's at home.''

''I understand. Thank you.'' The water was metallic-
tasting but wonderfully cool.

I wouldn't know a potato or green bean plant if it stood
up and took a bite out of my ankle, but I knew how to
walk a half-meter step. So I resolved to count to 3800 and
take a deep breath. I supposed I could tell the difference
between the smell of chicken manure and the absence
thereof.

At 3650 there was a rutted path leading to a complex of plastic domes and rectangular buildings apparently made of sod. There was a pen enclosing a small population explosion of chickens. They had a smell but it wasn't strong.

Halfway down the path, a door opened and Marygay came running out, wearing one tiny wisp of cloth. After a slippery but gratifying greeting, she asked what I was doing here so early.

"Oh, my mother had friends staying with her. I didn't want to put them out. Suppose I should have called."

"Indeed you should have . . . save you a long dusty walk—but we've got plenty of room, don't worry about that."

She took me inside to meet her parents, who greeted me warmly and made me feel definitely overdressed. Their faces showed their age but their bodies had no sag and few wrinkles.

Since dinner was an occasion, they let the chickens live and instead opened a can of beef, steaming it along with a cabbage and some potatoes. To my plain tastes it was equal to most of the gourmet fare we'd had on the dirigible and in London.

Over coffee and goat cheese (they apologized for not having wine; the commune would have a new vintage out in a couple of weeks), I asked what kind of work I could do.

"Will," Mr. Potter said, "I don't mind telling you that your coming here is a godsend. We've got five acres that are just sitting out there, fallow, because we don't have enough hands to work them. You can take the plow tomorrow and start breaking up an acre at a time."

"More potatoes, Daddy?" Marygay asked.

"No, no . . . not this season. Soybeans—cash crop and good for the soil. And Will, at night we all take turns standing guard. With four of us, we ought to be able to do a lot more sleeping." He took a big slurp of coffee. "Now, what else . . ."

"Richard," Mrs. Potter said, "tell him about the greenhouse."

"That's right, yes, the greenhouse. The commune has a

two-acre greenhouse down about a click from here, by the recreation center. Mostly grapes and tomatoes. Everybody spends one morning or one afternoon a week there.

"Why don't you children go down there tonight . . show Will the night life in fabulous Freehold? Sometimes you can get a real exciting game of checkers going."

"Oh, Daddy. It's not that bad."

"Actually, it isn't. They've got a fair library and a coin-op terminal to the Library of Congress. Marygay tells me you're a reader. That's good."

"Sounds fascinating." It did. "But what about guard?"

"No problem. Mrs. Potter—April—and I'll take the first four hours—oh," he said, standing, "let me show you the setup."

We went out back to "the tower," a sandbag hut on stilts. Climbed up a rope ladder through a hole in the middle of the hut.

"A little crowded in here, with two," Richard said. "Have a seat." There was an old piano stool beside the hole in the floor. I sat on it. "It's handy to be able to see all the field without getting a crick in your neck. Just don't keep turning in the same direction all the time."

He opened a wooden crate and uncovered a sleek rifle, wrapped in oily rags. "Recognize this?"

"Sure." I'd had to sleep with one in basic training. "Army standard issue T-sixteen. Semi-automatic, twelve-caliber tumblers—where the hell did you get it?"

"Commune went to a government auction. It's an antique now, son." He handed it to me and I snapped it apart. Clean, too clean.

"Has it ever been used?"

"Not in almost a year. Ammo costs too much for target practice. Take a couple of practice shots, though, convince yourself that it works."

I turned on the scope and just got a washed-out bright green. Set for nighttime. Clicked it back to log zero, set the magnification at ten, reassembled it.

"Marygay didn't want to try it out. Said she'd had her fill of that. I didn't press her, but a person's got to have confidence in ther tools."

I clicked off the safety and found a clod of dirt that the
range-finder said was between 100 and 120 meters away.
Set it at 110, rested the barrel of the rifle on the sandbags,
centered the clod in the crosshairs, and squeezed. The round
hissed out and kicked up dirt about five centimeters low.

"Fine." I reset it for night use and safetied it and handed
it back. "What happened a year ago?"

He wrapped it up carefully, keeping the rags away from
the eyepiece. "Had some jumpers come in. Fired a few
rounds and scared 'em away."

"All right, what's a jumper?"

"Yeah, you wouldn't know." He shook out a tobacco
cigarette and passed me the box. "I don't know why they
don't just call 'em thieves, that's what they are. Murderers,
too, sometimes.

"They know that a lot of the commune members are
pretty well off. If you raise cash crops you get to keep half
the cash; besides, a lot of our members were prosperous
when they joined.

"Anyhow, the jumpers take advantage of our relative
isolation. They come out from the city and try to sneak in,
usually hit one place, and run. Most of the time, they don't
get this far in, but the farms closer to the road . . . we hear
gunfire every couple of weeks. Usually just scaring off kids.
If it keeps up, a siren goes off and the commune goes on
alert."

"Doesn't sound fair to the people living close to the
road."

"There're compensations. They only have to donate half
as much of their crop as the rest of us do. And they're
issued heavier weapons."

Marygay and I took the family's two bicycles and ped-
aled down to the recreation center. I only fell off twice,
negotiating the bumpy road in the dark.

It was a little livelier than Richard had described it. A
young nude girl was dancing sensuously to an assortment
of homemade drums near the far side of the dome. Turned
out she was still in school; it was a project for a "cultural
relativity" class.

Most of the people there, in fact, were young and therefore still in school. They considered it a joke, though. After you had learned to read and write and could pass the Class I literacy test, you only had to take one course per year, and some of those you could pass just by signing up. So much for the "eighteen years' compulsory education" they had startled us with at Stargate.

Other people were playing board games, reading, watching the girl gyrate, or just talking. There was a bar that served soya, coffee, or thin homemade beer. Not a ration ticket to be seen; all made by the commune or purchased outside with commune tickets.

We got into a discussion about the war, with a bunch of people who knew Marygay and I were veterans. It's hard to describe their attitude, which was pretty uniform. They were angry in an abstract way that it took so much tax money to support; they were convinced that the Taurans would never be any danger to Earth; but they all knew that nearly half the jobs in the world were associated with the war, and if it stopped, everything would fall apart.

I thought everything was in shambles already, but then I hadn't grown up in this world. And they had never known "peacetime."

We went home about midnight and Marygay and I each stood two hours' guard. By the middle of the next morning, I was wishing I had gotten a little more sleep.

The plow was a big blade on wheels with two handles for steering, atomic powered. Not very much power, though; enough to move it forward at a slow crawl if the blade was in soft earth. Needless to say, there was little soft earth in the unused five acres. The plow would go a few centimeters, get stuck, freewheel until I put some back into it, then move a few more centimeters. I finished a tenth of an acre the first day and eventually got it up to a fifth of an acre a day.

It was hard, hardening work, but pleasant. I had an earclip that piped music to me, old tapes from Richard's collection, and the sun browned me all over. I was beginning to think I could live that way forever, when suddenly it was finished.

Marygay and I were reading up at the recreation center one evening when we heard faint gunfire down by the road. We decided it'd be smart to get back to the house. We were less than halfway there when firing broke out all along our left, on a line that seemed to extend from the road to far past the recreation center: a coordinated attack. We had to abandon the bikes and crawl on hands and knees in the drainage ditch by the side of the road, bullets hissing over our heads. A heavy vehicle rumbled by, shooting left and right. It took a good twenty minutes to crawl home. We passed two farmhouses that were burning brightly. I was glad ours didn't have any wood.

I noticed there was no return fire coming from our tower, but didn't say anything. There were two dead strangers in front of the house as we rushed inside.

April was lying on the floor, still alive but bleeding from a hundred tiny fragment wounds. The living room was rubble and dust; someone must have thrown a bomb through a door or window. I left Marygay with her mother and ran out back to the tower. The ladder was pulled up, so I had to shinny up one of the stilts.

Richard was sitting slumped over the rifle. In the pale green glow from the scope I could see a perfectly round hole above his left eye. A little blood had trickled down the bridge of his nose and dried.

I laid his body on the floor and covered his head with my shirt. I filled my pockets with clips and took the rifle back to the house.

Marygay had tried to make her mother comfortable. They were talking quietly. She was holding my shotgun-pistol and had another gun on the floor beside her. When I came in she looked up and nodded soberly, not crying.

April whispered something and Marygay asked, "Mother wants to know whether . . . Daddy had a hard time of it. She knows he's dead."

"No. I'm sure he didn't feel anything."

"That's good."

"It's something." I should keep my mouth shut. "It is good, yes."

I checked the doors and windows for an effective vantage

point. I couldn't find anyplace that wouldn't allow a whole platoon to sneak up behind me.

"I'm going to go outside and get on top of the house." Couldn't go back to the tower. "Don't you shoot unless somebody gets inside . . . maybe they'll think the place is deserted."

By the time I had clambered up to the sod roof, the heavy truck was coming back down the road. Through the scope I could see that there were five men on it, four in the cab and one who was on the open bed, cradling a machine gun, surrounded by loot. He was crouched between two refrigerators, but I had a clear shot at him. Held my fire, not wanting to draw attention. The truck stopped in front of the house, sat for a minute, and turned in. The window was probably bulletproof, but I sighted on the driver's face and squeezed off a round. He jumped as it ricocheted, whining, leaving an opaque star on the plastic, and the man in back opened up. A steady stream of bullets hummed over my head; I could hear them thumping into the sandbags of the tower. He didn't see me.

The truck wasn't ten meters away when the shooting stopped. He was evidently reloading, hidden behind the refrigerator. I took careful aim and when he popped up to fire I shot him in the throat. The bullet being a tumbler, it exited through the top of his skull.

The driver pulled the truck around in a long arc so that, when it stopped, the door to the cab was flush with the door of the house. This protected them from the tower and also from me, though I doubted they yet knew where I was; a T-16 makes no flash and very little noise. I kicked off my shoes and stepped cautiously onto the top of the cab, hoping the driver would get out on his side. Once the door opened I could fill the cab with ricocheting bullets.

No good. The far door, hidden from me by the roof's overhang, opened first. I waited for the driver and hoped that Marygay was well hidden. I shouldn't have worried.

There was a deafening roar, then another and another. The heavy truck rocked with the impact of thousands of tiny flechettes. One short scream that the second shot ended.

I jumped from the truck and ran around to the back door.
Marygay had her mother's head on her lap, and someone
was crying softly. I went to them and Marygay's cheeks
were dry under my palms.

"Good work, dear."

She didn't say anything. There was a steady heavy dripping sound from the door and the air was acrid with smoke
and the smell of fresh meat. We huddled together until
dawn.

I had thought April was sleeping, but in the dim light
her eyes were wide open and filmed. Her breath came in
shallow rasps. Her skin was gray parchment and dried
blood. She didn't answer when we talked to her.

A vehicle was coming up the road, so I took the rifle
and went outside. It was a dump truck with a white sheet
draped over one side and a man standing in the back with
a megaphone repeating, "Wounded . . . wounded." I
waved and the truck came in. They took April out on a
makeshift litter and told us which hospital they were going
to. We wanted to go along but there was simply no room;
the bed of the truck was covered with people in various
stages of disrepair.

Marygay didn't want to go back inside because it was
getting light enough to see the men she had killed so completely. I went back in to get some cigarettes and forced
myself to look. It was messy enough, but just didn't disturb
me that much. *That* bothered me, to be confronted with a
pile of human hamburger and mainly notice the flies and
ants and smell. Death is so much neater in space.

We buried her father behind the house, and when the
truck came back with April's small body wrapped in a
shroud, we buried her beside him. The commune's sanita-
tion truck came by a little later, and gas-masked men took
care of the jumpers' bodies.

We sat in the baking sun, and finally Marygay wept, for
a long time, silently.

11

We got off the plane at Dulles and found a monorail to Columbia.

It was a pleasingly diverse jumble of various kinds of buildings, arranged around a lake, surrounded by trees. All of the buildings were connected by slidewalk to the largest place, a fullerdome with stores and schools and offices.

We could have taken the enclosed slidewalk to Mom's place, but instead walked alongside it in the good cold air that smelled of fallen leaves. People slid by on the other side of the plastic, carefully not staring.

Mom didn't answer her door, but she'd given me an entry card. Mom was asleep in the bedroom, so Marygay and I settled in the living room and read for a while.

We were startled suddenly by a loud fit of coughing from the bedroom. I raced over and knocked on the door.

"William? I didn't—" coughing "—come in, I didn't know you were . . ."

She was propped up in bed, the light on, surrounded by various nostrums. She looked ghastly, pale and lined.

She lit a joint and it seemed to quell the coughing. "When did you get in? I didn't know . . ."

"Just a few minutes ago. . . . How long has this . . . have you been . . ."

"Oh, it's just a bug I picked up after Rhonda went to see her kids. I'll be fine in a couple of days." She started coughing again, drank some thick red liquid from a bottle. All of her medicines seemed to be the commercial, patent variety.

"Have you seen a doctor?"

"Doctor? Heavens no, Willy. They don't have . . . it's not serious . . . don't—"

"Not serious?" At eighty-four. "For Chrissake, mother." I went to the phone in the kitchen and with some difficulty managed to get the hospital.

A plain girl in her twenties formed in the cube. "Nurse Donalson, general services." She had a fixed smile, professional sincerity. But then everybody smiled.

"My mother needs to be looked at by a doctor. She has a—"

"Name and number, please."

"Beth Mandella." I spelled it. "What number?"

"Medical services number, of course," she smiled.

I called into Mom and asked her what her number was. "She says she can't remember."

"That's all right, sir, I'm sure I can find her records." She turned her smile to a keyboard beside her and punched out a code.

"Beth Mandella?" she said, her smile turning quizzical. "*You're* her son? She must be in her eighties."

"Please. It's a long story. She really has to see a doctor."

"Is this some kind of joke?"

"What do you mean?" Strangled coughing from the other room, the worst yet. "Really—this might be very serious, you've got to—"

"But sir, Mrs. Mandella got a zero priority rating way back in 2010."

"*What the hell is that supposed to mean?*"

"S-i-r . . ." The smile was hardening in place.

"Look. Pretend that I came from another planet. What is a 'zero priority rating'?"

"Another—oh! I know you!" She looked off to the left. "Sonya—come over here a second. You'd never guess who . . ." Another face crowded the cube, a vapid blonde girl whose smile was twin to the other nurse's. "Remember? On the stat this morning?"

"Oh, yeah," she said. "One of the soldiers—hey, that's really max, really max." The head withdrew.

"Oh, Mr. Mandella," she said, effusive. "No wonder you're confused. It's really very simple."

"Well?"

"It's part of the Universal Medical Security System. Everybody gets a rating on their seventieth birthday. It comes in automatically from Geneva."

"What does it rate? What does it mean?" But the ugly truth was obvious.

"Well, it tells how important a person is and what level of treatment he's allowed. Class three is the same as anybody else's; class two is the same except for certain life-extending—"

"And class zero is no treatment at all."

"That's correct, Mr. Mandella." And in her smile was not a glimmer of pity or understanding.

"Thank you." I disconnected. Marygay was standing behind me, crying soundlessly with her mouth wide open.

I found mountaineer's oxygen at a sporting goods store and even managed to get some black-market antibiotics through a character in a bar downtown in Washington. But Mom was beyond being able to respond to amateur treatment. She lived four days. The people from the crematorium had the same fixed smile.

I tried to get through to my brother, Mike, on the Moon, but the phone company wouldn't let me place the call until I had signed a contract and posted a $25,000 bond. I had to get a credit transfer from Geneva. The paperwork took half a day.

I finally got through to him. Without preamble:

"Mother's dead."

For a fraction of a second, the radio waves wandered up to the moon, and in another fraction, came back. He started and then nodded his head slowly. "No surprise. Every time I've come down to Earth the past ten years, I've wondered whether she'd still be there. Neither of us had enough money to keep in very close touch." He had told us in Geneva that a letter from Luna to Earth cost $100 postage—plus $5,000 tax. It discouraged communication with what the UN considered to be a bunch of regrettably necessary anarchists.

We commiserated for a while and then Mike said, "Willy, Earth is no place for you and Marygay; you know that by now. Come to Luna. Where you can still be an individual. Where we don't throw people out the airlock on their seventieth birthday.''

"We'd have to rejoin UNEF.''

"True, but you wouldn't have to fight. They say they need you more for training. You could study in your spare time, bring your physics up to date—maybe wind up eventually in research.''

We talked some more, a total of three minutes. I got $1000 back.

Marygay and I talked about it through the night. Maybe our decision would have been different if we hadn't been staying there, surrounded by Mother's life and death, but when the dawn came the proud, ambitious, careful beauty of Columbia had turned sinister and foreboding.

We packed our bags and had our money transferred to the Tycho Credit Union and took a monorail to the Cape.

"In case you're interested, you aren't the first combat veterans to come back.'' The recruiting officer was a muscular lieutenant of indeterminate sex. I flipped a coin mentally and it came up tails.

"Last I heard, there had been nine others,'' she said in her husky tenor. "All of them opted for the moon ... maybe you'll find some of your friends there.'' She slid two simple forms across the desk. "Sign these and you're in again. Second lieutenants.''

The form was a simple request to be assigned to active duty; we had never really gotten out of the Force, since they extended the draft law, but had just been on inactive status. I scrutinized the paper.

"There's nothing on this about the guarantees we were given at Stargate.''

"That won't be necessary. The Force will—''

"I think it is necessary, Lieutenant.'' I handed back the form. So did Marygay.

"Let me check.'' She left the desk and disappeared into an office. After a while we heard a printer rattle.

She brought back the same two sheets, with an addition typed under our names: GUARANTEED LOCATION OF CHOICE

[LUNA] AND ASSIGNMENT OF CHOICE [COMBAT TRAINING SPECIALIST].

We got a thorough physical checkup and were fitted for new fighting suits, made our financial arrangements, and caught the next morning's shuttle. We laid over at Earthport, enjoying zero gravity for a few hours, and then caught a ride to Luna, setting down at the Grimaldi base.

On the door to the Transient Officers' Billet, some wag had scraped "abandon hope all ye who enter." We found our two-man cubicle and began changing for chow.

Two raps on the door. "Mail call, sirs."

I opened the door and the sergeant standing there saluted. I just looked at him for a second and then remembered I was an officer and returned the salute. He handed me two identical faxes. I gave one to Marygay and we both gasped at the same time:

ORDERSORDERS**ORDERS**

THE FOLLOWING NAMED PERSONNEL:
Mandella, William 2LT [11 575 278] COCOMM D CO GRITRABN
AND
Potter, Marygay 2LT [17 386 907] COCOMM B CO GRITRABN ARE HEREBY REASSIGNED TO:
LT Mandella: PLCOMM 2 PL STFTHETA STARGATE
LT Potter: PLCOMM 3 PL STFTHETA STARGATE.
DESCRIPTION OF DUTIES:
Command infantry platoon in Tet-2 Campaign.
THE ABOVE NAMED PERSONNEL WILL REPORT IMMEDIATELY TO GRIMALDI TRANSPORTATION BATTALION TO BE MANIFESTED TO STARGATE.
ISSUED STARGATE TACBD/1298-8684-1450/20 Aug 2019 SG:
BY AUTHO STFCOM Commander.

ORDERSORDERS**ORDERS**

"They didn't waste any time, did they?" Marygay said bitterly.

"Must be a standing order. Strike Force Command's light-weeks away; they can't even know we've re-upped yet."

"What about our . . ." She let it trail off.

"The guarantee. Well, we were given our assignment of choice. Nobody guaranteed we'd have the assignment for more than an hour."

"It's so dirty."

I shrugged. "It's so army."

But I couldn't shake the feeling that we were going home.

LIEUTENANT
MANDELLA
2024–2389 A.D.

"Quick and dirty." I was looking at my platoon sergeant, Santesteban, but talking to myself. And anybody else who was listening.

"Yeah," he said. "Gotta do it in the first coupla minutes or we're screwed tight." He was matter-of-fact, laconic. Drugged.

Private Collins came up with Halliday. They were holding hands unself-consciously. "Lieutenant Mandella?" Her voice broke a little. "Can we have just a minute?"

"One minute," I said, too abruptly. "We have to leave in five, I'm sorry."

Hard to watch those two together now. Neither one had any combat experience. But they knew what everybody did; how slim their chances were of ever being together again. They slumped in a corner and mumbled words and traded mechanical caresses, no passion or even comfort. Collins's eyes shone but she wasn't weeping. Halliday just looked grim, numb. She was normally by far the prettier of the two, but the sparkle had gone out of her and left a well-formed dull shell.

I'd gotten used to open female homosex in the months since we'd left Earth. Even stopped resenting the loss of potential partners. The men together still gave me a chill, though.

I stripped and backed into the clamshelled suit. The new ones were a hell of a lot more complicated, with all the new biometrics and trauma maintenance. But well worth the trouble of hooking up, in case you got blown apart just a little bit. Go home to a comfortable pension with heroic prosthesis. They were even talking about the possibility of regeneration, at least for missing arms and legs. Better get it soon, before Heaven filled up with fractional people. Heaven was the new hospital/rest-and-recreation planet.

I finished the set-up sequence and the suit closed by itself. Gritted my teeth against the pain that never came, when the internal sensors and fluid tubes poked into your body. Conditioned neural bypass, so you felt only a slight puzzling dislocation. Rather than the death of a thousand cuts.

Collins and Halliday were getting into their suits now and the other dozen were almost set, so I stepped over to the third platoon's staging area. Say goodbye again to Marygay.

She was suited and heading my way. We touched helmets instead of using the radio. Privacy.

"Feeling OK, honey?"

"All right," she said. "Took my pill."

"Yeah, happy times." I'd taken mine too, supposed to make you feel optimistic without interfering with your sense of judgment. I knew most of us would probably die, but I didn't feel too bad about it. "Sack with me tonight?"

"If we're both here," she said neutrally. "Have to take a pill for that, too." She tried to laugh. "Sleep, I mean. How're the new people taking it? You have ten?"

"Ten, yeah, they're OK. Doped up, quarter-dose."

"I did that, too; try to keep them loose."

In fact, Santesteban was the only other combat veteran in my platoon; the four corporals had been in UNEF for a while but hadn't ever fought.

The speaker in my cheekbone crackled and Commander Cortez said, "Two minutes. Get your people lined up."

We had our goodbye and I went back to check my flock. Everybody seemed to have gotten suited up without any problems, so I put them on line. We waited for what seemed like a long time.

"All right, load 'em up." With the word "up," the bay door in front of me opened—the staging area having already been bled of air—and I led my men and women through to the assault ship.

These new ships were ugly as hell. Just an open framework with clamps to hold you in place, swiveled lasers fore and aft, small tachyon powerplants below the lasers. Everything automated; the machine would land us as quickly as possible and then zip off to harass the enemy. It was a one-use, throwaway drone. The vehicle that would come pick us up if we survived was cradled next to it, much prettier.

We clamped in and the assault ship cast off from the *Sangre y Victoria* with twin spurts from the yaw jets. Then the voice of the machine gave us a short countdown and we sped off at four gees' acceleration, straight down.

The planet, which we hadn't bothered to name, was a chunk of black rock without any normal star close enough to give it heat. At first it was visible only by the absence of stars where its bulk cut off their light, but as we dropped closer we could see subtle variations in the blackness of its surface. We were coming down on the hemisphere opposite the Taurans' outpost.

Our recon had shown that their camp sat in the middle of a flat lava plain several hundred kilometers in diameter. It was pretty primitive compared to other Tauran bases UNEF had encountered, but there wouldn't be any sneaking up on it. We were going to career over the horizon some fifteen klicks from the place, four ships converging simultaneously from different directions, all of us decelerating like mad, hopefully to drop right in their laps and come up shooting. There would be nothing to hide behind.

I wasn't worried, of course. Abstractedly, I wished I hadn't taken the pill.

We leveled off about a kilometer from the surface and sped along much faster than the rock's escape velocity, constantly correcting to keep from flying away. The surface rolled below us in a dark gray blur; we shed a little light from the pseudo-cerenkov glow made by our tachyon exhaust, scooting away from our reality into its own.

The ungainly contraption skimmed and jumped along for some ten minutes; then suddenly the front jet glowed and we were snapped forward inside our suits, eyeballs trying to escape from their sockets in the rapid deceleration.

"Prepare for ejection," the machine's female-mechanical voice said. "Five, four . . ."

The ship's lasers started firing, millisecond flashes freezing the land below in jerky stroboscopic motion. It was a twisted, pock-marked jumble of fissures and random black rocks, a few meters below our feet. We were dropping, slowing.

"Three—" It never got any farther. There was a too-bright flash and I saw the horizon drop away as the ship's tail pitched down—then clipped the ground, and we were rolling, horribly, pieces of people and ship scattering. Then we slid pinwheeling to a bumpy halt, and I tried to pull free but my leg was pinned under the ship's bulk: excruciating pain and a dry crunch as the girder crushed my leg; shrill whistle of air escaping my breached suit; then the trauma maintenance turned on *snick*, more pain, then no pain and I was rolling free, short stump of a leg trailing blood that froze shiny black on the dull black rock. I tasted brass and a red haze closed everything out, then deepened to the brown of river clay, then loam and I passed out, with the pill thinking *this is not so bad. . . .*

The suit is set up to save as much of your body as possible. If you lose part of an arm or a leg, one of sixteen razor-sharp irises closes around your limb with the force of a hydraulic press, snipping it off neatly and sealing the suit before you can die of explosive decompression. Then "trauma maintenance" cauterizes the stump, replaces lost blood, and fills you full of happy-juice and No-shock. So you will either die happy or, if your comrades go on to win the battle, eventually be carried back up to the ship's aid station.

We'd won that round, while I slept swaddled in dark cotton. I woke up in the infirmary. It was crowded. I was in the middle of a long row of cots, each one holding someone who had been three-fourths (or less) saved by his suit's trauma maintenance feature. We were being ignored by the ship's two doctors, who stood in bright light at operating tables, absorbed in blood rituals. I watched them for a long time. Squinting into the bright light, the blood on their green tunics could have been grease, the swathed bodies, odd soft machines that they were fixing. But the machines would cry out in their sleep, and the mechanics muttered reassurances while they plied their greasy tools. I watched and slept and woke up in different places.

Finally I woke up in a regular bay. I was strapped down and being fed through a tube, biosensor electrodes attached here and there, but no medics around. The only other person in the little room was Marygay, sleeping on the bunk next to me. Her right arm was amputated just above the elbow.

I didn't wake her up, just looked at her for a long time and tried to sort out my feelings. Tried to filter out the effect of the mood drugs. Looking at her stump, I could feel neither empathy nor revulsion. I tried to force one reaction, and then the other, but nothing real happened. It was as if she had always been that way. Was it drugs, conditioning, love? Have to wait to see.

Her eyes opened suddenly and I knew she had been awake for some time, had been giving me time to think. "Hello, broken toy," she said.

"How—how do you feel?" Bright question.

She put a finger to her lips and kissed it, a familiar gesture, reflection. "Stupid, numb. Glad not to be a soldier anymore." She smiled. "Did they tell you? We're going to Heaven."

"No. I knew it would be either there or Earth."

"Heaven will be better." Anything would. "I wish we were there now."

"How long?" I asked. "How long before we get there?"

She rolled over and looked at the ceiling. "No telling. You haven't talked to anybody?"

"Just woke up."

"There's a new directive they didn't bother to tell us about before. The *Sangre y Victoria* got orders for four missions. We have to keep on fighting until we've done all four. Or until we've sustained so many casualties that it wouldn't be practical to go on."

"How many is that?"

"I wonder. We lost a good third already. But we're headed for Aleph-7. Panty raid." New slang term for the type of operation whose main object was to gather Tauran artifacts, and prisoners if possible. I tried to find out where the term came from, but the one explanation I got was really idiotic.

One knock on the door and Dr. Foster barged in. He fluttered his hands. "Still in separate *beds*? Marygay, I thought you were more recovered than that." Foster was all right. A flaming mariposa, but he had an amused tolerance for heterosexuality.

He examined Marygay's stump and then mine. He stuck thermometers in our mouths so we couldn't talk. When he spoke, he was serious and blunt.

"I'm not going to sugarcoat anything for you. You're both on happyjuice up to your ears, and the loss you've sustained isn't going to bother you until I take you off the stuff. For my own convenience I'm keeping you drugged until you get to Heaven. I have twenty-one amputees to take care of. We can't handle twenty-one psychiatric cases.

"Enjoy your peace of mind while you still have it. You two especially, since you'll probably want to stay together. The prosthetics you get on Heaven will work just fine, but every time you look at his mechanical leg or you look at her arm, you're going to think of how lucky the other one is. You're going to constantly trigger memories of pain and loss for each other. . . . You may be at each other's throats in a week. Or you may share a sullen kind of love for the rest of your lives.

"Or you may be able to transcend it. Give each other strength. Just don't kid yourselves if it doesn't work out."

He checked the readout on each thermometer and made a notation in his notebook. "Doctor knows best, even if he is a little weird by your own old-fashioned standards. Keep it in mind." He took the thermometer out of my mouth and gave me a little pat on the shoulder. Impartially, he did the same to Marygay. At the door, he said, "We've got collapsar insertion in about six hours. One of the nurses will take you to the tanks."

We went into the tanks—so much more comfortable and safer than the old individual acceleration shells—and dropped into the Tet-2 collapsar field already starting the crazy fifty-gee evasive maneuvers that would protect us from enemy cruisers when we popped out by Aleph-7, a microsecond later.

Predictably, the Aleph-7 campaign was a dismal failure, and we limped away from it with a two-campaign total of fifty-four dead and thirty-nine cripples bound for Heaven. Only twelve soldiers were still able to fight, but they weren't exactly straining at the leash.

It took three collapsar jumps to get to Heaven. No ship ever went there directly from a battle, even though the delay sometimes cost extra lives. It was the one place besides Earth that the Taurans could not be allowed to find.

Heaven was a lovely, unspoiled Earth-like world; what Earth might have been like if men had treated her with compassion instead of lust. Virgin forests, white beaches, pristine deserts. The few dozen cities there either blended perfectly with the environment (one was totally underground) or were brazen statements of human ingenuity; Oceanus, in a coral reef with six fathoms of water over its transparent roof; Boreas, perched on a sheared-off mountaintop in the polar wasteland; and the fabulous Skye, a huge resort city that floated from continent to continent on the trade winds.

We landed, as everyone does, at the jungle city, Threshold. Three-fourths hospital, it's by far the planet's largest city, but you couldn't tell that from the air, flying down from orbit. The only sign of civilization was a short runway that suddenly appeared, a small white patch dwarfed to insignificance by the stately rain forest that crowded in from the east and an immense ocean that dominated the other horizon.

Once under the arboreal cover, the city was very much in evidence. Low buildings of native stone and wood rested among ten-meter-thick tree trunks. They were connected by unobtrusive stone paths, with one wide promenade meandering off to the beach. Sunlight filtered down in patches, and the air held a mixture of forest sweetness and salt tang.

I later learned that the city sprawled out over 200 square kilometers, that you could take a subway to anyplace that was too far to walk. The ecology of Threshold was very carefully balanced and maintained so as to resemble the jungle outside, with all the dangerous and uncomfortable elements eliminated. A powerful pressor field kept out large predators and such insect life as was not necessary for the health of the plants inside.

We walked, limped and rolled into the nearest building, which was the hospital's reception area. The rest of the hospital was underneath, thirty subterranean stories. Each person was examined and assigned his own room; I tried to get a double with Marygay, but they weren't set up for that.

"Earth-year" was 2189. So I was 215 years old, God, look at that old codger. Somebody pass the hat—no, not necessary. The doctor who examined me said that my accumulated pay would be transferred from Earth to Heaven. With compound interest, I was just shy of being a billionaire. He remarked that I'd find lots of ways to spend my billion on Heaven.

They took the most severely wounded first, so it was several days before I went into surgery. Afterwards, I woke up in my room and found that they had grafted a prosthesis onto my stump, an articulated structure of shiny metal that to my untrained eye looked exactly like the skeleton of a leg and foot. It looked creepy as hell, lying there in a transparent bag of fluid, wires running out of it to a machine at the end of the bed.

An aide came in. "How you feelin', sir?" I almost told him to forget the "sir" bullshit, I was out of the army and staying out this time. But it might be nice for the guy to keep feeling that I outranked him.

"I don't know. Hurts a little."

"Gonna hurt like a sonuvabitch. Wait'll the nerves start to grow."

"Nerves?"

"Sure." He was fiddling with the machine, reading dials on the other side. "How you gonna have a leg without nerves? It'd just sit there."

"Nerves? Like regular nerves? You mean I can just think 'move' and the thing moves?"

" 'Course you can." He looked at me quizzically, then went back to his adjustments.

What a wonder. "Prosthetics has sure come a long way."

"Pross-what-ics?"

"You know, artificial—"

"*Oh* yeah, like in books. Wooden legs, hooks and stuff."

How'd he ever get a job? "Yeah, prosthetics. Like this thing on the end of my stump."

"Look, sir." He set down the clipboard he'd been scribbling on. "You've been away a long time. That's gonna be a leg, just like the other leg except it can't break."

"They do it with arms, too?"

"Sure, any limb." He went back to his writing. "Livers, kidneys, stomachs, all kinds of things. Still working on hearts and lungs, have to use mechanical substitutes."

"Fantastic." Marygay would be whole again, too.

He shrugged. "Guess so. They've been doing it since before I was born. How old are you, sir?"

I told him, and he whistled. "God *damn*. You musta been in it from the beginning." His accent was very strange. All the words were right but all the sounds were wrong.

"Yeah. I was in the Epsilon attack. Aleph-null." They'd started naming collapsars after letters of the Hebrew alphabet, in order of discovery, then ran out of letters when the damn things started cropping up all over the place. So they added numbers after the letters; last I heard, they were up to Yod-42.

"Wow, ancient history. What was it like back then?"

"I don't know. Less crowded, nicer. Went back to Earth a year ago—hell, a century ago. Depends on how you look at it. It was so bad I re-enlisted, you know? Bunch of zombies. No offense."

He shrugged. "Never been there, myself. People who come from there seem to miss it. Maybe it got better."

"What, you were born on another planet? Heaven?" No wonder I couldn't place his accent.

"Born, raised and drafted." He put the pen back in his pocket and folded the clipboard up to a wallet-sized package. "Yes, sir. Third-generation angel. Best damned planet in all UNEF." He spelled it out, didn't say "youneff" the way I'd always heard it.

"Look, I've gotta run, lieutenant. Two other monitors to

check, this hour." He backed out the door. "You need anything, there's a buzzer on the table there."

Third-generation angel. His grandparents came from Earth, probably when I was a young punk of a hundred. I wondered how many other worlds they'd colonized while my back was turned. Lose an arm, grow a new one?

It was going to be good to settle down and live a whole year for every year that went by.

The guy wasn't kidding about the pain. And it wasn't just the new leg, though that hurt like boiling oil. For the new tissues to "take," they'd had to subvert my body's resistance to alien cells; cancer broke out in a half-dozen places and had to be treated separately, painfully.

I was feeling pretty used up, but it was still kind of fascinating to watch the leg grow. White threads turned into blood vessels and nerves, first hanging a little slack, then moving into place as the musculature grew up around the metal bone.

I got used to seeing it grow, so the sight never repelled me. But when Marygay came to visit, it was a jolt—she was ambulatory before the skin on her new arm had started to grow; looked like a walking anatomy demonstration. I got over the shock, though, and she eventually came in for a few hours every day to play games or trade gossip or just sit and read, her arm slowly growing inside the plastic cast.

I'd had skin for a week before they uncased the new leg and trundled the machine away. It was ugly as hell, hairless and dead white, stiff as a metal rod. But it worked, after a fashion. I could stand up and shuffle along.

They transferred me to orthopedics, for "range and motion repatterning"—a fancy name for slow torture. They strap you into a machine that bends both the old and new legs simultaneously. The new one resists.

Marygay was in a nearby section, having her arm twisted methodically. It must have been even worse on her; she looked gray and haggard every afternoon, when we met to go upstairs and sunbathe in the broken shade.

As the days went by, the therapy became less like torture and more like strenuous exercise. We both began swimming for an hour or so every clear day, in the calm, pressor-guarded water off the beach. I still limped on land, but in the water I could get around pretty well.

The only real excitement we had on Heaven—excitement to our combat-blunted sensibilities—was in that carefully guarded water.

They have to turn off the pressor field for a split second every time a ship lands; otherwise it would just ricochet off over the ocean. Every now and then an animal slips in, but the dangerous land animals are too slow to get through. Not so in the sea.

The undisputed master of Heaven's oceans is an ugly customer that the angels, in a fit of originality, named the "shark." It could eat a stack of earth sharks for breakfast, though.

The one that got in was an average-sized white shark who had been bumping around the edge of the pressor field for days, tormented by all that protein splashing around inside. Fortunately, there's a warning siren two minutes before the pressor is shut down, so nobody was in the water when he came streaking through. And streak through he did, almost beaching himself in the fury of his fruitless attack.

He was twelve meters of flexible muscle with a razor-sharp tail at one end and a collection of arm-length fangs at the other. His eyes, big yellow globes, were set on stalks more than a meter out from his head. His mouth was so wide that, open, a man could comfortably stand in it. Make an impressive photo for his heirs.

They couldn't just turn off the pressor field and wait for the thing to swim away. So the Recreation Committee organized a hunting party.

I wasn't too enthusiastic about offering myself up as an hors d'oeuvre to a giant fish, but Marygay had spearfished a lot as a kid growing up in Florida and was really excited by the prospect. I went along with the gag when I found out how they were doing it; seemed safe enough.

These "sharks" supposedly never attack people in boats. Two people who had more faith in fishermen's stories than I had gone out to the edge of the pressor field in a rowboat, armed only with a side of beef. They kicked the meat overboard and the shark was there in a flash.

This was the cue for us to step in and have our fun. There were twenty-three of us fools waiting on the beach with flippers, masks, breathers and one spear each. The spears were pretty formidable, though, jet-propelled and with high-explosive heads.

We splashed in and swam in phalanx, underwater, toward the feeding creature. When it saw us at first, it didn't attack. It tried to hide its meal, presumably so that some of us wouldn't be able to sneak around and munch on it while the shark was dealing with the others. But every time he tried for the deep water, he'd bump into the pressor field. He was obviously getting pissed off.

Finally, he just let go of the beef, whipped around and charged. Great sport. He was the size of your finger one second, way down there at the other end of the field, then suddenly as big as the guy next to you and closing fast.

Maybe ten of the spears hit him—mine didn't—and they tore him to shreds. But even after an expert, or lucky, brain shot that took off the top of his head and one eye, even with half his flesh and entrails scattered in a bloody path behind him, he slammed into our line and clamped his jaws around a woman, grinding off both of her legs before it occurred to him to die.

We carried her, barely alive, back to the beach, where an ambulance was waiting. They poured her full of blood surrogate and No-shock and rushed her to the hospital, where she survived to eventually go through the agony of growing new legs. I decided that I would leave the hunting of fish to other fish.

Most of our stay at Threshold, once the therapy became bearable, was pleasant enough. No military discipline, lots of reading and things to potter around with. But there was a pall over it, since it was obvious that we weren't out of the army; just pieces of broken equipment that they were fixing up to throw back into the fray. Marygay and I each had another three years to serve in our lieutenancies.

But we did have six months of rest and recreation coming once our new limbs were pronounced in good working

order. Marygay was released two days before I was but
waited around for me.

My back pay came to $892,746,012. Not in the form of
bales of currency, fortunately; on Heaven they used an electronic credit exchange, so I carried my fortune around in a
little machine with a digital readout. To buy something you
punched in the vendor's credit number and the amount of
purchase; the sum was automatically shuffled from your
account to his. The machine was the size of a slender wallet
and coded to your thumbprint.

Heaven's economy was governed by the continual presence of thousands of resting, recreating millionaire soldiers.
A modest snack would cost a hundred bucks, a room for a
night at least ten times that. Since UNEF built and owned
Heaven, this runaway inflation was pretty transparently a
simple way of getting our accumulated pay back into the
economic mainstream.

We had fun, desperate fun. We rented a flyer and camp-
ing gear and went off for weeks, exploring the planet. There
were icy rivers to swim and lush jungles to crawl through;
meadows and mountains and polar wastes and deserts.

We could be totally protected from the environment by
adjusting our individual pressor fields—sleep naked in a
blizzard—or we could take nature straight. At Marygay's
suggestion, the last thing we did before coming back to
civilization was to climb a pinnacle in the desert, fasting
for several days to heighten our sensibilities (or warp our
perceptions, I'm still not sure), and sit back-to-back in the
searing heat, contemplating the languid flux of life.

Then off to the fleshpots. We toured every city on the
planet, and each had its own particular charm, but we finally returned to Skye to spend the rest of our leave time.

The rest of the planet was bargain-basement compared
to Skye. In the four weeks we were using the airborne plea-
sure dome as our home base, Marygay and I each went
through a good half-billion dollars. We gambled—sometimes losing a million dollars or more in a night—ate and
drank the finest the planet had to offer, and sampled every
service and product that wasn't too bizarre for our admittedly archaic tastes. We each had a personal servant whose

salary was rather more than that of a major general.

Desperate fun, as I said. Unless the war changed radically, our chances of surviving the next three years were microscopic. We were remarkably healthy victims of a terminal disease, trying to cram a lifetime of sensation into a half of a year.

We did have the consolation, not small, that however short the remainder of our lives would be, we would at least be together. For some reason it never occurred to me that even that could be taken from us.

We were enjoying a light lunch in the transparent ''first floor'' of Skye, watching the ocean glide by underneath us, when a messenger bustled in and gave us two envelopes: our orders.

Marygay had been bumped to captain, and I to major, on the basis of our military records and tests we had taken at Threshold. I was a company commander and she was a company's executive officer.

But they weren't the same company.

She was going to muster with a new company being formed right here on Heaven. I was going back to Stargate for ''indoctrination and education'' before taking command.

For a long time we couldn't say anything. ''I'm going to protest,'' I said finally, weakly. ''They can't make me a commander. Into a commander.''

She was still struck dumb. This was not just a separation. Even if the war was over and we left for Earth only a few minutes apart, in different ships, the geometry of the collapsar jump would pile up years between us. When the second one arrived on Earth, his partner would probably be a half-century older; more probably dead.

We sat there for some time, not touching the exquisite food, ignoring the beauty around us and beneath us, only conscious of each other and the two sheets of paper that separated us with a gulf as wide and real as death.

We went back to Threshold. I protested but my arguments were shrugged off. I tried to get Marygay assigned to my company, as my exec. They said my personnel had all been allotted. I pointed out that most of them probably hadn't even been born yet. Nevertheless, allotted, they said. It would be almost a century, I said, before I even get to Stargate. They replied that Strike Force Command *plans* in terms of centuries.

Not in terms of people.

We had a day and a night together. The less said about that, the better. It wasn't just losing a lover. Marygay and I were each other's only link to real life, the Earth of the 1980s and 90s. Not the perverse grotesquerie we were supposedly fighting to preserve. When her shuttle took off it was like a casket rattling down into a grave.

I commandeered computer time and found out the orbital elements of her ship and its departure time; found out I could watch her leave from "our" desert.

I landed on the pinnacle where we had starved together and, a few hours before dawn, watched a new star appear over the western horizon, flare to brilliance and fade as it moved away, becoming just another star, then a dim star, and then nothing. I walked to the edge and looked down the sheer rock face to the dim frozen rippling of dunes half a kilometer below. I sat with my feet dangling over the edge, thinking nothing, until the sun's oblique rays illuminated the dunes in a soft, tempting chiaroscuro of low relief. Twice I shifted my weight as if to jump. When I didn't, it was not for fear of pain or loss. The pain would be only a bright spark and the loss would be only the army's. And it would be their ultimate victory over me— having ruled my life for so long, to force an end to it.

That much, I owed to the enemy.

MAJOR
MANDELLA
2458–3143 A.D.

1

What was that old experiment they told us about in high school biology? Take a flatworm and teach it how to swim through a maze. Then mash it up and feed it to a stupid flatworm, and lo! the stupid flatworm would be able to swim the maze, too.

I had a bad taste of major general in my mouth.

Actually, I supposed they had refined the techniques since my high school days. With time dilation, that was about 450 years for research and development.

At Stargate, my orders said, I was to undergo "indoctrination and education" prior to taking command of my very own Strike Force. Which was what they still called a company.

For my education on Stargate, they didn't mince up major generals and serve them to me with hollandaise. They didn't feed me *anything* except glucose for three weeks. Glucose and electricity.

They shaved every hair off my body, gave me a shot that turned me into a dishrag, attached dozens of electrodes to my head and body, immersed me in a tank of oxygenated fluorocarbon, and hooked me up to an ALSC. That's an "accelerated life situation computer." It kept me busy.

I guess it took the machine about ten minutes to review everything I had learned previously about the martial (excuse the expression) arts. Then it started in on the new stuff.

I learned the best way to use every weapon from a rock to a nova bomb. Not just intellectually; that's what all those electrodes were for. Cybernetically-controlled negative feedback kinesthesia; I felt the weapons in my hands and watched my performance with them. And did it over and over until I did it right. The illusion of reality was total. I used a spear-thrower with a band of Masai warriors on a village raid, and when I looked down at my body it was

long and black. I relearned epee from a cruel-looking man
in foppish clothes, in an eighteenth-century French court-
yard. I sat quietly in a tree with a Sharps rifle and sniped
at blue-uniformed men as they crawled across a muddy
field toward Vicksburg. In three weeks I killed several reg-
iments of electronic ghosts. It seemed more like a year to
me, but the ALSC does strange things to your sense of time.

Learning to use useless exotic weapons was only a small
part of the training. In fact, it was the relaxing part. Because
when I wasn't in kinesthesia, the machine kept my body
totally inert and zapped my brain with four millennia's
worth of military facts and theories. And I couldn't forget
any of it! Not while I was in the tank.

Want to know who Scipio Aemilianus was? I don't.
Bright light of the Third Punic War. *War is the province
of danger and therefore courage above all things is the first
quality of a warrior*, von Clausewitz maintained. And I'll
never forget the poetry of "the advance party minus normally moves in a column formation with the platoon headquarters leading, followed by a laser squad, the heavy
weapons squad, and the remaining laser squad; the column
relies on observation for its flank security except when the
terrain and visibility dictate the need for small security de-
tachments to the flanks, in which case the advance party
commander will detail one platoon sergeant . . ." and so on.
That's from *Strike Force Command Small Unit Leader's
Handbook*, as if you could call something a handbook when
it takes up two whole microfiche cards, 2,000 pages.

If you want to become a thoroughly eclectic expert in a
subject that repels you, join UNEF and sign up for officer
training.

One hundred nineteen people, and I was responsible for
118 of them. Counting myself but not counting the Commodore, who could presumably take care of herself.

I hadn't met any of my company during the two weeks
of physical rehabilitation that followed the ALSC session.
Before our first muster I was supposed to report to the
Temporal Orientation Officer. I called for an appointment
and his clerk said the Colonel would meet me at the Level
Six Officers' Club after dinner.

TABLE OF ORGANIZATION

Strike Force Gamma

Sade—138 Campaign

1ECHN:	*MAJ Mandella*		*COMM Antopol*
2ECHN:	*CAPT Moore*		
3ECHN:	*1LT Hilleboe*		
4ECHN:	*2LT Riland*		
	2LT Rusk		
	2LT Alsever MD		

5ECHN:	*2LT Borgstedt*	*2LT Brill*	*2LT Gainor*	*2LT Heimoff*
6ECHN:	*SSgt Webster*	*SSgt Gillies*	*SSgt Abrams*	*SSgt Dole*
7ECHN:	Sgt Dolins	Sgt Bell	Sgt Anderson	Sgt Noyes
	Cpl Geller	Cpl Kahn	Cpl Kalvin	Cpl Spraggs
8ECHN:	Pvt Boas	Cpl Weiner	Pvt Miller	Pvt Conroy
	Pvt Lingeman	Pvt Ikle	Pvt Reisman	Pvt Yakata
	Pvt Rosevear	Pvt Schon	Pvt Coupling	Pvt Burris
	Pvt Wolfe, R.	Pvt Shubik	Pvt Rostow	Pvt Cohen
	Pvt Lin	Pvt Duhl	Pvt Huntington	Pvt Graham
	Pvt Simmons	Pvt Perloff	Pvt De Sola	Pvt Schoellple
	Pvt Winograd	Pvt Moynihan	Pvt Pool	Pvt Wolfe, E.
	Pvt Brown	Pvt Frank	Pvt Nepala	Pvt Karkoshka
	Pvt Bloomquist	Pvt Graubard	Pvt Schuba	Pvt Majer
	Pvt Wong	Pvt Orlans	Pvt Ulanov	Pvt Dioujova
	Pvt Louria	Pvt Mayr	Pvt Shelley	Pvt Armaing
	Pvt Gross	Pvt Quarton	Pvt Lynn	Pvt Baulez
	Pvt Asadi	Pvt Hin	Pvt Slaer	Pvt Johnson
	Pvt Horman	Pvt Stendahl	Pvt Schenk	Pvt Orbrecht
	Pvt Fox	Pvt Erikson	Pvt Deelstra	Pvt Kayibanda
		Pvt Bora	Pvt Levy	Pvt Tschudi

Supporting: 1LT Williams (NAV), 2LTs Jarvil (MED), Laasonen (MED), Wilber (PSY), Szydlowska (MAINT), Gaptchenko (ORD), Gedo (COMM), Gim (COMP); 1SGTs Evans (MED), Rodriguez (MED), Kostidinov (MED), Rwabwogo (PSY), Blazynski (MAINT), Turpin (ORD); SSGTs Carreras (MED), Kousnetzov (MED), Waruinge (MED), Rojas (MED), Botos (MAINT), Orban (CK), Mbugua (COMP); SGTs Perez (MED), Seales (MAINT), Anghelov (ORD), Vugin (COMP); CPLs Daborg (MED), Correa (MED), Kajdi (SEX), Valdez (SEX), Muranga (ORD); PVTs Kottysch (MAINT), Rudkoski (CK), Minter (ORD).

APPROVED STFCOM STARGATE 12 Mar 2458. FOR THE COMMANDER:

Olga Torischeva BGEN STFCOM

I went down to Six early, thinking to eat dinner there, but they had nothing but snacks. So I munched on a fungus thing that vaguely resembled escargots and took the rest of my calories in the form of alcohol.

"Major Mandella?" I'd been busily engaged in my seventh beer and hadn't seen the Colonel approach. I started to rise but he motioned for me to stay seated and dropped heavily into the chair opposite me.

"I'm in your debt," he said. "You saved me from at least half of a boring evening." He offered his hand. "Jack Kynock, at your service."

"Colonel—"

"Don't Colonel me and I won't Major you. We old fossils have to . . . keep our perspective. William."

"All right with me."

He ordered a kind of drink I'd never heard of. "Where to start? Last time you were on Earth was 2007, according to the records."

"That's right."

"Didn't like it much, did you?"

"No." Zombies, happy robots.

"Well, it got better. Then it got worse, thank you." A private brought his drink, a bubbling concoction that was green at the bottom of the glass and lightened to chartreuse at the top. He sipped. "Then they got better again, then worse, then . . . I don't know. Cycles."

"What's it like now?"

"Well . . . I'm not really sure. Stacks of reports and such, but it's hard to filter out the propaganda. I haven't been back in almost two hundred years; it was pretty bad then. Depending on what you like."

"What do you mean?"

"Oh, let me see. There was lots of excitement. Ever hear of the Pacifist movement?"

"I don't think so."

"Hmn, the name's deceptive. Actually, it was a war, a guerrilla war."

"I thought I could give you name, rank and serial number of every war from Troy on up." He smiled. "They must have missed one."

"For good reason. It was run by veterans—survivors of Yod-38 and Aleph-40, I hear; they got discharged together and decided they could take on all of UNEF, Earthside. They got lots of support from the population."

"But didn't win."

"We're still here." He swirled his drink and the colors shifted. "Actually, all I know is hearsay. Last time I got to Earth, the war was over, except for some sporadic sabotage. And it wasn't exactly a safe topic of conversation."

"It surprises me a little," I said, "well, more than a little. That Earth's population would do anything at all . . . against the government's wishes."

He made a noncommittal sound.

"Least of all, revolution. When we were there, you couldn't get anybody to say a damned thing against the UNEF—or any of the local governments, for that matter. They were conditioned from ear to ear to accept things as they were."

"Ah. That's a cyclic thing, too." He settled back in his chair. "It's not a matter of technique. If they wanted to, Earth's government could have total control over . . . every nontrivial thought and action of each citizen, from cradle to grave.

"They don't do it because it would be fatal. Because there's a war on. Take your own case: did you get any motivational conditioning while you were in the can?"

I thought for a moment. "If I did, I wouldn't necessarily know about it."

"That's true. Partially true. But take my word for it, they left that part of your brain alone. Any change in your attitude toward UNEF or the war, or war in general, comes only from new knowledge. Nobody's fiddled with your basic motivations. And you should know why."

Names, dates, figures rattled down through the maze of new knowledge. "Tet-17, Sed-21, Aleph-14. The Lazlo . . . 'The Lazlo Emergency Commission Report.' June, 2106."

"Right. And by extension, your own experience on Aleph-1. Robots don't make good soldiers."

"They would," I said. "Up to the twenty-first century. Behavioral conditioning would have been the answer to a

Joe Haldeman

general's dream. Make up an army with all the best features of the SS, the Praetorian Guard, the Golden Horde. Mosby's Raiders, the Green Berets.''

He laughed over his glass. ''Then put that army up against a squad of men in modern fighting suits. It'd be over in a couple of minutes.''

''So long as each man in the squad kept his head about him. And just fought like hell to stay alive.'' The generation of soldiers that had precipitated the Lazlo Reports had been conditioned from birth to conform to somebody's vision of the ideal fighting man. They worked beautifully as a team, totally bloodthirsty, placing no great importance on personal survival—and the Taurans cut them to ribbons. The Taurans also fought with no regard for self. But they were better at it, and there were always more of them.

Kynock took a drink and watched the colors. ''I've seen your psych profile,'' he said. ''Both before you got here and after your session in the can. It's essentially the same, before and after.''

''That's reassuring.'' I signaled for another beer.

''Maybe it shouldn't be.''

''What, it says I won't make a good officer? I told them that from the beginning. I'm no leader.''

''Right in a way, wrong in a way. Want to know what that profile says?''

I shrugged. ''Classified, isn't it?''

''Yes,'' he said. ''But you're a major now. You can pull the profile of anybody in your command.''

''I don't suppose it has any big surprises.'' But I was a little curious. What animal isn't fascinated by a mirror?

''No. It says you're a pacifist. A failed one at that, which gives you a mild neurosis. Which you handle by transferring the burden of guilt to the army.''

The fresh beer was so cold it hurt my teeth. ''No surprises yet.''

''And as far as being a leader, you do have a certain potential. But it would be along the lines of a teacher or a minister; you would have to lead from empathy, compassion. You have the desire to impose your ideas on other people, but not your will. Which means, you're right, you'll make one hell of a bad officer unless you shape up.''

I had to laugh. "UNEF must have known all of this when they ordered me to officer training.''

"There are other parameters," he said. "For instance, you're adaptable, reasonably intelligent, analytical. And you're one of the eleven people who's lived through the whole war.''

"Surviving is a virtue in a private." Couldn't resist it. "But an officer should provide gallant example. Go down with the ship. Stride the parapet as if unafraid.''

He harrumphed at that. "Not when you're a thousand light years from your replacement.''

"It doesn't add up, though. Why would they haul me all the way from Heaven to take a chance on my 'shaping up,' when probably a third of the people here on Stargate are better officer material? God, the military mind!''

"I suspect the bureaucratic mind, at least, had something to do with it. You have an embarrassing amount of seniority to be a footsoldier.''

"That's all time dilation. I've only been in three campaigns.''

"Immaterial. Besides, that's two-and-a-half more than the average soldier survives. The propaganda boys will probably make you into some kind of a folk hero.''

"Folk hero." I sipped at the beer. "Where is John Wayne now that we really need him?''

"John Wayne?" He shook his head. "I never went in the can, you know. I'm no expert at military history.''

"Forget it.''

Kynock finished his drink and asked the private to get him—I swear to God—a "rum Antares.''

"Well, I'm supposed to be your Temporal Orientation Officer. What do you want to know about the present? What passes for the present.''

Still on my mind: "You've never been in the can?''

"No, combat officers only. The computer facilities and energy you go through in three weeks would keep the Earth running for several days. Too expensive for us deskwarmers.''

"Your decorations say you're combat.''

"Honorary. I was." The rum Antares was a tall slender glass with a little ice floating at the top, filled with pale amber liquid. At the bottom was a bright red globule about the size of a thumbnail; crimson filaments waved up from it.

"What's that red stuff?"

"Cinnamon. Oh, some ester with cinnamon in it. Quite good . . . want a taste?"

"No, I'll stick to beer, thanks."

"Down at level one, the library machine has a temporal orientation file, that my staff updates every day. You can go to it for specific questions. Mainly I want to . . . prepare you for meeting your Strike Force."

"What, they're all cyborgs? Clones?"

He laughed. "No, it's illegal to clone humans. The main problem is with, uh, you're heterosexual."

"Oh, that's no problem. I'm tolerant."

"Yes, your profile shows that you . . . think you're tolerant, but that's not the problem, exactly."

"Oh," I knew what he was going to say. Not the details, but the substance.

"Only emotionally stable people are drafted into UNEF. I know this is hard for you to accept, but heterosexuality is considered an emotional dysfunction. Relatively easy to cure."

"If they think they're going to cure *me*—"

"Relax, you're too old." He took a delicate sip. "It won't be as hard to get along with them as you might—"

"Wait. You mean nobody . . . everybody in my company is homosexual? But me?"

"William, everybody on Earth is homosexual. Except for a thousand or so; veterans and incurables."

"Ah." What could I say? "Seems like a drastic way to solve the population problem."

"Perhaps. It does work, though; Earth's population is stable at just under a billion. When one person dies or goes offplanet, another is quickened."

"Not 'born.' "

"Born, yes, but not the old-fashioned way. Your old

term for it was 'test-tube babies,' but of course they don't use a test-tube.''

''Well, that's something.''

''Part of every creche is an artificial womb that takes care of a person the first eight or ten months after quickening. What you would call birth takes place over a period of days; it isn't the sudden, drastic event that it used to be.''

O brave new world, I thought. ''No birth trauma. A billion perfectly adjusted homosexuals.''

''Perfectly adjusted by present-day Earth standards. You and I might find them a little odd.''

''That's an understatement.'' I drank off the rest of my beer. ''Yourself, you, uh . . . are you homosexual?''

''Oh, no,'' he said. I relaxed. ''Actually, though, I'm not hetero anymore, either.'' He slapped his hip and it made an odd sound. ''Got wounded and it turned out that I had a rare disorder of the lymphatic system, can't regenerate. Nothing but metal and plastic from the waist down. To use your word, I'm a cyborg.''

Far out, as my mother used to say. ''Oh, Private,'' I called to the waiter, ''bring me one of those Antares things.'' Sitting here in a bar with an asexual cyborg who is probably the only other normal person on the whole goddamned planet.

''Make it a double, please.''

2

They looked normal enough, filing into the lecture hall where we held our first muster, the next day. Rather young and a little stiff.

Most of them had only been out of the creche for seven or eight years. The creche was a controlled, isolated environment to which only a few specialists—pediatricians and teachers, mostly—had access. When a person leaves the creche at age twelve or thirteen, he chooses a first name (his last name having been taken from the donor-parent with the higher genetic rating) and is legally a probationary adult, with schooling about equivalent to what I had after my first year of college. Most of them go on to more specialized education, but some are assigned a job and go right to work.

They're observed very closely and anyone who shows any signs of sociopathy, such as heterosexual leanings, is sent away to a correctional facility. He's either cured or kept there for the rest of his life.

Everyone is drafted into UNEF at the age of twenty. Most people work at a desk for five years and are discharged. A few lucky souls, about one in eight thousand, are invited to volunteer for combat training. Refusing is "sociopathic," even though it means signing up for an extra five years. And your chance of surviving the ten years is so small as to be negligible; nobody ever had. Your best chance is to have the war end before your ten (subjective) years of service are up. Hope that time dilation puts many years between each of your battles.

Since you can figure on going into battle roughly once every subjective year, and since an average of 34 percent survive each battle, it's easy to compute your chances of being able to fight it out for ten years. It comes to about two one-thousandths of one percent. Or, to put it another way, get an old-fashioned six-shooter and play Russian Roulette with four of the six chambers loaded. If you can do it ten times in a row without decorating the opposite wall, congratulations! You're a civilian.

There being some sixty thousand combat soldiers in UNEF, you could expect about 1.2 of them to survive for ten years. I didn't seriously plan on being the lucky one, even though I was halfway there.

How many of these young soldiers filing into the auditorium knew they were doomed? I tried to match faces up with the dossiers I'd been scanning all morning, but it was hard. They'd all been selected through the same battery of stringent parameters, and they looked remarkably alike: tall but not too tall, muscular but not heavy, intelligent but not in a brooding way ... and Earth was much more racially homogenous than it had been in my century. Most of them looked vaguely Polynesian. Only two of them, Kayibanda and Lin, seemed pure representatives of racial types. I wondered whether the others gave them a hard time.

Most of the women were achingly handsome, but I was in no position to be critical. I'd been celibate for over a year, ever since saying goodbye to Marygay, back on Heaven.

I wondered if one of them might have a trace of atavism, or might humor her commander's eccentricity. *It is absolutely forbidden for an officer to form sexual liaison with his subordinates.* Such a warm way of putting it. *Violation of this regulation is punishable by attachment of all funds and reduction to the rank of private or, if the relationship interferes with a unit's combat efficiency, summary execution.* If all of UNEF's regulations could be broken so casually and consistently as that one was, it would be a very easygoing army.

But not one of the boys appealed to me. How they'd look after another year, I wasn't sure.

"Tench-*hut!*" That was Lieutenant Hilleboe. It was a credit to my new reflexes that I didn't jump to my feet. Everybody in the auditorium snapped to.

"My name is Lieutenant Hilleboe and I am your Second Field Officer." That used to be "Field First Sergeant." A good sign that an army has been around too long is that it starts getting top-heavy with officers.

Hilleboe came on like a real hard-ass professional soldier. Probably shouted orders at the mirror every morning, while she was shaving. But I'd seen her profile and knew that she'd only been in action once, and only for a couple of minutes at that. Lost an arm and a leg and was commissioned, same as me, as a result of the tests they give at the regeneration clinic.

Hell, maybe she had been a very pleasant person before going through that trauma; it was bad enough just having one limb regrown.

She was giving them the usual first-sergeant peptalk, stern-but-fair: don't waste my time with little things, use the chain of command, most problems can be solved at the fifth echelon.

It made me wish I'd had more time to talk with her earlier. Strike Force Command had really rushed us into this first muster—we were scheduled to board ship the next day—and I'd only had a few words with my officers.

Not enough, because it was becoming clear that Hilleboe and I had rather disparate philosophies about how to run a company. It was true that *running* it was her job; I only commanded. But she was setting up a potential "good guy-bad guy" situation, using the chain of command to so isolate herself from the men and women under her. I had planned not to be quite so aloof, setting aside an hour every other day when any soldier could come to me directly with grievances or suggestions, without permission from his superiors.

We had both been given the same information during our three weeks in the can. It was interesting that we'd arrived at such different conclusions about leadership. This Open Door policy, for instance, had shown good results in "modern" armies in Australia and America. And it seemed especially appropriate to our situation, in which everybody would be cooped up for months or even years at a time. We'd used the system on the *Sangre y Victoria*, the last starship to which I'd been attached, and it had seemed to keep tensions down.

She had them at ease while delivering this organizational harangue; pretty soon she'd call them to attention and introduce me. What would I talk about? I'd planned just to say a few predictable words and explain my Open Door policy, then turn them over to Commodore Antopol, who would say something about the *Masaryk II*. But I'd better put off my explanation until after I'd had a long talk with Hilleboe; in fact, it would be best if she were the one to introduce the policy to the men and women, so it wouldn't look like the two of us were at loggerheads.

My executive officer, Captain Moore, saved me. He came rushing through a side door—he was always rushing, a pudgy meteor—threw a quick salute and handed me an envelope that contained our combat orders. I had a quick whispered conference with the Commodore, and she agreed that it wouldn't do any harm to tell them where we were going, even though the rank and file technically didn't have the "need to know."

One thing we didn't have to worry about in this war was enemy agents. With a good coat of paint, a Tauran might be able to disguise himself as an ambulatory mushroom. Bound to raise suspicions.

Hilleboe had called them to attention and was dutifully telling them what a good commander I was going to be; that I'd been in the war from the beginning, and if they intended to survive through their enlistment they had better follow my example. She didn't mention that I was a mediocre soldier with a talent for getting missed. Nor that I'd resigned from the army at the earliest opportunity and only got back in because conditions on Earth were so intolerable.

"Thank you, Lieutenant." I took her place at the podium. "At ease." I unfolded the single sheet that had our orders, and held it up. "I have some good news and some bad news." What had been a joke five centuries before was now just a statement of fact.

"These are our combat orders for the Sade-138 campaign. The good news is that we probably won't be fighting, not immediately. The bad news is that we're going to be a target."

They stirred a little bit at that, but nobody said anything

or took his eyes off me. Good discipline. Or maybe just
fatalism; I didn't know how realistic a picture they had of
their future. Their lack of a future, that is.

"What we are ordered to do . . . is to find the largest
portal planet orbiting the Sade-138 collapsar and build a
base there. Then stay at the base until we are relieved. That
will be two or three years, probably.

"During that time we will almost certainly be attacked.
As most of you probably know, Strike Force Command has
uncovered a pattern in the enemy's movements from collapsar to collapsar. They hope eventually to trace this complex pattern back through time and space and find the
Taurans' home planet. For the present, they can only send
out intercepting forces, to hamper the enemy's expansion.

"In a large perspective, this is what we're ordered to do.
We'll be one of several dozen strike forces employed in
these blocking maneuvers, on the enemy's frontier. I won't
be able to stress often enough or hard enough how important this mission is—if UNEF can keep the enemy from
expanding, we may be able to envelop him. And win the
war."

Preferably before we're all dead meat. "One thing I want
to be clear: we may be attacked the day we land, or we
may simply occupy the planet for ten years and come on
home." Fat chance. "Whatever happens, every one of us
will stay in the best fighting trim all the time. In transit, we
will maintain a regular program of calisthenics as well as
a review of our training. Especially construction techniques—we have to set up the base and its defense facilities
in the shortest possible time."

God, I was beginning to sound like an officer. "Any
questions?" There were none. "Then I'd like to introduce
Commodore Antopol. Commodore?"

The commodore didn't try to hide her boredom as she
outlined, to this room full of ground-pounders, the char-
acteristics and capabilities of *Masaryk II*. I had learned
most of what she was saying through the can's force-
feeding, but the last thing she said caught my attention.

"Sade-138 will be the most distant collapsar men have
gone to. It isn't even in the galaxy proper, but rather is part

of the Large Magellanic Cloud, some 150,000 light years distant.

"Our voyage will require four collapsar jumps and will last some four months, subjective. Maneuvering into collapsar insertion will put us about three hundred years behind Stargate's calendar by the time we reach Sade-138."

And another seven hundred years gone, if I lived to return. Not that it would make that much difference; Marygay was as good as dead and there wasn't another person alive who meant anything to me.

"As the major said, you mustn't let these figures lull you into complacency. The enemy is also headed for Sade-138; we may all get there the same day. The mathematics of the situation is complicated, but take our word for it; it's going to be a close race.

"Major, do you have anything more for them?"

I started to rise. "Well . . ."

"Tench-*hut!*" Hilleboe shouted. Had to learn to expect that.

"Only that I'd like to meet with my senior officers, echelon 4 and above, for a few minutes. Platoon sergeants, you're responsible for getting your troops to Staging Area 67 at 0400 tomorrow morning. Your time's your own until then. Dismissed."

I invited the five officers up to my billet and brought out a bottle of real French brandy. It had cost two months' pay, but what else could I do with the money? Invest it?

I passed around glasses but Alsever, the doctor, demurred. Instead she broke a little capsule under her nose and inhaled deeply. Then tried without too much success to mask her euphoric expression.

"First let's get down to one basic personnel problem," I said, pouring. "Do all of you know that I'm not homosexual?"

Mixed chorus of yes sirs and no sirs.

"Do you think this is going to . . . complicate my situation as commander? As far as the rank and file?"

"Sir, I don't—" Moore began.

"No need for honorifics," I said, "not in this closed

circle; I was a private four years ago, in my own time frame. When there aren't any troops around, I'm just Mandella, or William.'' I had a feeling that was a mistake even as I was saying it. ''Go on.''

''Well, William,'' he continued, ''it might have been a problem a hundred years ago. You know how people felt then.''

''Actually, I don't. All I know about the period from the twenty-first century to the present is military history.''

''Oh. Well, it was, uh, it was, how to say it?'' His hands fluttered.

''It was a crime,'' Alsever said laconically. ''That was when the Eugenics Council was first getting people used to the idea of universal homosex.''

''Eugenics Council?''

''Part of UNEF. Only has authority on Earth.'' She took a deep sniff at the empty capsule. ''The idea was to keep people from making babies the biological way. Because, A, people showed a regrettable lack of sense in choosing their genetic partner. And B, the Council saw that racial differences had an unnecessarily divisive effect on humanity; with total control over births, they could make everybody the same race in a few generations.''

I didn't know they had gone quite that far. But I suppose it was logical. ''You approve? As a doctor.''

''As a doctor? I'm not sure.'' She took another capsule from her pocket and rolled it between thumb and forefinger, staring at nothing. Or something the rest of us couldn't see. ''In a way, it makes my job simpler. A lot of diseases simply no longer exist. But I don't think they know as much about genetics as they think they do. It's not an exact science; they could be doing something very wrong, and the results wouldn't show up for centuries.''

She cracked the capsule under her nose and took two deep breaths. ''As a woman, though, I'm all in favor of it.'' Hilleboe and Rusk nodded vigorously.

''Not having to go through childbirth?''

''That's part of it.'' She crossed her eyes comically, looking at the capsule, gave it a final sniff. ''Mostly,

though, it's not . . . having to . . . have a man. Inside me.
You understand. It's disgusting.''

Moore laughed. ''If you haven't tried it, Diana, don't—''

''Oh, shut up.'' She threw the empty capsule at him play-
fully.

''But it's perfectly natural,'' I protested.

''So is swinging through trees. Digging for roots with a
blunt stick. Progress, my good major; progress.''

''Anyway,'' Moore said, ''it was only a crime for a short
period. Then it was considered a, oh, curable . . .''

''Dysfunction,'' Alsever said.

''Thank you. And now, well, it's so rare . . . I doubt that
any of the men and women have any strong feelings about
it, one way or the other.''

''Just an eccentricity,'' Diana said, magnanimously.
''Not as if you ate babies.''

''That's right, Mandella,'' Hilleboe said. ''I don't feel
any differently toward you because of it.''

''I—I'm glad.'' That was just great. It was dawning on
me that I had not the slightest idea of how to conduct myself socially. So much of my ''normal'' behavior was based
on a complex unspoken code of sexual etiquette. Was I
suppose to treat the men like women, and vice versa? Or
treat everybody like brothers and sisters? It was all very
confusing.

I finished off my glass and set it down. ''Well, thanks
for your reassurances. That was mainly what I wanted to
ask you about . . . I'm sure you all have things to do, good-
byes and such. Don't let me hold you prisoner.''

They all wandered off except for Charlie Moore. He and
I decided to go on a monumental binge, trying to hit every
bar and officer's club in the sector. We managed twelve
and probably could have hit them all, but I decided to get
a few hours' sleep before the next day's muster.

The one time Charlie made a pass at me, he was very
polite about it. I hoped my refusal was also polite—but
figured I'd be getting lots of practice.

3

UNEF's first starships had been possessed of a kind of spidery, delicate beauty. But with various technological improvements, structural strength became more important than conserving mass (one of the old ships would have folded up like an accordion if you'd tried a twenty-five-gee maneuver), and that was reflected in the design: stolid, heavy, functional-looking. The only decoration was the name MASARYK II, stenciled in dull blue letters across the obsidian hull.

Our shuttle drifted over the name on its way to the loading bay, and there was a crew of tiny men and women doing maintenance on the hull. With them as a reference, we could see that the letters were a good hundred meters tall. The ship was over a kilometer long (1036.5 meters, my latent memory said), and about a third that wide (319.4 meters).

That didn't mean there was going to be plenty of elbowroom. In its belly, the ship held six large tachyondrive fighters and fifty robot drones. The infantry was tucked off in a corner. *War is the province of friction*, Chuck von Clausewitz said; I had a feeling we were going to put him to the test.

We had about six hours before going into the acceleration tank. I dropped my kit in the tiny billet that would be my home for the next twenty months and went off to explore.

Charlie had beaten me to the lounge and to the privilege of being first to evaluate the quality of *Masaryk II*'s coffee.

"Rhinoceros bile," he said.

"At least it isn't soya," I said, taking a first cautious sip. Decided I might be longing for soya in a week.

The officers' lounge was a cubicle about three meters by four, metal floor and walls, with a coffee machine and a

190

library readout. Six hard chairs and a table with a typer on it.

"Jolly place, isn't it?" He idly punched up a general index on the library machine. "Lots of military theory."

"That's good. Refresh our memories."

"Sign up for officer training?"

"Me? No. Orders."

"At least you have an excuse." He slapped the on-off button and watched the green spot dwindle. "I signed up. They didn't tell me it'd feel like this."

"Yeah." He wasn't talking about any subtle problem: burden of responsibility or anything. "They say it wears off, a little at a time." All of that information they force into you; a constant silent whispering.

"Ah, there you are." Hilleboe came through the door and exchanged greetings with us. She gave the room a quick survey, and it was obvious that the Spartan arrangements met with her approval. "Will you be wanting to address the company before we go into the acceleration tanks?"

"No, I don't see why that would be . . . necessary." I almost said "desirable." The art of chastising subordinates is a delicate art. I could see that I'd have to keep reminding Hilleboe that she wasn't in charge.

Or I could just switch insignia with her. Let her experience the joys of command.

"You could, please, round up all platoon leaders and go over the immersion sequence with them. Eventually we'll be doing speed drills. But for now, I think the troops could use a few hours' rest." If they were as hungover as their commander.

"Yes, sir." She turned and left. A little miffed, because what I'd asked her to do should properly have been a job for Riland or Rusk.

Charlie eased his pudgy self into one of the hard chairs and sighed. "Twenty months on this greasy machine. With her. Shit."

"Well, if you're nice to me, I won't billet the two of you together."

"All right. I'm your slave forever. Starting, oh, next Friday." He peered into his cup and decided against drinking the dregs. "Seriously, she's going to be a problem. What are you going to do with her?"

"I don't know." Charlie was being insubordinate, too, of course. But he was my XO and out of the chain of command. Besides, I had to have *one* friend. "Maybe she'll mellow, once we're under weigh."

"Sure." Technically, we were already under weigh, crawling toward the Stargate collapsar at one gee. But that was only for the convenience of the crew; it's hard to batten down the hatches in free fall. The trip wouldn't really start until we were in the tanks.

The lounge was too depressing, so Charlie and I used the remaining hours of mobility to explore the ship.

The bridge looked like any other computer facility; they had dispensed with the luxury of viewscreens. We stood at a respectful distance while Antopol and her officers went through a last series of checks before climbing into the tanks and leaving our destiny to the machines.

Actually, there was a porthole, a thick plastic bubble, in the navigation room forward. Lieutenant Williams wasn't busy, the pre-insertion part of his job being fully automated, so he was glad to show us around.

He tapped the porthole with a fingernail. "Hope we don't have to use this, this trip."

"How so?" Charlie said.

"We only use it if we get lost." If the insertion angle was off by a thousandth of a radian, we were liable to wind up on the other side of the galaxy. "We can get a rough idea of our position by analyzing the spectra of the brightest stars. Thumbprints. Identify three and we can triangulate."

"Then find the nearest collapsar and get back on the rack," I said.

"That's the problem. Sade-138 is the only collapsar we know of in the Magellanic Clouds. We know of it only because of captured enemy data. Even if we could find another collapsar, assuming we got lost in the cloud, we wouldn't know how to insert."

"That's great."

"It's not as though we'd be actually lost," he said with

a rather wicked expression. "We could zip up in the tanks, aim for Earth and blast away at full power. We'd get there in about three months, ship time."

"Sure," I said. "But 150,000 years in the future." At twenty-five gees, you get to nine-tenths the speed of light in less than a month. From then on, you're in the arms of Saint Albert.

"Well, that is a drawback," he said. "But at least we'd find out who'd won the war."

It made you wonder how many soldiers had gotten out of the war in just that way. There were forty-two strike forces lost somewhere and unaccounted for. It was possible that all of them were crawling through normal space at near-lightspeed and would show up at Earth or Stargate one-by-one over the centuries.

A convenient way to go AWOL, since once you were out of the chain of collapsar jumps you'd be practically impossible to track down. Unfortunately, your jump sequence was pre-programmed by Strike Force Command; the human navigator only came into the picture if a miscalculation slipped you into the wrong "wormhole," and you popped out in some random part of space.

Charlie and I went on to inspect the gym, which was big enough for about a dozen people at a time. I asked him to make up a roster so that everyone could work out for an hour each day when we were out of the tanks.

The mess area was only a little larger than the gym— even with four staggered shifts, the meals would be shoulder-to-shoulder affairs—and the enlisted men and women's lounge was even more depressing than the officers'. I was going to have a real morale problem on my hands long before the twenty months were up.

The armorer's bay was as large as the gym, mess hall and both lounges put together. It had to be, because of the great variety of infantry weapons that had evolved over the centuries. The basic weapon was still the fighting suit, though it was much more sophisticated than that first model I had been squeezed into, just before the Aleph-Null campaign.

Lieutenant Riland, the armory officer, was supervising

his four subordinates, one from each platoon, who were doing a last-minute check of weapons storage. Probably the most important job on the whole ship, when you contemplate what could happen to all those tons of explosives and radioactives under twenty-five gees.

I returned his perfunctory salute. "Everything going all right, Lieutenant?"

"Yessir, except for those damned swords." For use in the stasis field. "No way we can orient them that they won't be bent. Just hope they don't break."

I couldn't begin to understand the principles behind the stasis field; the gap between present-day physics and my master's degree in the same subject was as long as the time that separated Galileo and Einstein. But I knew the effects.

Nothing could move at greater than 16.3 meters per second inside the field, which was a hemispherical (in space, spherical) volume about fifty meters in radius. Inside, there was no such thing as electromagnetic radiation; no electricity, no magnetism, no light. From inside your suit, you could see your surroundings in ghostly monochrome—which phenomenon was glibly explained to me as being due to "phase transference of quasi-energy leaking through from an adjacent tachyon reality," so much phlogiston to me.

The result of it, though, was to make all conventional weapons of warfare useless. Even a nova bomb was just an inert lump inside the field. And any creature, Terran or Tauran, caught inside the field without the proper insulation would die in a fraction of a second.

At first it looked as though we had come upon the ultimate weapon. There were five engagements where whole Tauran bases were wiped out without any human ground casualties. All you had to do was carry the field to the enemy (four husky soldiers could handle it in Earth-gravity) and watch them die as they slipped in through the field's opaque wall. The people carrying the generator were invulnerable except for the short periods when they might have to turn the thing off to get their bearings.

The sixth time the field was used, though, the Taurans were ready for it. They wore protective suits and were armed with sharp spears, with which they could breach the suits of the generator-carriers. From then on the carriers were armed.

Only three other such battles had been reported, although a dozen strike forces had gone out with the stasis field. The others were still fighting, or still en route, or had been totally defeated. There was no way to tell unless they came back. And they weren't encouraged to come back if Taurans were still in control of ''their'' real estate—supposedly that constituted ''desertion under fire,'' which meant execution for all officers (although rumor had it that they were simply brainwiped, imprinted and sent back into the fray).

''Will we be using the stasis field, sir?'' Riland asked.

''Probably. Not at first, not unless the Taurans are already there. I don't relish the thought of living in a suit, day in and day out.'' Neither did I relish the thought of using sword, spear, throwing knife; no matter how many electronic illusions I'd sent to Valhalla with them.

Checked my watch. ''Well, we'd better get on down to the tanks, Captain. Make sure everything's squared away.'' We had about two hours before the insertion sequence would start.

The room the tanks were in resembled a huge chemical factory; the floor was a good hundred meters in diameter and jammed with bulky apparatus painted a uniform, dull gray. The eight tanks were arranged almost symmetrically around the central elevator, the symmetry spoiled by the fact that one of the tanks was twice the size of the others. That would be the command tank, for all the senior officers and supporting specialists.

Sergeant Blazynski stepped out from behind one of the tanks and saluted. I didn't return his salute.

''What the hell is that?'' In all that universe of gray, there was one spot of color.

''It's a cat, sir.''

''Do tell.'' A big one, too, and bright calico. It looked ridiculous, draped over the sergeant's shoulder. ''Let me rephrase the question: what the hell is a cat doing here?''

''It's the maintenance squad's mascot, sir.'' The cat raised its head enough to hiss half-heartedly at me, then returned to its flaccid repose.

I looked at Charlie and he shrugged back. "It seems kind of cruel," he said. To the sergeant: "You won't get much use of it. After twenty-five gees, it'll be just so much fur and guts."

"Oh no, sir! Sirs." He ruffed back the fur between the creature's shoulders. It had a fluorocarbon fitting imbedded there, just like the one above my hipbone. "We bought it at a store on Stargate, already modified. Lots of ships have them now, sir. The Commodore signed the forms for us."

Well, that was her right; maintenance was under both of us equally. And it was her ship. "You couldn't have gotten a dog?" God, I hated cats. Always sneaking around.

"No, sir, they don't adapt. Can't take free fall."

"Did you have to make any special adaptations? In the tank?" Charlie asked.

"No sir. We had an extra couch." Great; that meant I'd be sharing a tank with the animal. "We only had to shorten the straps.

"It takes a different kind of drug for the cell-wall strengthening, but that was included in the price."

Charlie scratched it behind an ear. It purred softly but didn't move. "Seems kind of stupid. The animal, I mean."

"We drugged him ahead of time." No wonder it was so inert; the drug slows your metabolism down to a rate barely adequate to sustain life. "Makes it easier to strap him in."

"Guess it's all right," I said. Maybe good for morale. "But if it starts getting in the way, I'll personally recycle it."

"Yes, sir!" he said, visibly relieved, thinking that I couldn't really do anything like that to such a cute bundle of fur. Try me, buddy.

So we had seen it all. The only thing left, this side of the engines, was the huge hold where the fighters and drones waited, clamped in their massive cradles against the coming acceleration. Charlie and I went down to take a look, but there were no windows on our side of the airlock. I knew there'd be one on the inside, but the chamber was evacuated, and it wasn't worth going through the fill-and-warm cycle merely to satisfy our curiosity.

I was starting to feel really supernumerary. Called Hilleboe and she said everything was under control. With an hour to kill, we went back to the lounge and had the computer mediate a game of *Kriegspieler*, which was just starting to get interesting when the ten-minute warning sounded.

The acceleration tanks had a "half-life-to-failure" of five weeks; there was a fifty-fifty chance that you could stay immersed for five weeks before some valve or tube popped and you were squashed like a bug underfoot. In practice, it had to be one hell of an emergency to justify using the tanks for more than two weeks' acceleration. We were only going under for ten days, this first leg of our journey.

Five weeks or five hours, though, it was all the same as far as the tankee was concerned. Once the pressure got up to an operational level, you had no sense of the passage of time. Your body and brain were concrete. None of your senses provided any input, and you could amuse yourself for several hours just trying to spell your own name.

So I wasn't really surprised that no time seemed to have passed when I was suddenly dry, my body tingling with the return of sensation. The place sounded like an asthmatics' convention in the middle of a hay field: thirty-nine people and one cat all coughing and sneezing to get rid of the last residues of fluorocarbon. While I was fumbling with my straps, the side door opened, flooding the tank with painfully bright light. The cat was the first one out, with a general scramble right behind him. For the sake of dignity, I waited until last.

Over a hundred people were milling around outside, stretching and massaging out cramps. Dignity! Surrounded by acres of young female flesh, I stared into their faces and desperately tried to solve a third-order differential equation in my head, to circumvent the gallant reflex. A temporary expedient, but it got me to the elevator.

Hilleboe was shouting orders, getting people lined up, and as the doors closed I noticed that all of one platoon had a uniform light bruise, from head to foot. Twenty pairs of black eyes. I'd have to see both Maintenance and Medical about that.

After I got dressed.

4

We stayed at one gee for three weeks, with occasional periods of free fall for navigation check, while the *Masaryk II* made a long, narrow loop away from the collapsar Resh-10, and back again. That period went all right, the people adjusting pretty well to ship routine. I gave them a minimum of busy-work and a maximum of training review and exercise—for their own good, though I wasn't naive enough to think they'd see it that way.

After about a week of one gee, Private Rudkoski (the cook's assistant) had a still, producing some eight liters a day of 95 percent ethyl alcohol. I didn't want to stop him—life was cheerless enough; I didn't mind as long as people showed up for duty sober—but I was damned curious both how he managed to divert the raw materials out of our sealed-tight ecology, and how the people paid for their booze. So I used the chain of command in reverse, asking Alsever to find out. She asked Jarvil, who asked Carreras, who sat down with Orban, the cook. Turned out that Sergeant Orban had set the whole thing up, letting Rudkoski do the dirty work, and was aching to brag about it to a trustworthy person.

If I had ever taken meals with the enlisted men and women, I might have figured out that something odd was going on. But the scheme didn't extend up to officers' country.

Through Rudkoski, Orban had juryrigged a ship-wide economy based on alcohol. It went like this:

Each meal was prepared with one very sugary dessert—jelly, custard or flan—which you were free to eat if you could stand the cloying taste. But if it was still on your tray when you presented it at the recycling window, Rudkoski would give you a ten-cent chit and scrape the sugary stuff into a fermentation vat. He had two twenty-liter vats, one "working" while the other was being filled.

The ten-cent chit was at the bottom of a system that allowed you to buy a half-liter of straight ethyl (with your choice of flavoring) for five dollars. A squad of five people who skipped all of their desserts could buy about a liter a week, enough for a party but not enough to constitute a public health problem.

When Diana brought me this information, she also brought a bottle of Rudkoski's Worst—literally; it was a flavor that just hadn't worked. It came up through the chain of command with only a few centimeters missing.

Its taste was a ghastly combination of strawberry and caraway seed. With a perversity not uncommon to people who rarely drink, Diana loved it. I had some ice water brought up, and she got totally blasted within an hour. For myself, I made one drink and didn't finish it.

When she was more than halfway to oblivion, mumbling a reassuring soliloquy to her liver, she suddenly tilted her head up to stare at me with childlike directness.

"You have a real problem, Major William."

"Not half the problem you'll have in the morning, Lieutenant Doctor Diana."

"Oh not really." She waved a drunken hand in front of her face. "Some vitamins, some glu . . . cose, an eensy cc of adren . . . aline if all else fails. You . . . you . . . have . . . a real . . . problem."

"Look, Diana, don't you want me to—"

"What you need . . . is to get an appointment with that nice Corporal Valdez." Valdez was the male sex counselor. "He has empathy. Itsiz job. He'd make you—"

"We talked about this before, remember? I want to stay the way I am."

"Don't we all." She wiped away a tear that was probably one percent alcohol. "You know they call you the Old C'reer. No they don't."

She looked at the floor and then at the wall. "The Ol' Queer, that's what."

I had expected names worse than that. But not so soon. "I don't care. The commander always gets names."

"I know but." She stood up suddenly and wobbled a

little bit. "Too much t' drink. Lie down." She turned her
back to me and stretched so hard that a joint popped. Then
a seam whispered open and she shrugged off her tunic,
stepped out of it and tiptoed to my bed. She sat down and
patted the mattress. "Come on, William. Only chance."

"For Christ's sake, Diana. It wouldn't be fair."

"All's fair," she giggled. "And 'sides, I'm a doctor. I
can be clin'cal; won't bother me a bit. Help me with this."
After five hundred years, they were still putting brassiere
clasps in the back.

One kind of gentleman would have helped her get un-
dressed and then made a quiet exit. Another kind of gentleman might have bolted for the door. Being neither kind,
I closed in for the kill.

Perhaps fortunately, she passed out before we had made
any headway. I admired the sight and touch of her for a
long time before, feeling like a cad, I managed to gather
everything up and dress her.

I lifted her out of the bed, sweet burden, and then realized that if anyone saw me carrying her down to her billet,
she'd be the butt of rumors for the rest of the campaign. I
called up Charlie, told him we'd had some booze and Diana
was rather the worse for it, and asked him whether he'd
come up for a drink and help me haul the good doctor
home.

By the time Charlie knocked, she was draped innocently
in a chair, snoring softly.

He smiled at her. "Physician, heal thyself." I offered
him the bottle, with a warning. He sniffed it and made a
face.

"What is this, varnish?"

"Just something the cooks whipped up. Vacuum still."

He set it down carefully, as if it might explode if jarred.
"I predict a coming shortage of customers. Epidemic of
death by poisoning—she actually drank that vile stuff?"

"Well, the cooks admitted it was an experiment that
didn't pan out; their other flavors are evidently potable.
Yeah, she loved it."

"Well . . ." He laughed. "Damn! What, you take her
legs and I take her arms?"

"No, look, we each take an arm. Maybe we can get her to do part of the walking."

She moaned a little when we lifted her out of the chair, opened one eye and said, "Hello, Charlee." Then she closed the eye and let us drag her down to the billet. No one saw us on the way, but her bunkmate, Laasonen, was sitting up reading.

"She really drank the stuff, eh?" She regarded her friend with wry affection. "Here, let me help."

The three of us wrestled her into bed. Laasonen smoothed the hair out of her eyes. "She said it was in the nature of an experiment."

"More devotion to science than I have," Charlie said. "A stronger stomach, too."

We all wished he hadn't said that.

Diana sheepishly admitted that she hadn't remembered anything after the first drink, and talking to her, I deduced that she thought Charlie had been there all along. Which was all for the best, of course. But oh! Diana, my lovely latent heterosexual, let me buy you a bottle of good scotch the next time we come into port. Seven hundred years from now.

We got back into the tanks for the hop from Resh-10 to Kaph-35. That was two weeks at twenty-five gees; then we had another four weeks of routine at one gravity.

I had announced my open door policy, but practically no one ever took advantage of it. I saw very little of the troops and those occasions were almost always negative: testing them on their training review, handing out reprimands, and occasionally lecturing classes. And they rarely spoke intelligibly, except in response to a direct question.

Most of them either had English as their native tongue or as a second language, but it had changed so drastically over 450 years that I could barely understand it, not at all if it was spoken rapidly. Fortunately, they had all been taught early twenty-first century English during their basic training; that language, or dialect, served as a temporal *lingua franca* through which a twenty-fifth century soldier could communicate with someone who had been a contem-

porary of his nineteen-times-great-grandparents. If there
had still been such a thing as grandparents.

I thought of my first combat commander, Captain Stott—
whom I had hated just as cordially as the rest of the company did—and tried to imagine how I would have felt if
he had been a sexual deviate and I'd been forced to learn
a new language for his convenience.

So we had discipline problems, sure. But the wonder was
that we had any discipline at all. Hilleboe was responsible
for that; as little as I liked her personally, I had to give her
credit for keeping the troops in line.

Most of the shipboard graffiti concerned improbable sexual geometries between the Second Field Officer and her
commander.

From Kaph-35 we jumped to Samk-78, from there to
Ayin-129 and finally to Sade-138. Most of the jumps were
no more than a few hundred light years, but the last one
was 140,000—supposedly the longest collapsar jump ever
made by a manned craft.

The time spent scooting down the wormhole from one
collapsar to the next was always the same, independent of
the distance. When I'd studied physics, they thought the
duration of a collapsar jump was exactly zero. But a couple
of centuries later, they did a complicated wave-guide experiment that proved the jump actually lasted some small
fraction of a nanosecond. Doesn't seem like much, but
they'd had to rebuild physics from the foundation up when
the collapsar jump was first discovered; they had to tear the
whole damned thing down again when they found out it
took time to get from A to B. Physicists were still arguing
about it.

But we had more pressing problems as we flashed out
of Sade-138's collapsar field at three-quarters of the speed
of light. There was no way to tell immediately whether the
Taurans had beat us there. We launched a pre-programmed
drone that would decelerate at 300 gees and take a preliminary look around. It would warn us if it detected any other
ships in the system, or evidence of Tauran activity on any
of the collapsar's planets.

The drone launched, we zipped up in the tanks and the computers put us through a three-week evasive maneuver while the ship slowed down. No problems except that three weeks is a hell of a long time to stay frozen in the tank; for a couple of days afterward everybody crept around like aged cripples.

If the drone had sent back word that the Taurans were already in the system, we would immediately have stepped down to one gee and started deploying fighters and drones armed with nova bombs. Or we might not have lived that long: sometimes the Taurans could get to a ship only hours after it entered the system. Dying in the tank might not be the most pleasant way to go.

It took us a month to get back to within a couple of AUs of Sade-138, where the drone had found a planet that met our requirements.

It was an odd planet, slightly smaller than Earth but more dense. It wasn't quite the cryogenic deepfreeze that most portal planets were, both because of heat from its core and because S Doradus, the brightest star in the cloud, was only a third of a light year away.

The strangest feature of the planet was its lack of geography. From space it looked like a slightly damaged billiard ball. Our resident physicist, Lieutenant Gim, explained its relatively pristine condition by pointing out that its anomalous, almost cometary orbit probably meant that it had spent most of its life as a "rogue planet," drifting alone through interstellar space. The chances were good that it had never been struck by a large meteor until it wandered into Sade-138's bailiwick and was captured—forced to share space with all the other flotsam the collapsar dragged around with it.

We left the *Masaryk II* in orbit (it was capable of landing, but that would restrict its visibility and getaway time) and shuttled building materials down to the surface with the six fighters.

It was good to get out of the ship, even though the planet wasn't exactly hospitable. The atmosphere was a thin cold wind of hydrogen and helium, it being too cold even at noon for any other substance to exist as a gas.

"Noon" was when S Doradus was overhead, a tiny, painfully bright spark. The temperature slowly dropped at night, going from twenty-five degrees Kelvin down to seventeen degrees—which caused problems, because just before dawn the hydrogen would start to condense out of the air, making everything so slippery that it was useless to do anything other than sit down and wait it out. At dawn a faint pastel rainbow provided the only relief from the black-and-white monotony of the landscape.

The ground was treacherous, covered with little granular chunks of frozen gas that shifted slowly, incessantly in the anemic breeze. You had to walk in a slow waddle to stay on your feet; of the four people who would die during the base's construction, three would be the victims of simple falls.

The troops weren't happy with my decision to construct the anti-spacecraft and perimeter defenses before putting up living quarters. That was by the book, though, and they got two days of shipboard rest for every "day" planetside—which wasn't overly generous, I admit, since ship days were 24 hours long, and a day on the planet was 38.5 hours from dawn to dawn.

The base was completed in just less than four weeks, and it was a formidable structure indeed. The perimeter, a circle one kilometer in diameter, was guarded by twenty-five gigawatt lasers that would automatically aim and fire within a thousandth of a second. They would react to the motion of any significantly large object between the perimeter and the horizon. Sometimes when the wind was right and the ground damp with hydrogen, the little ice granules would stick together into a loose snowball and begin to roll. They wouldn't roll far.

For early protection, before the enemy came over our horizon, the base was in the center of a huge mine field. The buried mines would detonate upon sufficient distortion of their local gravitational fields: a single Tauran would set one off if he came within twenty meters of it; a small spacecraft a kilometer overhead would also detonate it. There were 2800 of them, mostly 100-microton nuclear bombs. Fifty of them were devastatingly powerful tachyon devices.

They were all scattered at random in a ring that extended from the limit of the lasers' effectiveness, out another five kilometers.

Inside the base, we relied on individual lasers, microton grenades, and a tachyon-powered repeating rocket launcher that had never been tried in combat, one per platoon. As a last resort, the stasis field was set up beside the living quarters. Inside its opaque gray dome, as well as enough paleolithic weaponry to hold off the Golden Horde, we'd stashed a small cruiser, just in case we managed to lose all our spacecraft in the process of winning a battle. Twelve people would be able to get back to Stargate.

It didn't do to dwell on the fact that the other survivors would have to sit on their hands until relieved by reinforcements or death.

The living quarters and administration facilities were all underground, to protect them from line-of-sight weapons. It didn't do too much for morale, though; there were waiting lists for every outside detail, no matter how strenuous or risky. I hadn't wanted the troops to go up to the surface in their free time, both because of the danger involved and the administrative headache of constantly checking equipment in and out and keeping track of who was where.

Finally I had to relent and allow people to go up for a few hours every week. There was nothing to see except the featureless plain and the sky (which was dominated by S Doradus during the day, and the huge dim oval of the galaxy at night), but that was an improvement over staring at the melted-rock walls and ceiling.

A favorite sport was to walk out to the perimeter and throw snowballs in front of the laser; see how small a snowball you could throw and still set the weapon off. It seemed to me that the entertainment value of this pastime was about equal to watching a faucet drip, but there was no real harm in it, since the weapons would only fire outward and we had power to spare.

For five months things went pretty smoothly. Such administrative problems as we had were similar to those we'd encountered on the *Masaryk II*. And we were in less danger as passive troglodytes than we had been scooting from collapsar to collapsar, at least until the enemy showed up.

I looked the other way when Rudkoski reassembled his still. Anything that broke the monotony of garrison duty was welcome, and the chits not only provided booze for the troops but gave them something to gamble with. I only interfered in two ways: nobody could go outside unless they were totally sober, and nobody could sell sexual favors. Maybe that was the Puritan in me, but it was, again, by the book. The opinion of the supporting specialists was split. Lieutenant Wilber, the psychiatric officer, agreed with me; the sex counselors Kajdi and Valdez didn't. But then, they were probably coining money, being the resident "professionals."

Five months of comfortably boring routine, and then along came Private Graubard.

For obvious reasons, no weapons were allowed in the living quarters. The way these people were trained, even a fistfight could be a duel to the death, and tempers were short. A hundred merely normal people would probably have been at each other's throats after a week in our caves, but these soldiers had been hand-picked for their ability to get along in close confinement.

Still there were fights. Graubard had almost killed his ex-lover Schon when that worthy made a face at him in the chow line. He had a week of solitary detention (so did Schon, for having precipitated it) and then psychiatric counseling and punitive details. Then I transferred him to the fourth platoon, so he wouldn't be seeing Schon every day.

The first time they passed in the halls, Graubard greeted Schon with a karate kick to the throat. Diana had to build him a new trachea. Graubard got a more intensive round of detention, counseling and details—hell, I couldn't transfer him to another *company*—and then he was a good boy for two weeks. I fiddled their work and chow schedules so the two would never be in the same room together. But they met in a corridor again, and this time it came out more even: Schon got two broken ribs, but Graubard got a ruptured testicle and lost four teeth.

If it kept up, I was going to have at least one less mouth to feed.

By the Universal Code of Military Justice I could have ordered Graubard executed, since we were technically in a state of combat. Perhaps I should have, then and there. But Charlie suggested a more humanitarian solution, and I accepted it.

We didn't have enough room to keep Graubard in solitary detention forever, which seemed to be the only humane yet practical thing to do, but they had plenty of room aboard the *Masaryk II*, hovering overhead in a stationary orbit. I called Antopol and she agreed to take care of him. I gave her permission to space the bastard if he gave her any trouble.

We called a general assembly to explain things, so that the lesson of Graubard wouldn't be lost on anybody. I was just starting to talk, standing on the rock dais with the company sitting in front of me, and the officers and Graubard behind me—when the crazy fool decided to kill me.

Like everybody else, Graubard was assigned five hours per week of training inside the stasis field. Under close supervision, the soldiers would practice using their swords and spears and whatnot on dummy Taurans. Somehow Graubard had managed to smuggle out a weapon, an Indian chakra, which is a circle of metal with a razor-keen outer edge. It's a tricky weapon, but once you know how to use it, it can be much more effective than a regular throwing knife. Graubard was an expert.

All in a fraction of a second, Graubard disabled the people on either side of him—hitting Charlie in the temple with an elbow while he broke Hilleboe's kneecap with a kick—and slid the chakra out of his tunic and spun it toward me in one smooth action. It had covered half the distance to my throat before I reacted.

Instinctively I slapped out to deflect it and came within a centimeter of losing four fingers. The razor edge slashed open the top of my palm, but I succeeded in knocking the thing off course. And Graubard was rushing me, teeth bared in an expression I hope I never see again.

Maybe he didn't realize that the *old queer* was really

only five years older than he; that the *old queer* had combat reflexes and three weeks of negative feedback kinesthesia training. At any rate, it was so easy I almost felt sorry for him.

His right toe was turning in; I knew he would take one more step and go into a savaté leap. I adjusted the distance between us with a short *ballestra* and, just as both his feet left the ground, gave him an ungentle side-kick to the solar plexus. He was unconscious before he hit the ground. But not dead.

If I'd merely killed him in self-defense, my troubles would have been over instead of suddenly being multiplied.

A simple psychotic troublemaker a commander can lock up and forget about. But not a failed assassin. And I didn't have to take a poll to know that executing him was not going to improve my relationship with the troops.

I realized that Diana was on her knees beside me, trying to pry open my fingers. "Check Hilleboe and Moore," I mumbled, and to the troops: "Dismissed."

5

"Don't be an ass," Charlie said. He was holding a damp rag to the bruise on the side of his head.

"You don't think I have to execute him?"

"Stop twitching!" Diana was trying to get the lips of my wound to line up together so she could paint them shut. From the wrist down, the hand felt like a lump of ice.

"Not by your own hand, you don't. You can detail someone. At random."

"Charlie's right," Diana said. "Have everybody draw a slip of paper out of a bowl."

I was glad Hilleboe was sound asleep on the other cot. I didn't need her opinion. "And if the person so chosen refuses?"

"Punish him and get another," Charlie said. "Didn't you learn anything in the can? You can't abrogate your authority by publicly doing a job . . . that obviously should be detailed."

"Any other job, sure. But for this . . . nobody in the company has ever killed. It would look like I was getting somebody else to do my moral dirty work."

"If it's so damned complicated," Diana said, "why not just get up in front of the troops and tell them how complicated it is. Then have them draw straws. They aren't children."

There had been an army in which that sort of thing was done, a strong quasi-memory told me. The Marxist POUM militia in the Spanish Civil War, early twentieth. You obeyed an order only after it had been explained in detail; you could refuse if it didn't make sense. Officers and men got drunk together and never saluted or used titles. They lost the war. But the other side didn't have any fun.

"Finished." Diana set the limp hand in my lap. "Don't

try to use it for a half-hour. When it starts to hurt, you can use it."

I inspected the wound closely. "The lines don't match up. Not that I'm complaining."

"You shouldn't. By all rights, you ought to have just a stump. And no regeneration facilities this side of Stargate."

"Stump ought to be at the top of your neck," Charlie said. "I don't see why you have any qualms. You should have killed the bastard outright."

"*I know that, goddammit!*" Both Charlie and Diana jumped at my outburst. "Sorry, shit. Look, just let me do the worrying."

"Why don't you both talk about something else for a while." Diana got up and checked the contents of her medical bag. "I've got another patient to check. Try to keep from exciting each other."

"Graubard?" Charlie asked.

"That's right. To make sure he can mount the scaffold without assistance."

"What if Hilleboe—"

"She'll be out for another half-hour. I'll send Jarvil down, just in case." She hurried out the door.

"The scaffold . . ." I hadn't given that any thought. "How the hell are we going to execute him? We can't do it indoors: morale. Firing squad would be pretty grisly."

"Chuck him out the airlock. You don't owe him any ceremony."

"You're probably right. I wasn't thinking about him." I wondered whether Charlie had ever seen the body of a person who'd died that way. "Maybe we ought to just stuff him into the recycler. He'd wind up there eventually."

Charlie laughed. "That's the spirit."

"We'd have to trim him up a little bit. Door's not very wide." Charlie had a few suggestions as to how to get around that. Jarvil came in and more-or-less ignored us.

Suddenly the infirmary door banged open. A patient on a cart; Diana rushing alongside pressing on the man's chest, while a private pushed. Two other privates were following, but hung back at the door. "Over by the wall," she ordered.

It was Graubard. "Tried to kill himself," Diana said, but that was pretty obvious. "Heart stopped." He'd made a noose out of his belt; it was still hanging limply around his neck.

There were two big electrodes with rubber handles hanging on the wall. Diana snatched them with one hand while she ripped his tunic open with the other. "Get your hands off the cart!" She held the electrodes apart, kicked a switch, and pressed them down onto his chest. They made a low hum while his body trembled and flopped. Smell of burning flesh.

Diana was shaking her head. "Get ready to crack him," she said to Jarvil. "Get Doris down here." The body was gurgling, but it was a mechanical sound, like plumbing.

She kicked off the power and let the electrodes drop, pulled a ring off her finger and crossed to stick her arms in the sterilizer. Jarvil started to rub an evil-smelling fluid over the man's chest.

There was a small red mark between the two electrode burns. It took me a moment to recognize what it was. Jarvil wiped it away. I stepped closer and checked Graubard's neck.

"Get out of the way, William, you aren't sterile." Diana felt his collarbone, measured down a little ways and made an incision straight down to the bottom of his breastbone. Blood welled out and Jarvil handed her an instrument that looked like big chrome-plated bolt-cutters. I looked away but couldn't help hearing the thing crunch through his ribs. She asked for retractors and sponges and so on while I wandered back to where I'd been sitting. With the corner of my eye I saw her working away inside his thorax, massaging his heart directly.

Charlie looked the way I felt. He called out weakly, "Hey, don't knock yourself out, Diana." She didn't answer. Jarvil had wheeled up the artificial heart and was holding out two tubes. Diana picked up a scalpel and I looked away again.

He was still dead a half-hour later. They turned off the machine and threw a sheet over him. Diana washed the blood off her arms and said, "Got to change. Back in a minute."

I got up and walked to her billet, next door. Had to know. I raised my hand to knock but it was suddenly hurting like there was a line of fire drawn across it. I rapped with my left and she opened the door immediately.

"What—oh, you want something for your hand." She was half-dressed, unself-conscious. "Ask Jarvil."

"No, that's not it. What happened, Diana?"

"Oh. Well," she pulled a tunic over her head and her voice was muffled. "It was my fault, I guess. I left him alone for a minute."

"And he tried to hang himself."

"That's right." She sat on the bed and offered me the chair. "I went off to the head and he was dead by the time I got back. I'd already sent Jarvil away because I didn't want Hilleboe to be unsupervised for too long."

"But, Diana . . . there's no mark on his neck. No bruise, nothing."

She shrugged. "The hanging didn't kill him. He had a heart attack."

"Somebody gave him a shot. Right over his heart."

She looked at me curiously. "I did that, William. Adrenaline. Standard procedure."

You get that red dot of expressed blood if you jerk away from the projector while you're getting a shot. Otherwise the medicine goes right through the pores, doesn't leave a mark. "He was dead when you gave him the shot?"

"That would be my professional opinion." Deadpan. "No heartbeat, pulse, respiration. Very few other disorders show these symptoms."

"Yeah. I see."

"Is something . . . what's the matter, William?"

Either I'd been improbably lucky or Diana was a very good actress. "Nothing. Yeah, I better get something for this hand." I opened the door. "Saved me a lot of trouble."

She looked straight into my eyes. "That's true."

Actually, I'd traded one kind of trouble for another. Despite the fact that there were several disinterested witnesses to Graubard's demise, there was a persistent rumor that I'd had Doc Alsever simply exterminate him—since I'd botched the job myself and didn't want to go through a troublesome court-martial.

The fact was that, under the Universal Code of Military "Justice," Graubard hadn't deserved any kind of trial at all. All I had to do was say "You, you and you. Take this man out and kill him, please." And woe betide the private who refused to carry out the order.

My relationship with the troops did improve, in a sense. At least outwardly, they showed more deference to me. But I suspected it was at least partly the cheap kind of respect you might offer any ruffian who had proved himself to be dangerous and volatile.

So *Killer* was my new name. Just when I'd gotten used to *Old Queer*.

The base quickly settled back into its routine of training and waiting. I was almost impatient for the Taurans to show up, just to get it over with one way or the other.

The troops had adjusted to the situation much better than I had, for obvious reasons. They had specific duties to perform and ample free time for the usual soldierly anodynes to boredom. My duties were more varied but offered little satisfaction, since the problems that percolated up to me were of the "the buck stops here" type; those with pleasing, unambiguous solutions were taken care of in the lower echelons.

I'd never cared much for sports or games, but found myself turning to them more and more as a kind of safety valve. For the first time in my life, in these tense, claustrophobic surroundings, I couldn't escape into reading or study. So I fenced, quarterstaff and saber, with the other officers, worked myself to exhaustion on the exercise machines and even kept a jump-rope in my office. Most of the other officers played chess, but they could usually beat me—whenever I won it gave me the feeling I was being humored. Word games were difficult because my language was an archaic dialect that they had trouble manipulating. And I lacked the time and talent to master "modern" English.

For a while I let Diana feed me mood-altering drugs, but the cumulative effect of them was frightening—I was getting addicted in a way that was at first too subtle to bother me—so I stopped short. Then I tried some systematic psychoanalysis with Lieutenant Wilber. It was impossible. Although he knew all about my problem in an academic kind of way, we didn't speak the same cultural language; his counseling me about love and sex was like me telling a fourteenth-century serf how best to get along with his priest and landlord.

And that, after all, was the root of my problem. I was sure I could have handled the pressures and frustrations of command; of being cooped up in a cave with these people who at times seemed scarcely less alien than the enemy; even the near-certainty that it could lead only to painful death in a worthless cause—if only I could have had Marygay with me. And the feeling got more intense as the months crept by.

He got very stern with me at this point and accused me of romanticizing my position. He knew what love was, he said; he had been in love himself. And the sexual polarity of the couple made no difference—all right, I could accept that; that idea had been a cliché in my parents' generation (though it had run into some predictable resistance in my own). But love, he said, love was a fragile blossom; love was a delicate crystal; love was an unstable reaction with a half-life of about eight months. Bullshit, I said, and accused him of wearing cultural blinders; thirty centuries of prewar society taught that love was one thing that could last to the grave and even beyond *and if he had been born instead of hatched he would know that without being told*! Whereupon he would assume a wry, tolerant expression and reiterate that I was merely a victim of self-imposed sexual frustration and romantic delusion.

In retrospect, I guess we had a good time arguing with each other. Cure me, he didn't.

I did have a new friend who sat in my lap all the time. It was the cat, who had the usual talent for hiding from people who like cats and cleaving unto those who have sinus trouble or just don't like sneaky little animals. We did have something in common, though, since to my knowledge he was the only other heterosexual male mammal within any reasonable distance. He'd been castrated, of course, but that didn't make much difference under the circumstances.

6

It was exactly 400 days since the day we had begun construction. I was sitting at my desk not checking out Hilleboe's new duty roster. The cat was on my lap, purring loudly even though I refused to pet it. Charlie was stretched out in a chair reading something on the viewer. The phone buzzed and it was the Commodore.

"They're here."

"What?"

"I said they're here. A Tauran ship just exited the collapsar field. Velocity .80c. Deceleration thirty gees. Give or take."

Charlie was leaning over my desk. "What?" I dumped the cat.

"How long? Before you can pursue?" I asked.

"Soon as you get off the phone." I switched off and went over to the logistic computer, which was a twin to the one on *Masaryk II* and had a direct data link to it. While I tried to get numbers out of the thing, Charlie fiddled with the visual display.

The display was a hologram about a meter square by half a meter thick and was programmed to show the positions of Sade-138, our planet, and a few other chunks of rock in the system. There were green and red dots to show the positions of our vessels and the Taurans'.

The computer said that the minimum time it could take the Taurans to decelerate and get back to this planet would be a little over eleven days. Of course, that would be straight maximum acceleration and deceleration all the way; we could pick them off like flies on a wall. So, like us, they'd mix up their direction of flight and degree of acceleration in a random way. Based on several hundred past records of enemy behavior, the computer was able to give us a probability table:

216

Days to Contact	Probability
11	.000001
15	.001514
20	.032164
25	.103287
30	.676324
35	.820584
40	.982685
45	.993576
50	.999369
MEDIAN	
28.9554	.500000

Unless, of course, Antopol and her gang of merry pirates managed to make a kill. The chances of that, I had learned in the can, were slightly less than fifty-fifty.

But whether it took 28.9554 days or two weeks, those of us on the ground had to just sit on our hands and watch. If Antopol was successful, then we wouldn't have to fight until the regular garrison troops replaced us here and we moved on to the next collapsar.

"Haven't left yet." Charlie had the display cranked down to minimum scale; the planet was a white ball the size of a large melon and *Masaryk II* was a green dot off to the right some eight melons away; you couldn't get both on the screen at the same time.

While we were watching a small green dot popped out of the ship's dot and drifted away from it. A ghostly number 2 drifted beside it, and a key projected on the display's lower left-hand corner identified it as 2—*Pursuit Drone*. Other numbers in the key identified the *Masaryk II*, a planetary defense fighter and fourteen planetary defense drones. Those sixteen ships were not yet far enough away from one another to have separate dots.

The cat was rubbing against my ankle; I picked it up and stroked it. "Tell Hilleboe to call a general assembly. Might as well break it to everyone at once."

*   *   *

The men and women didn't take it very well, and I
couldn't blame them. We had all expected the Taurans to
attack much sooner—and when they persisted in not coming, the feeling grew that Strike Force Command had made
a mistake and that they'd never show up at all.

I wanted the company to start weapons training in ear-
nest; they hadn't used any high-powered weapons in almost
two years. So I activated their laser-fingers and passed out
the grenade and rocket launchers. We couldn't practice inside the base for fear of damaging the external sensors and
defensive laser ring. So we turned off half the circle of
gigawatt lasers and went out about a klick beyond the perimeter, one platoon at a time, accompanied by either me
or Charlie. Rusk kept a close watch on the early-warning
screens. If anything approached, she would send up a flare,
and the platoon would have to get back inside the ring
before the unknown came over the horizon, at which time
the defensive lasers would come on automatically. Besides
knocking out the unknown, they would fry the platoon in
less than .02 second.

We couldn't spare anything from the base to use as a
target, but that turned out to be no problem. The first tachyon rocket we fired scooped out a hole twenty meters long
by ten wide by five deep; the rubble gave us a multitude
of targets from twice-man-sized on down.

The soldiers were good, a lot better than they had been
with the primitive weapons in the stasis field. The best laser
practice turned out to be rather like skeetshooting: pair up
the people and have one stand behind the other, throwing
rocks at random intervals. The one who was shooting had
to gauge the rock's trajectory and zap it before it hit the
ground. Their eye-hand coordination was impressive
(maybe the Eugenics Council had done something right).
Shooting at rocks down to pebble-size, most of them could
do better than nine out of ten. Old non-bioengineered me
could hit maybe seven out of ten, and I'd had a good deal
more practice than they had.

They were equally facile at estimating trajectories with
the grenade launcher, which was a more versatile weapon
than it had been in the past. Instead of shooting one-

microton bombs with a standard propulsive charge, it had four different charges and a choice of one-, two-, three- or four-microton bombs. And for really close in-fighting, where it was dangerous to use the lasers, the barrel of the launcher would unsnap, and you could load it with a magazine of "shotgun" rounds. Each shot would send out an expanding cloud of a thousand tiny flechettes that were instant death out to five meters and turned to harmless vapor at six.

The tachyon rocket launcher required no skill whatsoever. All you had to do was to be careful no one was standing behind you when you fired it; the backwash from the rocket was dangerous for several meters behind the launching tube. Otherwise, you just lined your target up in the crosshairs and pushed the button. You didn't have to worry about trajectory; the rocket traveled in a straight line for all practical purposes. It reached escape velocity in less than a second.

It improved the troops' morale to get out and chew up the landscape with their new toys. But the landscape wasn't fighting back. No matter how physically impressive the weapons were, their effectiveness would depend on what the Taurans could throw back. A Greek phalanx must have looked pretty impressive, but it wouldn't do too well against a single man with a flamethrower.

And as with any engagement, because of time dilation, there was no way to tell what sort of weaponry they would have. They might have never heard of the stasis field. Or they might be able to say a magic word and make us disappear.

I was out with the fourth platoon, burning rocks, when Charlie called and asked me to come back in, urgent. I left Heimoff in charge.

"Another one?" The scale of the holograph display was such that our planet was pea-sized, about five centimeters from the X that marked the position of Sade-138. There were forty-one red and green dots scattered around the field; the key identified number *41* as *Tauran Cruiser* (2).

"You called Antopol?"

"Yeah." He anticipated the next question. "It'll take

almost a day for the signal to get there and back."

"It's never happened before," but of course Charlie knew that.

"Maybe this collapsar is especially important to them."

"Likely." So it was almost certain we'd be fighting on the ground. Even if Antopol managed to get the first cruiser, she wouldn't have a fifty-fifty chance on the second one. Low on drones and fighters. "I wouldn't like to be Antopol now."

"She'll just get it earlier."

"I don't know. We're in pretty good shape."

"Save it for the troops, William." He turned down the display's scale to where it showed only two objects: Sade-138 and the new red dot, slowly moving.

We spent the next two weeks watching dots blink out. And if you knew when and where to look, you could go outside and see the real thing happening, a hard bright speck of white light that faded in about a second.

In that second, a nova bomb had put out over a million times the power of a gigawatt laser. It made a miniature star half a klick in diameter and as hot as the interior of the sun. Anything it touched it would consume. The radiation from a near miss could botch up a ship's electronics beyond repair—two fighters, one of ours and one of theirs, had evidently suffered that fate, silently drifting out of the system at a constant velocity, without power.

We had used more powerful nova bombs earlier in the war, but the degenerate matter used to fuel them was unstable in large quantities. The bombs had a tendency to explode while they were still inside the ship. Evidently the Taurans had the same problem—or they had copied the process from us in the first place—because they had also scaled down to nova bombs that used less than a hundred kilograms of degenerate matter. And they deployed them much the same way we did, the warhead separating into dozens of pieces as it approached the target, only one of which was the nova bomb.

They would probably have a few bombs left over after they finished off *Masaryk II* and her retinue of fighters and drones. So it was likely that we were wasting time and energy in weapons practice.

The thought did slip by my conscience that I could gather up eleven people and board the fighter we had hidden safe behind the stasis field. It was pre-programmed to take us back to Stargate.

I even went to the extreme of making a mental list of the eleven, trying to think of eleven people who meant more to me than the rest. Turned out I'd be picking six at random.

I put the thought away, though. We did have a chance, maybe a damned good one, even against a fully-armed cruiser. It wouldn't be easy to get a nova bomb close enough to include us inside its kill-radius.

Besides, they'd space me for desertion. So why bother?

Spirits rose when one of Antopol's drones knocked out the first Tauran cruiser. Not counting the ships left behind for planetary defense, she still had eighteen drones and two fighters. They wheeled around to intercept the second cruiser, by then a few light-hours away, still being harassed by fifteen enemy drones.

One of the Tauran drones got her. Her ancillary crafts continued the attack, but it was a rout. One fighter and three drones fled the battle at maximum acceleration, looping up over the plane of the ecliptic, and were not pursued. We watched them with morbid interest while the enemy cruiser inched back to do battle with us. The fighter was headed back for Sade-138, to escape. Nobody blamed them. In fact, we sent them a farewell-good luck message; they didn't respond, naturally, being zipped up in the tanks. But it would be recorded.

It took the enemy five days to get back to the planet and be comfortably ensconced in a stationary orbit on the other side. We settled in for the inevitable first phase of the attack, which would be aerial and totally automated: their drones against our lasers. I put a force of fifty men and women inside the stasis field, in case one of the drones got through. An empty gesture, really; the enemy could just stand by and wait for them to turn off the field, fry them the second it flickered out.

Charlie had a weird idea that I almost went for.

"We could boobytrap the place."

"What do you mean?" I said. "This place *is* booby-trapped, out to twenty-five klicks."

"No, not the mines and such. I mean the base itself, here, underground."

"Go on."

"There are two nova bombs in that fighter." He pointed at the stasis field through a couple of hundred meters of rock. "We can roll them down here, boobytrap them, then hide everybody in the stasis field and wait."

In a way it was tempting. It would relieve me from any responsibility for decision-making, leave everything up to chance. "I don't think it would work, Charlie."

He seemed hurt. "Sure it would."

"No, look. For it to work, you have to get every single Tauran inside the kill-radius before it goes off—but they wouldn't all come charging in here once they breached our defenses. Least of all if the place seemed deserted. They'd suspect something, send in an advance party. And after the advance party set off the bombs—"

"We'd be back where we started, yeah. Minus the base. Sorry."

I shrugged. "It was an idea. Keep thinking, Charlie." I turned my attention back to the display, where the lopsided space war was in progress. Logically enough, the enemy wanted to knock out that one fighter overhead before he started to work on us. About all we could do was watch the red dots crawl around the planet and try to score. So far the pilot had managed to knock out all the drones; the enemy hadn't sent any fighters after him yet.

I'd given the pilot control over five of the lasers in our defensive ring. They couldn't do much good, though. A gigawatt laser pumps out a billion kilowatts per second at a range of a hundred meters. A thousand klicks up, though, the beam was attenuated to ten kilowatts. Might do some damage if it hit an optical sensor. At least confuse things.

"We could use another fighter. Or six."

"Use up the drones," I said. We did have a fighter, of course, and a swabbie attached to us who could pilot it. It might turn out to be our only hope, if they got us cornered in the stasis field.

"How far away is the other guy?" Charlie asked, meaning the fighter pilot who had turned tail. I cranked down the scale, and the green dot appeared at the right of the display. "About six light-hours." He had two drones left, too near to him to show as separate dots, having expended one in covering his getaway. "He's not accelerating any more, but he's doing point nine gee."

"Couldn't do us any good if he wanted to." Need almost a month to slow down.

At that low point, the light that stood for our own defensive fighter faded out. "Shit."

"Now the fun starts. Should I tell the troops to get ready, stand by to go topside?"

"No . . . have them suit up, in case we lose air. But I expect it'll be a little while before we have a ground attack." I turned the scale up again. Four red dots were already creeping around the globe toward us.

I got suited up and came back to Administration to watch the fireworks on the monitors.

The lasers worked perfectly. All four drones converged on us simultaneously; were targeted and destroyed. All but one of the nova bombs went off below our horizon (the visual horizon was about ten kilometers away, but the lasers were mounted high and could target something at twice that distance). The bomb that detonated on our horizon had melted out a semicircular chunk that glowed brilliantly white for several minutes. An hour later, it was still glowing dull orange, and the ground temperature outside had risen to fifty degrees Absolute, melting most of our snow, exposing an irregular dark gray surface.

The next attack was also over in a fraction of a second, but this time there had been eight drones, and four of them got within ten klicks. Radiation from the glowing craters raised the temperature to nearly 300 degrees. That was above the melting point of water, and I was starting to get worried. The fighting suits were good to over a thousand degrees, but the automatic lasers depended on low-temperature superconductors for their speed.

I asked the computer what the lasers' temperature limit was, and it printed out *TR 398-734-009-265, "Some Aspects Concerning the Adaptability of Cryogenic Ordnance to Use in Relatively High-Temperature Environments,"* which had lots of handy advice about how we could insulate the weapons if we had access to a fully-equipped armorer's shop. It did note that the response time of automatic-aiming devices increased as the temperature increased, and that above some "critical temperature," the weapons would not aim at all. But there was no way to predict any individual weapon's behavior, other than to note that the highest critical temperature recorded was 790 degrees and the lowest was 420 degrees.

Charlie was watching the display. His voice was flat over the suit's radio. "Sixteen this time."

"Surprised?" One of the few things we knew about Tauran psychology was a certain compulsiveness about numbers, especially primes and powers of two.

"Let's just hope they don't have 32 left." I queried the computer on this; all it could say was that the cruiser had thus far launched a total of 44 drones and that some cruisers had been known to carry as many as 128.

We had more than a half-hour before the drones would strike. I could evacuate everybody to the stasis field, and they would be temporarily safe if one of the nova bombs got through. Safe, but trapped. How long would it take the crater to cool down, if three or four—let alone sixteen—of the bombs made it through? You couldn't live forever in a fighting suit, even though it recycled everything with remorseless efficiency. One week was enough to make you thoroughly miserable. Two weeks, suicidal. Nobody had ever gone three weeks, under field conditions.

Besides, as a defensive position, the stasis field could be a death-trap. The enemy has all the options since the dome is opaque; the only way you can find out what they're up to is to stick your head out. They didn't have to wade in with primitive weapons unless they were impatient. They could keep the dome saturated with laser fire and wait for you to turn off the generator. Meanwhile harassing you by throwing spears, rocks, arrows into the dome—you could return fire, but it was pretty futile.

Of course, if one man stayed inside the base, the others could wait out the next half-hour in the stasis field. If he didn't come get them, they'd know the outside was hot. I chinned the combination that would give me a frequency available to everybody echelon 5 and above.

"This is Major Mandella." That still sounded like a bad joke.

I outlined the situation to them and asked them to tell their troops that everyone in the company was free to move into the stasis field. I would stay behind and come retrieve them if things went well—not out of nobility, of course; I preferred taking the chance of being vaporized in a nano-second, rather than almost certain slow death under the gray dome.

I chinned Charlie's frequency. "You can go, too. I'll take care of things here."

"No, thanks," he said slowly. "I'd just as soon . . . Hey, look at this."

The cruiser had launched another red dot, a couple of minutes behind the others. The display's key identified it as being another drone. "That's curious."

"Superstitious bastards," he said without feeling.

It turned out that only eleven people chose to join the fifty who had been ordered into the dome. That shouldn't have surprised me, but it did.

As the drones approached, Charlie and I stared at the monitors, carefully not looking at the holograph display, tacitly agreeing that it would be better not to know when they were one minute away, thirty seconds . . . And then, like the other times, it was over before we knew it had started. The screens glared white and there was a yowl of static, and we were still alive.

But this time there were fifteen new holes on the horizon—or closer!—and the temperature was rising so fast that the last digit in the readout was an amorphous blur.

The number peaked in the high 800s and began to slide
back down.

We had never seen any of the drones, not during that
tiny fraction of a second it took the lasers to aim and fire.
But then the seventeenth one flashed over the horizon, zig-
zagging crazily, and stopped directly overhead. For an instant it seemed to hover, and then it began to fall. Half the
lasers had detected it, and they were firing steadily, but
none of them could aim; they were all stuck in their last
firing position.

It glittered as it dropped, the mirror polish of its sleek
hull reflecting the white glow from the craters and the eerie
flickering of the constant, impotent laser fire. I heard Charlie take one deep breath, and the drone fell so close you
could see spidery Tauran numerals etched on the hull and
a transparent porthole near the tip—then its engine flared
and it was suddenly gone.

"What the hell?" Charlie said, quietly.

The porthole. "Maybe reconnaissance."

"I guess. So we can't touch them, and they know it."

"Unless the lasers recover." Didn't seem likely. "We
better get everybody under the dome. Us, too."

He said a word whose vowel had changed over the centuries, but whose meaning was clear. "No hurry. Let's see
what they do."

We waited for several hours. The temperature outside
stabilized at 690 degrees—just under the melting point of
zinc, I remembered to no purpose—and I tried the manual
controls for the lasers, but they were still frozen.

"Here they come," Charlie said. "Eight again."

I started for the display. "Guess we'll—"

"Wait! They aren't drones." The key identified all eight
with the legend *Troop Carrier*.

"Guess they want to take the base," he said. "Intact."

That, and maybe try out new weapons and techniques.
"It's not much of a risk for them. They can always retreat
and drop a nova bomb in our laps."

I called Brill and had her go get everybody who was in
the stasis field, set them up with the remainder of her platoon as a defensive line circling around the northeast and

northwest quadrants. I'd put the rest of the people on the other half-circle.

"I wonder," Charlie said. "Maybe we shouldn't put everyone topside at once. Until we know how many Taurans there are."

That was a point. Keep a reserve, let the enemy underestimate our strength. "It's an idea . . . There might be just 64 of them in eight carriers." Or 128 or 256. I wished our spy satellites had a finer sense of discrimination. But you can only cram so much into a machine the size of a grape.

I decided to let Brill's seventy people be our first line of defense and ordered them into a ring in the ditches we had made outside the base's perimeter. Everybody else would stay downstairs until needed.

If it turned out that the Taurans, either through numbers or new technology, could field an unstoppable force, I'd order everyone into the stasis field. There was a tunnel from the living quarters to the dome, so the people underground could go straight there in safety. The ones in the ditches would have to fall back under fire. If any of them were still alive when I gave the order.

I called in Hilleboe and had her and Charlie keep watch over the lasers. If they came unstuck, I'd call Brill and her people back. Turn on the automatic aiming system again, then sit back and watch the show. But even stuck, the lasers could be useful. Charlie marked the monitors to show where the rays would go; he and Hilleboe could fire them manually whenever something moved into a weapon's line-of-sight.

We had about twenty minutes. Brill was walking around the perimeter with her men and women, ordering them into the ditches a squad at a time, setting up overlapping fields of fire. I broke in and asked her to set up the heavy weapons so that they could be used to channel the enemy's advance into the path of the lasers.

There wasn't much else to do but wait. I asked Charlie to measure the enemy's progress and try to give us an accurate count-down, then sat at my desk and pulled out a pad, to diagram Brill's arrangement and see whether I could improve on it.

The cat jumped up on my lap, mewling piteously. He'd evidently been unable to tell one person from the other, suited up. But nobody else ever sat at this desk. I reached up to pet him and he jumped away.

The first line that I drew ripped through four sheets of paper. It had been some time since I'd done any delicate work in a suit. I remembered how in training, they'd made us practice controlling the strength-amplification circuits by passing eggs from person to person, messy business. I wondered if they still had eggs on Earth.

The diagram completed, I couldn't see any way to add to it. All those reams of theory crammed in my brain; there was plenty of tactical advice about envelopment and encirclement, but from the wrong point of view. If you were the one who was being encircled, you didn't have many options. Sit tight and fight. Respond quickly to enemy concentrations of force, but stay flexible so the enemy can't employ a diversionary force to divert strength from some predictable section of your perimeter. *Make full use of air and space support*, always good advice. Keep your head down and your chin up and pray for the cavalry. Hold your position and don't contemplate Dienbienphu, the Alamo, the Battle of Hastings.

"Eight more carriers out," Charlie said. "Five minutes. Until the first eight get here."

So they were going to attack in two waves. At least two. What would I do, in the Tauran commander's position? That wasn't too far-fetched; the Taurans lacked imagination in tactics and tended to copy human patterns.

The first wave could be a throwaway, a kamikaze attack to soften us up and evaluate our defenses. Then the second would come in more methodically, and finish the job. Or vice versa: the first group would have twenty minutes to get entrenched; then the second could skip over their heads and hit us hard at one spot—breach the perimeter and over-run the base.

Or maybe they sent out two forces simply because two was a magic number. Or they could launch only eight troop carriers at a time (that would be bad, implying that the carriers were large; in different situations they had used carriers holding as few as 4 troops or as many as 128).

"Three minutes." I stared at the cluster of monitors that showed various sectors of the mine field. If we were lucky, they'd land out there, out of caution. Or maybe pass over it low enough to detonate mines.

I was feeling vaguely guilty. I was safe in my hole, doodling, ready to start calling out orders. How did those seventy sacrificial lambs feel about their absentee commander?

Then I remembered how I had felt about Captain Stott that first mission, when he'd elected to stay safely in orbit while we fought on the ground. The rush of remembered hate was so strong I had to bite back nausea.

"Hilleboe, can you handle the lasers by yourself?"

"I don't see why not, sir."

I tossed down the pen and stood up. "Charlie, you take over the unit coordination; you can do it as well as I could. I'm going topside."

"I wouldn't advise that, sir."

"Hell no, William. Don't be an idiot."

"I'm not taking orders, I'm giv—"

"You wouldn't last ten seconds up there," Charlie said.

"I'll take the same chance as everybody else."

"Don't you hear what I'm saying. *They'll* kill you!"

"The troops? Nonsense. I know they don't like me especially, but—"

"You haven't listened in on the squad frequencies?" No, they didn't speak my brand of English when they talked among themselves. "They think you put them out on the line for punishment, for cowardice. After you'd told them anyone was free to go into the dome."

"Didn't you, sir?" Hilleboe said.

"To punish them? No, of course not." Not consciously. "They were just up there when I needed . . . Hasn't Lieutenant Brill said anything to them?"

"Not that I've heard," Charlie said. "Maybe she's been too busy to tune in."

Or she agreed with them. "I'd better get—"

"There!" Hilleboe shouted. The first enemy ship was visible in one of the mine field monitors; the others appeared in the next second. They came in from random directions and weren't evenly distributed around the base. Five in the northeast quadrant and only one in the southwest. I relayed the information to Brill.

But we had predicted their logic pretty well; all of them were coming down in the ring of mines. One came close enough to one of the tachyon devices to set it off. The blast caught the rear end of the oddly streamlined craft, causing it to make a complete flip and crash nose-first. Side ports opened up and Taurans came crawling out. Twelve of them; probably four left inside. If all the others had sixteen as well, there were only slightly more of them than of us.

In the first wave.

The other seven had landed without incident, and yes, there were sixteen each. Brill shuffled a couple of squads to conform to the enemy's troop concentration, and she waited.

They moved fast across the mine field, striding in unison like bowlegged, top-heavy robots, not even breaking stride when one of them was blown to bits by a mine, which happened eleven times.

When they came over the horizon, the reason for their apparently random distribution was obvious: they had analyzed beforehand which approaches would give them the most natural cover, from the rubble that the drones had kicked up. They would be able to get within a couple of kilometers of the base before we got any clear line-of-sight of them. And their suits had augmentation circuits similar to ours, so they could cover a kilometer in less than a minute.

Brill had her troops open fire immediately, probably more for morale than out of any hope of actually hitting the enemy. They probably were getting a few, though it was hard to tell. At least the tachyon rockets did an impressive job of turning boulders into gravel.

The Taurans returned fire with some weapon similar to the tachyon rocket, maybe exactly the same. They rarely found a mark, though; our people were at and below ground level, and if the rocket didn't hit something, it would keep going on forever, amen. They did score a hit on one of the gigawatt lasers, though, and the concussion that filtered down to us was strong enough to make me wish we had burrowed a little deeper than twenty meters.

The gigawatts weren't doing us any good. The Taurans must have figured out the lines of sight ahead of time, and gave them wide berth. That turned out to be fortunate, because it caused Charlie to let his attention wander from the laser monitors for a moment.

"What the hell?"

"What's that, Charlie?" I didn't take my eyes off the monitors. Waiting for something to happen.

"The ship, the cruiser—it's gone." I looked at the holograph display. He was right; the only red lights were those that stood for the troop carriers.

"Where did it go?" I asked inanely.

"Let's play it back." He programmed the display to go back a couple of minutes and cranked out the scale to where both planet and collapsar showed on the cube. The cruiser showed up, and with it, three green dots. Our "coward," attacking the cruiser with only two drones.

But he had a little help from the laws of physics.

Instead of going into collapsar insertion, he had skimmed *around* the collapsar field in a slingshot orbit. He had come out going nine-tenths of the speed of light; the drones were going .99c, headed straight for the enemy cruiser. Our planet was about a thousand light-seconds from the collapsar, so the Tauran ship had only ten seconds to detect and stop both drones. And at that speed, it didn't matter whether you'd been hit by a nova-bomb or a spitball.

The first drone disintegrated the cruiser, and the other one, .01 second behind, glided on down to impact on the planet. The fighter missed the planet by a couple of hundred kilometers and hurtled on into space, decelerating with the maximum twenty-five gees. He'd be back in a couple of months.

But the Taurans weren't going to wait. They were getting close enough to our lines for both sides to start using lasers, but they were also within easy grenade range. A good-size rock could shield them from laser fire, but the grenades and rockets were slaughtering them.

At first, Brill's troops had the overwhelming advantage;

fighting from ditches, they could only be harmed by an occasional lucky shot or an extremely well-aimed grenade (which the Taurans threw by hand, with a range of several hundred meters). Brill had lost four, but it looked as if the Tauran force was down to less than half its original size.

Eventually, the landscape had been torn up enough so that the bulk of the Tauran force was able to fight from holes in the ground. The fighting slowed down to individual laser duels, punctuated occasionally by heavier weapons. But it wasn't smart to use up a tachyon rocket against a single Tauran, not with another force of unknown size only a few minutes away.

Something had been bothering me about that holographic replay. Now, with the battle's lull, I knew what it was.

When that second drone crashed at near-lightspeed, how much damage had it done to the planet? I stepped over to the computer and punched it up; found out how much energy had been released in the collision, and then compared it with geological information in the computer's memory.

Twenty times as much energy as the most powerful earthquake ever recorded. On a planet three-quarters the size of Earth.

On the general frequency: "Everybody-topside! Right now!" I palmed the button that would cycle and open the airlock and tunnel that led from Administration to the surface.

"What the hell, Will—"

"Earthquake!" How long? "Move!"

Hilleboe and Charlie were right behind me. The cat was sitting on my desk, licking himself unconcernedly. I had an irrational impulse to put him inside my suit, which was the way he'd been carried from the ship to the base, but knew he wouldn't tolerate more than a few minutes of it. Then I had the more reasonable impulse to simply vaporize him with my laser-finger, but by then the door was closed and we were swarming up the ladder. All the way up, and for some time afterward, I was haunted by the image of that helpless animal, trapped under tons of rubble, dying slowly as the air hissed away.

"Safer in the ditches?" Charlie said.

"I don't know," I said. "Never been in an earthquake."
Maybe the walls of the ditch would close up and crush us.

I was surprised at how dark it was on the surface. S
Doradus had almost set; the monitors had compensated for
the low light level.

An enemy laser raked across the clearing to our left,
making a quick shower of sparks when it flicked by a gigawatt mounting. We hadn't been seen yet. We all decided
yes, it would be safer in the ditches, and made it to the
nearest one in three strides.

There were four men and women in the ditch, one of
them badly wounded or dead. We scrambled down the
ledge and I turned up my image amplifier to log two, to
inspect our ditchmates. We were lucky; one was a grenadier
and they also had a rocket launcher. I could just make out
the names on their helmets. We were in Brill's ditch, but
she hadn't noticed us yet. She was at the opposite end,
cautiously peering over the edge, directing two squads in a
flanking movement. When they were safely in position, she
ducked back down. "Is that you, Major?"

"That's right," I said cautiously. I wondered whether
any of the people in the ditch were among the ones after
my scalp.

"What's this about an earthquake?"

She had been told about the cruiser being destroyed, but
not about the other drone. I explained in as few words as
possible.

"Nobody's come out of the airlock," she said. "Not yet.
I guess they all went into the stasis field."

"Yeah, they were just as close to one as the other."
Maybe some of them were still down below, hadn't taken
my warning seriously. I chinned the general frequency to
check, and then all hell broke loose.

The ground dropped away and then flexed back up;
slammed us so hard that we were airborne, tumbling out of
the ditch. We flew several meters, going high enough to
see the pattern of bright orange and yellow ovals, the craters where nova bombs had been stopped. I landed on my
feet but the ground was shifting and slithering so much that
it was impossible to stay upright.

With a basso grinding I could feel through my suit, the cleared area above our base crumbled and fell in. Part of the stasis field's underside was exposed when the ground subsided; it settled to its new level with aloof grace.

Well, minus one cat. I hoped everybody else had time and sense enough to get under the dome.

A figure came staggering out of the ditch nearest to me and I realized with a start that it wasn't human. At that range, my laser burned a hole straight through his helmet; he took two steps and fell over backward. Another helmet peered over the edge of the ditch. I sheared the top of it off before he could raise his weapon.

I couldn't get my bearings. The only thing that hadn't changed was the stasis dome, and it looked the same from any angle. The gigawatt lasers were all buried, but one of them had switched on, a brilliant flickering searchlight that illuminated a swirling cloud of vaporized rock.

Obviously, though, I was in enemy territory. I started across the trembling ground toward the dome.

I couldn't raise any platoon leaders. All of them but Brill were probably inside the dome. I did get Hilleboe and Charlie; told Hilleboe to go inside the dome and roust everybody out. If the next wave also had 128, we were going to need everybody.

The tremors died down and I found my way into a "friendly" ditch—the cooks' ditch, in fact, since the only people there were Orban and Rudkoski.

"Looks like you'll have to start from scratch again, Private."

"That's all right, sir. Liver needed a rest."

I got a beep from Hilleboe and chinned her on. "Sir . . . there were only ten people there. The rest didn't make it."

"They stayed behind?" Seemed like they'd had plenty of time.

"I don't know, sir."

"Never mind. Get me a count, how many people we have, all totalled." I tried the platoon leaders' frequency again and it was still silent.

The three of us watched for enemy laser fire for a couple

of minutes, but there was none. Probably waiting for reinforcements.

Hilleboe called back. "I only get fifty-three, sir. Some
may be unconscious."

"All right. Have them sit tight until—" Then the second
wave showed up, the troop carriers roaring over the horizon
with their jets pointed our way, decelerating. *"Get some
rockets on those bastards!"* Hilleboe yelled to everyone in
particular. But nobody had managed to stay attached to a
rocket launcher while he was being tossed around. No grenade launchers, either, and the range was too far for the
hand lasers to do any damage.

These carriers were four or five times the size of the ones
in the first wave. One of them grounded about a kilometer
in front of us, barely stopping long enough to disgorge its
troops. Of which there were over 50, probably 64—times
8 made 512. No way we could hold them back.

"Everybody listen, this is Major Mandella." I tried to
keep my voice even and quiet. "We're going to retreat back
into the dome, quickly but in an orderly way. I know we're
scattered all over hell. If you belong to the second or fourth
platoon, stay put for a minute and give covering fire while
the first and third platoons, and support, fall back.

"First and third and support, fall back to about half your
present distance from the dome, then take cover and defend
the second and fourth as they come back. They'll go to the
edge of the dome and cover you while you come back the
rest of the way." I shouldn't have said "retreat"; that word
wasn't in the book. Retrograde action.

There was a lot more retrograde than action. Eight or
nine people were firing, and all the rest were in full flight.
Rudkoski and Orban had vanished. I took a few carefully
aimed shots, to no great effect, then ran down to the other
end of the ditch, climbed out and headed for the dome.

The Taurans started firing rockets, but most of them
seemed to be going too high. I saw two of us get blown
away before I got to my halfway point; found a nice big
rock and hid behind it. I peeked out and decided that only
two or three of the Taurans were close enough to be even
remotely possible laser targets, and the better part of valor

would be in not drawing unnecessary attention to myself. I
ran the rest of the way to the edge of the field and stopped
to return fire. After a couple of shots, I realized that I was
just making myself a target; as far as I could see there was
only one other person who was still running toward the
dome.

A rocket zipped by, so close I could have touched it. I
flexed my knees and kicked, and entered the dome in a
rather undignified posture.

Inside, I could see the rocket that had missed me drifting lazily through the gloom, rising slightly as it passed through to the other side of the dome. It would vaporize the instant it came out the other side, since all of the kinetic energy it had lost in abruptly slowing down to 16.3 meters per second would come back in the form of heat.

Nine people were lying dead, facedown just inside of the field's edge. It wasn't unexpected, though it wasn't the sort of thing you were supposed to tell the troops.

Their fighting suits were intact—otherwise they wouldn't have made it this far—but sometime during the past few minutes' rough-and-tumble, they had damaged the coating of special insulation that protected them from the stasis field. So as soon as they entered the field, all electrical activity in their bodies ceased, which killed them instantly. Also, since no molecule in their bodies could move faster than 16.3 meters per second, they instantly froze solid, their body temperature stabilized at a cool 0.426 degrees Absolute.

I decided not to turn any of them over to find out their names, not yet. We had to get some sort of defensive position worked out before the Taurans came through the dome. If they decided to slug it out rather than wait.

With elaborate gestures, I managed to get everybody collected in the center of the field, under the fighter's tail, where the weapons were racked.

There were plenty of weapons, since we had been prepared to outfit three times this number of people. After giving each person a shield and short-sword, I traced a question in the snow: GOOD ARCHERS? RAISE HANDS. I got five volunteers, then picked out three more so that all the bows would be in use. Twenty arrows per bow. They were the most effective long-range weapons we had; the arrows were almost invisible in their slow flight, heavily weighted and tipped with a deadly sliver of diamond-hard crystal.

I arranged the archers in a circle around the fighter (its landing fins would give them partial protection from missiles coming in from behind) and between each pair of archers put four other people: two spear-throwers, one quarterstaff, and a person armed with battleax and a dozen throwing knives. This arrangement would theoretically take care of the enemy at any range, from the edge of the field to hand-to-hand combat.

Actually, at some 600-to-42 odds, they could probably walk in with a rock in each hand, no shields or special weapons, and still beat the shit out of us.

Assuming they knew what the stasis field was. Their technology seemed up to date in all other respects.

For several hours nothing happened. We got about as bored as anyone could, waiting to die. No one to talk to, nothing to see but the unchanging gray dome, gray snow, gray spaceship and a few identically gray soldiers. Nothing to hear, taste or smell but yourself.

Those of us who still had any interest in the battle were keeping watch on the bottom edge of the dome, waiting for the first Taurans to come through. So it took us a second to realize what was going on when the attack did start. It came from above, a cloud of catapulted darts swarming in through the dome some thirty meters above the ground, headed straight for the center of the hemisphere.

The shields were big enough that you could hide most of your body behind them by crouching slightly; the people who saw the darts coming could protect themselves easily. The ones who had their backs to the action, or were just asleep at the switch, had to rely on dumb luck for survival; there was no way to shout a warning, and it took only three seconds for a missile to get from the edge of the dome to its center.

We were lucky, losing only five. One of them was an archer, Shubik. I took over her bow and we waited, expecting a ground attack immediately.

It didn't come. After a half-hour, I went around the circle and explained with gestures that the first thing you were supposed to do, if anything happened, was to touch the person on your right. He'd do the same, and so on down the line.

That might have saved my life. The second dart attack, a couple of hours later, came from behind me. I felt the nudge, slapped the person on my right, turned around and saw the cloud descending. I got the shield over my head, and they hit a split-second later.

I set down my bow to pluck three darts from the shield and the ground attack started.

It was a weird, impressive sight. Some three hundred of them stepped into the field simultaneously, almost shoulder-to-shoulder around the perimeter of the dome. They advanced in step, each one holding a round shield barely large enough to hide his massive chest. They were throwing darts similar to the ones we had been barraged with.

I set up the shield in front of me—it had little extensions on the bottom to keep it upright—and with the first arrow I shot, I knew we had a chance. It struck one of them in the center of his shield, went straight through and penetrated his suit.

It was a one-sided massacre. The darts weren't very effective without the element of surprise—but when one came sailing over my head from behind, it did give me a crawly feeling between the shoulder blades.

With twenty arrows I got twenty Taurans. They closed ranks every time one dropped; you didn't even have to aim. After running out of arrows, I tried throwing their darts back at them. But their light shields were quite adequate against the small missiles.

We'd killed more than half of them with arrows and spears, long before they got into range of the hand-to-hand weapons. I drew my sword and waited. They still outnumbered us by better than three to one.

When they got within ten meters, the people with the chakram throwing knives had their own field day. Although the spinning disc was easy enough to see and took more

than a half-second to get from thrower to target, most of
the Taurans reacted in the same ineffective way, raising up
the shield to ward it off. The razor-sharp, tempered heavy
blade cut through the light shield like a buzz-saw through
cardboard.

The first hand-to-hand contact was with the quarterstaffs, which were metal rods two meters long that tapered
at the ends to a double-edged, serrated knife blade. The
Taurans had a cold-blooded—or valiant, if your mind
works that way—method for dealing with them. They
would simply grab the blade and die. While the human was
trying to extricate his weapon from the frozen death-grip,
a Tauran swordsman, with a scimitar over a meter long,
would step in and kill him.

Besides the swords, they had a bolo-like thing that was
a length of elastic cord that ended with about ten centimeters of something like barbed wire, and a small weight
to propel it. It was a dangerous weapon for all concerned;
if they missed their target it would come snapping back
unpredictably. But they hit their target pretty often, going
under the shields and wrapping the thorny wire around an-
kles.

I stood back-to-back with Private Erikson, and with our
swords we managed to stay alive for the next few minutes.
When the Taurans were down to a couple of dozen survivors, they just turned around and started marching out. We
threw some darts after them, getting three, but we didn't
want to chase after them. They might turn around and start
hacking again.

There were only twenty-eight of us left standing. Nearly
ten times that number of dead Taurans littered the ground,
but there was no satisfaction in it.

They could do the whole thing over, with a fresh 300.
And this time it would work.

We moved from body to body, pulling out arrows and
spears, then took up places around the fighter again. Nobody bothered to retrieve the quarterstaffs. I counted noses:
Charlie and Diana were still alive (Hilleboe had been one
of the quarterstaff victims), as well as two supporting of-

ficers. Wilber and Szydlowska. Rudkoski was still alive but Orban had taken a dart.

After a day of waiting, it looked as though the enemy had decided on a war of attrition rather than repeating the ground attack. Darts came in constantly, not in swarms anymore, but in twos and threes and tens. And from all different angles. We couldn't stay alert forever; they'd get somebody every three or four hours.

We took turns sleeping, two at a time, on top of the stasis field generator. Sitting directly under the bulk of the fighter, it was the safest place in the dome.

Every now and then, a Tauran would appear at the edge of the field, evidently to see whether any of us were left. Sometimes we'd shoot an arrow at him, for practice.

The darts stopped falling after a couple of days. I supposed it was possible that they'd simply run out of them. Or maybe they'd decided to stop when we were down to twenty survivors.

There was a more likely possibility. I took one of the quarterstaffs down to the edge of the field and poked it through, a centimeter or so. When I drew it back, the point was melted off. When I showed it to Charlie, he rocked back and forth (the only way you can nod in a suit); this sort of thing had happened before, one of the first times the stasis field hadn't worked. They simply saturated it with laser fire and waited for us to go stir-crazy and turn off the generator. They were probably sitting in their ships playing the Tauran equivalent of pinochle.

I tried to think. It was hard to keep your mind on something for any length of time in that hostile environment, sense-deprived, looking over your shoulder every few seconds. Something Charlie had said. Only yesterday. I couldn't track it down. It wouldn't have worked then; that was all I could remember. Then finally it came to me.

I called everyone over and wrote in the snow:

GET NOVA BOMBS FROM SHIP.
CARRY TO EDGE OF FIELD.
MOVE FIELD.

Szydlowska knew where the proper tools would be aboard ship. Luckily, we had left all of the entrances open before turning on the stasis field; they were electronic and would have been frozen shut. We got an assortment of wrenches from the engine room and climbed up to the cockpit. He knew how to remove the access plate that exposed a crawl space into the bomb-bay. I followed him in through the meter-wide tube.

Normally, I supposed, it would have been pitch-black. But the stasis field illuminated the bomb-bay with the same dim, shadowless light that prevailed outside. The bomb-bay was too small for both of us, so I stayed at the end of the crawl space and watched.

The bomb-bay doors had a "manual override" so they were easy; Szydlowska just turned a hand-crank and we were in business. Freeing the two nova bombs from their cradles was another thing. Finally, he went back down to the engine room and brought back a crowbar. He pried one loose and I got the other, and we rolled them out the bomb-bay.

Sergeant Anghelov was already working on them by the time we climbed back down. All you had to do to arm the bomb was to unscrew the fuse on the nose of it and poke something around in the fuse socket to wreck the delay mechanism and safety restraints.

We carried them quickly to the edge, six people per bomb, and set them down next to each other. Then we waved to the four people who were standing by at the field generator's handles. They picked it up and walked ten paces in the opposite direction. The bombs disappeared as the edge of the field slid over them.

There was no doubt that the bombs went off. For a couple of seconds it was hot as the interior of a star outside, and even the stasis field took notice of the fact: about a third of the dome glowed a dull pink for a moment, then was gray again. There was a slight acceleration, like you would feel in a slow elevator. That meant we were drifting down to the bottom of the crater. Would there be a solid bottom? Or would we sink down through molten rock to

be trapped like a fly in amber—didn't pay to even think
about that. Perhaps if it happened, we could blast our way
out with the fighter's gigawatt laser.

Twelve of us, anyhow.

HOW LONG? Charlie scraped in the snow at my feet.

That was a damned good question. About all I knew was
the amount of energy two nova bombs released. I didn't
know how big a fireball they would make, which would
determine the temperature at detonation and the size of the
crater. I didn't know the heat capacity of the surrounding
rock, or its boiling point. I wrote: ONE WEEK, SHRUG?
HAVE TO THINK.

The ship's computer could have told me in a thousandth
of a second, but it wasn't talking. I started writing equations
in the snow, trying to get a maximum and minimum figure
for the length of time it would take for the outside to cool
down to 500 degrees. Anghelov, whose physics was much
more up-to-date, did his own calculations on the other side
of the ship.

My answer said anywhere from six hours to six days
(although for six hours, the surrounding rock would have
to conduct heat like pure copper), and Anghelov got five
hours to 4½ days. I voted for six and nobody else got a
vote.

We slept a lot. Charlie and Diana played chess by scraping symbols in the snow; I was never able to hold the shifting positions of the pieces in my mind. I checked my
figures several times and kept coming up with six days. I
checked Anghelov's computations, too, and they seemed
all right, but I stuck to my guns. It wouldn't hurt us to stay
in the suits an extra day and a half. We argued good-
naturedly in terse shorthand.

There had been nineteen of us left the day we tossed the
bombs outside. There were still nineteen, six days later,
when I paused with my hand over the generator's cutoff
switch. What was waiting for us out there? Surely we had
killed all the Taurans within several klicks of the explosion.
But there might have been a reserve force farther away,
now waiting patiently on the crater's lip. At least you could

push a quarterstaff through the field and have it come back whole.

I dispersed the people evenly around the area, so they might not get us with a single shot. Then, ready to turn it back on immediately if anything went wrong, I pushed.

8

My radio was still tuned to the general frequency; after more than a week of silence my ears were suddenly assaulted with loud, happy babbling.

We stood in the center of a crater almost a kilometer wide and deep. Its sides were a shiny black crust shot through with red cracks, hot but no longer dangerous. The hemisphere of earth that we rested on had sunk a good forty meters into the floor of the crater, while it had still been molten, so now we stood on a kind of pedestal.

Not a Tauran in sight.

We rushed to the ship, sealed it and filled it with cool air and popped our suits. I didn't press seniority for the one shower; just sat back in an acceleration couch and took deep breaths of air that didn't smell like recycled Mandella.

The ship was designed for a maximum crew of twelve, so we stayed outside in shifts of seven to keep from straining the life support systems. I sent a repeating message to the other fighter, which was still over six weeks away, that we were in good shape and waiting to be picked up. I was reasonably certain he would have seven free berths, since the normal crew for a combat mission was only three.

It was good to walk around and talk again. I officially suspended all things military for the duration of our stay on the planet. Some of the people were survivors of Brill's mutinous bunch, but they didn't show any hostility toward me.

We played a kind of nostalgia game, comparing the various eras we'd experienced on Earth, wondering what it would be like in the 700-years-future we were going back to. Nobody mentioned the fact that we would at best go back to a few months' furlough and then be assigned to another strike force, another turn of the wheel.

Wheels. One day Charlie asked me from what country

245

my name originated; it sounded weird to him. I told him it
originated from the lack of a dictionary and that if it were
spelled right, it would look even weirder.

I got to kill a good half-hour explaining all the peripheral
details to that. Basically, though, my parents were "hippies" (a kind of subculture in the late-twentieth-century
America, that rejected materialism and embraced a broad
spectrum of odd ideas) who lived with a group of other
hippies in a small agricultural community. When my
mother got pregnant, they wouldn't be so conventional as
to get married: this entailed the woman taking the man's
name, and implied that she was his property. But they got
all intoxicated and sentimental and decided they would both
change their names to be the same. They rode into the nearest town, arguing all the way as to what name would be
the best symbol for the love-bond between them—I nar-
rowly missed having a much shorter name—and they settled on Mandala.

A mandala is a wheel-like design the hippies had bor-
rowed from a foreign religion, that symbolized the cosmos,
the cosmic mind, God, or whatever needed a symbol. Neither my mother nor my father knew how to spell the word,
and the magistrate in town wrote it down the way it
sounded to him.

They named me William in honor of a wealthy uncle,
who unfortunately died penniless.

The six weeks passed rather pleasantly: talking, reading,
resting. The other ship landed next to ours and did have
nine free berths. We shuffled crews so that each ship had
someone who could get it out of trouble if the pre-
programmed jump sequence malfunctioned. I assigned myself to the other ship, in hopes it would have some new
books. It didn't.

We zipped up in the tanks and took off simultaneously.

We wound up spending a lot of time in the tanks, just
to keep from looking at the same faces all day long in the
crowded ship. The added periods of acceleration got us
back to Stargate in ten months, subjective. Of course, it

was 340 years (minus seven months) to the hypothetical objective observer.

There were hundreds of cruisers in orbit around Stargate. Bad news: with that kind of backlog we probably wouldn't get any furlough at all.

I supposed I was more likely to get a court-martial than a furlough, anyhow. Losing 88 percent of my company, many of them because they didn't have enough confidence in me to obey the direct earthquake order. And we were back where we'd started on Sade-138; no Taurans there, but no base either.

We got landing instructions and went straight down, no shuttle. There was another surprise waiting at the spaceport. Dozens of cruisers were standing around on the ground (they'd never done that before for fear that Stargate would be hit)—and two captured Tauran cruisers as well. We'd never managed to get one intact.

Seven centuries could have brought us a decisive advantage, of course. Maybe we were winning.

We went through an airlock under a "returnees" sign. After the air cycled and we'd popped our suits, a beautiful young woman came in with a cartload of tunics and told us, in perfectly-accented English, to get dressed and go to the lecture hall at the end of the corridor to our left.

The tunic felt odd, light yet warm. It was the first thing I'd worn besides a fighting suit or bare skin in almost a year.

The lecture hall was about a hundred times too big for the twenty-two of us. The same woman was there and asked us to move down to the front. That was unsettling; I could have sworn she had gone down the corridor the other way—I *knew* she had; I'd been captivated by the sight of her clothed behind.

Hell, maybe they had matter transmitters. Or teleportation. Wanted to save herself a few steps.

We sat for a minute and a man, clothed in the same kind of unadorned tunic the woman and we were wearing, walked across the stage with a stack of thick notebooks under each arm.

The woman followed him on, also carrying notebooks.

I looked behind me and she was still standing in the aisle. To make things even more odd, the man was virtually a twin to both of them.

The man riffled through one of the notebooks and cleared his throat. "These books are for your convenience," he said, also with perfect accent, "and you don't have to read them if you don't want to. You don't have to do anything you don't want to do, because . . . you're free men and women. The war is over."

Disbelieving silence.

"As you will read in this book, the war ended 221 years ago. Accordingly, this is the year 220. Old style, of course, it is 3138 A.D.

"You are the last group of soldiers to return. When you leave here, I will leave as well. And destroy Stargate. It exists only as a rendezvous point for returnees and as a monument to human stupidity. And shame. As you will read. Destroying it will be a cleansing."

He stopped speaking and the woman started without a pause. "I am sorry for what you've been through and wish I could say that it was for good cause, but as you will read, it was not.

"Even the wealth you have accumulated, back salary and compound interest, is worthless, as I no longer use money or credit. Nor is there such a thing as an economy, in which to use these . . . things."

"As you must have guessed by now," the man took over, "I am, we are, clones of a single individual. Some two hundred and fifty years ago, my name was Kahn. Now it is Man.

"I had a direct ancestor in your company, a Corporal Larry Kahn. It saddens me that he didn't come back."

"I am over ten billion individuals but only one con-sciousness," she said. "After you read, I will try to clarify this. I know that it will be difficult to understand.

"No other humans are quickened, since I am the perfect pattern. Individuals who die are replaced.

"There are some planets, however, on which humans are born in the normal, mammalian way. If my society is too alien for you, you may go to one of these planets. If you wish to take part in procreation, I will not discourage it. Many veterans ask me to change their polarity to heterosexual so that they can more easily fit into these other societies. This I can do very easily."

Don't worry about that, Man, just make out my ticket.

"You will be my guest here at Stargate for ten days, after which you will be taken wherever you want to go," he said. "Please read this book in the meantime. Feel free to ask any questions, or request any service." They both stood and walked off the stage.

Charlie was sitting next to me. "Incredible," he said. "They let . . . they encourage . . . men and women to do *that* again? Together?"

The female aisle-Man was sitting behind us, and she answered before I could frame a reasonably sympathetic, hypocritical reply. "It isn't a judgment on your society," she said, probably not seeing that he took it a little more personally than that. "I only feel that it's necessary as a eugenic safety device. I have no evidence that there is anything wrong with cloning only one ideal individual, but if it turns out to have been a mistake, there will be a large genetic pool with which to start again."

She patted him on the shoulder. "Of course, you don't have to go to these breeder planets. You can stay on one of my planets. I make no distinction between heterosexual play and homosexual."

She went up on the stage to give a long spiel about where we were going to stay and eat and so forth while we were on Stargate, "Never been seduced by a computer before," Charlie muttered.

The 1143-year-long war had been begun on false pretenses and only continued because the two races were unable to communicate.

Once they could talk, the first question was "Why did you start this thing?" and the answer was "Me?"

The Taurans hadn't known war for millennia, and toward the beginning of the twenty-first century it looked as though mankind was ready to outgrow the institution as well. But the old soldiers were still around, and many of them were in positions of power. They virtually ran the United Nations Exploratory and Colonization Group, that was taking advantage of the newly-discovered collapsar jump to explore interstellar space.

Many of the early ships met with accidents and disappeared. The ex-military men were suspicious. They armed the colonizing vessels, and the first time they met a Tauran ship, they blasted it.

They dusted off their medals and the rest was going to be history.

You couldn't blame it all on the military, though. The evidence they presented for the Taurans' having been responsible for the earlier casualties was laughably thin. The few people who pointed this out were ignored.

The fact was, Earth's economy needed a war, and this one was ideal. It gave a nice hole to throw buckets of money into, but would unify humanity rather than dividing it.

The Taurans relearned war, after a fashion. They never got really good at it, and would eventually have lost.

The Taurans, the book explained, couldn't communicate with humans because they had no concept of the individual; they had been natural clones for millions of years. Eventually, Earth's cruisers were manned by Man, Kahn-clones, and they were for the first time able to get through to each other.

The book stated this as a bald fact. I asked a Man to explain what it meant, what was special about clone-to-clone communication, and he said that I *a priori* couldn't understand it. There were no words for it, and my brain wouldn't be able to accommodate the concepts even if there were words.

All right. It sounded a little fishy, but I was willing to accept it. I'd accept that up was down if it meant the war was over.

Man was a pretty considerate entity. Just for us twenty-two, he went to the trouble of rejuvenating a little restaurant-tavern and staffing it at all hours (I never saw a Man eat or drink—guess they'd discovered a way around it). I was sitting in there one evening, drinking beer and reading their book, when Charlie came in and sat down next to me.

Without preamble, he said, "I'm going to give it a try."

"Give what a try?"

"Women. Hetero." He shuddered. "No offense . . . it's not really very appealing." He patted my hand, looking distracted. "But the alternative . . . have you tried it?"

"Well . . . no, I haven't." Female Man was a visual treat, but only in the same sense as a painting or a piece of sculpture. I just couldn't see them as human beings.

"Don't." He didn't elaborate. "Besides, they say—he says, she says, it says—that they can change me back just as easily. If I don't like it."

"You'll like it, Charlie."

"Sure that's what *they* say." He ordered a stiff drink. "Just seems unnatural. Anyway, since, uh, I'm going to make the switch, do you mind if . . . why don't we plan on going to the same planet?"

"Sure, Charlie, that'd be great." I meant it. "You know where you're going?"

"Hell, I don't care. Just away from here."

"I wonder if Heaven's still as nice—"

"No." Charlie jerked a thumb at the bartender. "He lives there."

"I don't know. I guess there's a list."

A man came into the tavern, pushing a cart piled high with folders. "Major Mandella? Captain Moore?"

"That's us," Charlie said.

"These are your military records. I hope you find them of interest. They were transferred to paper when your strike force was the only one outstanding, because it would have been impractical to keep the normal data retrieval networks running to preserve so few data."

They always anticipated your questions, even when you didn't have any.

My folder was easily five times as thick as Charlie's. Probably thicker than any other, since I seemed to be the only trooper who'd made it through the whole duration. Poor Marygay. "Wonder what kind of report old Stott filed about me." I flipped to the front of the folder.

Stapled to the front page was a small square of paper.

All the other pages were pristine white, but this one was tan with age and crumbling around the edges.

The handwriting was familiar, too familiar even after so long. The date was over 250 years old.

I winced and was blinded by sudden tears. I'd had no reason to suspect that she might be alive. But I hadn't really known she was dead, not until I saw that date.

"William? What's—"

"Leave me be, Charlie. Just for a minute." I wiped my eyes and closed the folder. I shouldn't even read the damned note. Going to a new life, I should leave the old ghosts behind.

But even a message from the grave was contact of a sort. I opened the folder again.

11 Oct 2878

William—

All this is in your personnel file. But knowing you, you might just chuck it. So I made sure you'd get this note.

Obviously, I lived. Maybe you will, too. Join me.

I know from the records that you're out at Sade-138 and won't be back for a couple of centuries. No problem.

I'm going to a planet they call Middle Finger, the fifth planet out from Mizar. It's two collapsar jumps, ten months subjective. Middle Finger is a kind of Coventry for heterosexuals. They call it a "eugenic control baseline."

No matter. It took all of my money, and all the money of five other old-timers, but we bought a cruiser from UNEF. And we're using it as a time machine.

So I'm on a relativistic shuttle, waiting for you. All it does is go out five light years and come back to Middle Finger, very fast. Every ten years I age about a month. So if you're on schedule and still alive, I'll only be twenty-eight when you get here. Hurry!

I never found anybody else and I don't want anybody else. I don't care whether you're ninety years old or thirty. If I can't be your lover, I'll be your nurse.

—Marygay.

"Say, bartender."

"Yes, Major?"

"Do you know of a place called Middle Finger? Is it still there?"

"Of course it is. Where else would it be?" Reasonable question. "A very nice place. Garden planet. Some people don't think it's exciting enough."

"What's this all about?" Charlie said.

I handed the bartender my empty glass. "I just found out where we're going."

9
EPILOGUE

From *The New Voice*, Paxton, Middle Finger 24-6

14/2/3143

OLD-TIMER HAS FIRST BOY

Marygay Potter-Mandella (24 Post Road, Paxton) gave birth Friday last to a fine baby boy, 3.1 kilos.

Marygay lays claim to being the second-"oldest" resident of Middle Finger, having been born in 1977. She fought through most of the Forever War and then waited for her mate on the time shuttle, 261 years.

The baby, not yet named, was delivered at home with the help of a friend of the family, Dr. Diana Alsever-Moore.

ABOUT THE AUTHOR

Joe Haldeman was born in the USA in 1943. At college he studied physics and astronomy. He then served as a combat engineer in Vietnam from 1967 to 1969. He was severely wounded during the war and received a Purple Heart. Haldeman's first SF story was 'Out of Phase', published in 1969. *The Forever War* was published in 1974 and became a huge success, winning both a Nebula award in 1975 and a Hugo in 1976. He wrote two other novels in the 1970s, *Mindbridge* and *All My Sins Remembered*, before starting the *Worlds* sequence in 1981. A novella version of *The Hemingway Hoax* (1990) won both Nebula and Hugo awards in '90 and '91 respectively. More recent titles include *None So Blind* and *1968*. Haldeman now combines his writing career with a position as adjunct professor teaching writing at MIT. His latest novel, *Forever Peace*, won the 1998 Hugo award, and will be published in 1999 by Millennium. He is presently working on a sequel to *The Forever War*, entitled *Forever Free*.

SF MASTERWORKS

'An amazing list – genuinely the best novels from sixty years of SF' – Iain M. Banks

ONE BOOK WILL BE PUBLISHED PER MONTH.
THE FIRST 6 MONTHS OF THE 2001 PROGRAMME
ARE AS FOLLOWS:

#37 NOVA Samuel R. Delany
'The best science fiction writer in the world' Algis Budrys

**#38 THE FIRST MEN IN THE MOON
H. G. Wells**
'Wells' scientific romances were works of art'
Arthur C. Clarke

**#39 THE CITY AND THE STARS
Arthur C. Clarke**
*'One of the most imaginative novels of the
far future ever written'* Sunday Times

#40 BLOOD MUSIC Greg Bear
'Classic science fiction' New Scientist

#41 JEM Frederik Pohl
*'The most consistently able writer science fiction
has yet produced'* Kingsley Amis

#42 BRING THE JUBILEE Ward Moore
'A classic alternative world story'
Brian Aldiss

Fantasy Masterworks